THE THERAPIST

S.A. FALK

Storm
PUBLISHING

To request permissions, contact the publisher at rights@stormpublishing.co

Ebook ISBN: 978-1-80508-186-9
Paperback ISBN: 978-1-80508-188-3

Cover design by: Dissect Designs
Cover images by: Shutterstock

Published by Storm Publishing.
For further information, visit:
www.stormpublishing.co

ALSO BY S.A. FALK

The Patient's Secret

ONE

I feel hollow sitting in the church pew. I see, but I do not watch. I hear, but I do not listen. My disbelief has numbed all of my senses.

I know that this is real. I saw her in the hospital, brain-dead and unresponsive. I saw her at the wake, lifeless and rotten. I know that she is gone, and yet, I do not want to accept it. I *cannot* accept it.

I don't know how many times I have called her cell phone just to hear her on the voicemail greeting. To trick myself into believing that she is still alive. *You have reached Dr. Maynard. I'm sorry I missed your call, but if you leave your name, number, and a brief message, I will get back to you as soon as possible. If this is an emergency, please call 9-1-1.*

She will never get back to me though.

I have felt grief before, but not like this. This is not a loss. This is a void.

At her funeral service, I hear the pastor speak about her in such a sterile, anesthetized way. How this should be a celebration of her life. How her spirit lives on in all of us. How God has called her home. Then her family members say their piece, and although their words are heartfelt, they do not comfort me. The emptiness remains.

During the reception, I mingle with the other mourners as if I am a fog creeping from one mire to the next.

"How did you know Lacey?" they ask me.

I don't want to tell complete strangers the truth about my relationship with her. That she was my therapist for the last thirty years. That she dragged me out of a pit when I was a teenager and I saw no way out. That she is the reason I am alive, and the inspiration for what I have dedicated my life to.

"She was my professional mentor," I tell them. "I'm a correctional psychiatrist."

I can try to tell myself that she was just my therapist, but that will only degrade the impact that she had on my life. Dr. Maynard was my mentor. My dearest friend. My surrogate mother. My savior.

My employer, the California Department of Corrections, only grants me the time off to attend her funeral service. "Bereavement leave only applies for immediate family," my human resources representative tells me.

I feel like telling her that I have no immediate family. My mother and father have both long since passed, and I have no siblings. Aside from a handful of distant relatives that I lost contact with years ago, I am alone. Dr. Maynard *was* my family.

But I don't. I simply nod at her and choke down my grief.

That following Monday, the last thing I want to do is return to work. But I don't have much of an option as the lead psychiatrist at Pantano State Hospital, the state-run forensic psychiatric facility. Today in particular, since we have a new patient arriving that will require our utmost attention.

I arrive at the hospital early, long before the sun has risen and the day shift crew has arrived. A couple of guards monitor the shadowed hallways, peeking into the windows of room doors to make sure that everyone is quiet or asleep.

"How did it go?" I ask one of the guards as I walk past him toward my office.

"Quiet as the grave," he answers tiredly.

The comment hits an exposed nerve, but I hide my reaction. The guard doesn't know I lost someone so recently. As a matter of fact, nobody but HR and my boss knows.

I would like to say that my non-disclosure is a direct result of my occupation, but I know that's not true. I am an extremely private person by nature, and my personal life, in my opinion, is of little consequence to my colleagues.

The day shift workers arrive around five thirty. Guards, caseworkers, and therapists. The screeching of metal folding chairs on the linoleum floor tears through the early morning air of the central day room and reverberates down the corridors. The musk of cheap coffee rises out of styrofoam cups as the staff shuffle about the room groggily, waiting for the caffeine to hit their respective bloodstreams and smother the fatigue that lingers in their systems.

Their motions are so ingrained in them that they may as well be hypnotized. Routine can have that effect on people, sane or not.

But Pantano State Hospital thrives on routine. It is what curbs the chaos and squelches the insanity. If not for routine, this place would be engulfed in pandemonium.

This particular morning feels different though. An anxious energy has taken hold of the staff as if the caffeine is being pumped into the room through the HVAC system. The caseworkers and guards chatter among themselves as they drag their chairs to form the oval in which we meet. I cannot discern exactly what is being said, but I have a pretty good guess as to what all the fuss is about.

"Alright, everyone," I call out, knowing that we have more to go over this morning than usual. "Let's get settled in so we can get started."

Their murmurs hush as they take their seats. Their nervous-ness remains. Several of them fidget in their seats to dispel the energy.

"For the sake of time, we'll skip the pleasantries. We have a lot to cover this morning." I motion to the caseworker nearest me and add, "Michael, you want to start?"

"Sure," Michael says, flipping to a dog-eared page in his legal pad. He begins by debriefing the group about some of the incidents from the previous week and the safety plans that will be in place to prevent them happening again. One of his patients has been refusing to eat and will likely get a feeding tube if he keeps it up. Another tried to assault a guard over the weekend, so he will be spending the next forty-eight hours on the confinement unit upstairs.

"We need to keep a close eye on Edgar as well," he adds. "He's been withdrawing more lately and I am concerned he's on the verge of a breakdown. Those of you who see him regularly, try to engage with him as best you can."

Across the oval, one of the guards mumbles something to the guard next to him. I look around and see that most of the group is distracted. I can see it on their faces and in their flick-ering eyes.

"Darrel?" I call across the oval to the guard. "Do you have a question?"

"No, Dr. Fletcher," he replies quickly.

"You sure?" I add, knowing full well that something is on his mind.

"Well..." He hesitates, glancing at some of the other guards. "When are we going to talk about Trent Davis?"

"We do not talk about new arrivals until we've debriefed from the previous week," I answer.

"Yeah, but most new arrivals aren't guys like Trent Davis."

"We've had serial killers here before," I reply flatly as if this fact is anything but spectacular.

"I understand," he says. "It just seems like we should be extra vigilant with him, is all."

I ignore the comment, partly because it is pointing out the obvious but also because I want to maintain the routine of the meeting. "We will talk about Mr. Davis when we're done debriefing last week," I answer with finality.

Darrel acquiesces to my firmness and the energy within the oval abates.

I turn the floor over to the other caseworkers and they continue to report back on the previous week.

I would be lying if I told you I was not a little anxious about Trent Davis myself. Like I said, we have had serial killers on the unit before, not to mention the lion's share of violent offenders. But Trent Davis is unique even for our standards.

Pantano State Hospital is not your garden variety psychiatric facility. We serve a very specific clientele. Patients who have committed heinous crimes but are insane within every definition of the law. Those with temporary insanity are here for as few as six months until they are psychologically ready to stand trial and face a jury of their peers. Those with indefinite insanity are here for as long as the courts deem necessary. Years. Decades. Centuries even.

Trent Davis is one of the latter, and today marks the beginning of six consecutive life sentences for him.

As extraordinary as this is though, it is not what makes guards like Darrel uneasy. For one thing, Trent Davis is a celebrity. Not in the sense of Richard Ramirez or Ted Bundy, who created media frenzies during their trials. Trent Davis is a famous musician, and up until a few months ago, a very successful one as the singer, songwriter, multi-instrumentalist, and producer of the heavy metal band SOS.

The other part that makes his case extraordinary is *how* he earned six consecutive life sentences. By his own account, he murdered six hitchhikers that he picked up along deserted sections of Interstate 5 between San Francisco and Bakersfield. He incapacitated them before taking them back to his home in Bakersfield where he ritualistically killed them in his basement, drinking their blood and removing their major organs. When he was done, he dumped their remains in the same spot on the shoulder of the interstate where he had picked them up. Trent never actually said what he did with the excised organs, but because the remains were never found, the media and the masses have assumed he ate them.

The last caseworker has finished discussing her patients, and the figurative conch shell has made its way back to me. Everyone is staring at me eagerly, waiting for me to talk about what they have been waiting for since they stepped onto the unit.

"Questions or comments before we go on to new arrivals?" I ask. After a silent pause, I open the manila folder in my lap and continue, "Our new arrival is Trent Davis. Popularly known as The Vampire of Bakersfield, although I do not want to hear anyone refer to him by that. From this point forward, he is either Mr. Davis or Trent. Understood?" I stop briefly and several of the staff nod. "Mr. Davis was recently found not guilty by reason of insanity for six murders committed between 2019 and 2023. His official diagnosis is schizoaffective disorder paired with post-traumatic stress and substance abuse.

"Mr. Davis was a musician prior to his crimes. As the lead member of the heavy metal band SOS, he made it a point to be as controversial as he could be with both his lyrics and his performances. His music has been cited as influencing a number of suicides, in addition to a school shooting in Des Moines, Iowa. Although charges were never brought against him, each accusation afforded him a great deal of publicity and notoriety from news outlets and social media, and he had no issue provoking it."

"As this relates to our work with Mr. Davis—" Officer

Williams' hand goes into the air and interrupts me. "Yes, Officer Williams?"

"Isn't it true that he cannibalized his victims?" he asks.

"Allegedly," I answer, slightly annoyed because of the interruption. "Why is that relevant?"

"Well, that seems like a pretty significant safety hazard."

"You afraid he's going to try to drink your blood?" another guard snipes in jest.

"We all know what he did," I reply curtly. "I have no interest in sensationalizing the gore of his crimes this morning, understand?"

"Yes, ma'am," responds Williams.

"Alright," I say. "Now we need to be extremely vigilant about confidentiality as it relates to his case. Especially in these early days, the press is going to be swarming the perimeter of the hospital wanting to know everything that he's doing and saying. Do not talk to them. What happens in this unit stays in this unit.

"In terms of safety protocols, we are going to start Mr. Davis on restricted privileges. His room is to be locked at all times, and when he is in communal areas, he will wear wrist shackles for the safety of staff and patients. He is not to be within ten feet of any other patient until he proves to us that he is capable of appropriate, safe behavior. If another patient tries to get near him, separate them immediately. Do not get close to him unless you are being watched by another staff member.

"Related to his substance abuse, Mr. Davis has been addicted to meth and barbiturates for over a decade, so he experienced significant withdrawals during his time in custody. Unless he's been getting fixes in prison, however, he should be past the worst of it. Even so, bear in mind that he's been self-medicating for years, so the more sober he gets, the more the schizoaffective symptoms are going to emerge. Hallucinations, depression, mania, and delusional thinking. I am going to do what I can to medicate him appropriately, but it will take some time to get the cocktail right. In the meantime, keep a close eye on him and document all of your observations.

"As for his arrival later this morning, I would like Officers Nunez and Clark to accompany him through admission. Warden Moreno and I will be joining you as well. Once his intake has been completed, we'll bring him up to the unit and get him settled in. Questions?"

I scan the oval, but nobody raises their hand or speaks up.

"Good," I reply. "Let's put the room back together and get ready for the morning."

The metal chairs screech on the linoleum floor again and the hum of conversation returns.

As I gather my things, Officer Williams approaches me.

"I wanted to apologize for what I said earlier, Dr. Fletcher," he tells me. "I wasn't trying to be gratuitous."

"But you were," I say firmly. "What he has done is unimaginable and repulsive, but they're sending him to us for a reason. He is incredibly afflicted, and it is our job to treat him to the best of our ability without bias or judgment."

"Yes, ma'am," he responds. "If I am being honest though, it gives me the creeps. I mean, drinking their blood and eating their organs? That's some fucked-up shit."

Coldly, I say, "That's who we serve, Officer. If you're not comfortable with it, this unit is not for you."

Before he can respond, I walk away and leave the day room.

I realize my response was probably calloused, but I have little patience for that kind of frailty, especially from one of the guards. In order for this unit to operate smoothly and safely, I need the guards to delicately tow the line between therapeutic and domineering. I want them to treat the patients with dignity and sympathy, but if push comes to shove, they need to be able to assume control with an iron fist.

TWO

Warden Moreno stands beside me in the foyer of the admissions office while the two guards wait outside for the transport van to arrive. The office is positioned at the back of the hospital so that neither the press nor any other prying eyes can catch glimpses of patients as they arrive.

"I've been fielding calls from the news all morning," Moreno says to me. "Leave it to the press to turn this into a goddamn freak show."

"The freak show began long before this morning," I respond. "It started long before he was even arrested."

Moreno keeps his eyes honed on the windows before us. "You buy the diagnosis?" he asks.

"Not my place to say yet," I answer. "But I am going to find out, I'll guarantee that. How about you?"

Moreno scoffs slightly. "Judge Groban is about as soft-hearted as they come. Any other judge would've flushed that plea down the toilet and sent that psychopath to San Quentin. Instead, we get to put up with this circus."

I nod my head, but I do not reply. I understand where Moreno is coming from, but he has worked corrections and law enforcement his entire life, and his view of rehabilitation is distorted.

I purposely curb my assumptions with new patients because I want to see them and evaluate them for myself. It's not that I don't trust the diagnoses or opinions of other psychiatrists, but psychosis is complicated, especially when multiple conditions are involved. Evaluating a patient in the heat of substance withdrawal skews results, in my experience, not to mention that a lot of severe diagnoses require months of observable behavior, not a couple of hours with survey questions.

"You be sure to keep me in the loop with what's going on," Moreno adds. "Davis so much as smiles at someone, I want to know about it."

"Understood," I say.

A Department of Corrections van soon pulls up in front of the foyer, and a guard climbs out of the passenger seat and slides open the back door. Nunez and Clark step forward, blocking the view of Davis as they guide him out of the van. The guards soon step aside and assume their posts behind him, nudging him forward toward the foyer doors.

Trent Davis looks nothing like he does in the pictures and video clips that I have seen. As a musician, his appearance was theatrical if not campy. Dark lipstick, heavy eye shadow, white or red contact lenses, and jet-black hair made him look like the title character of a Tim Burton film. Now, he looks like a blanched corpse in a pale green jumpsuit and shackles around his wrists and ankles.

His eyes are hollow and his face is expressionless as the guards open the foyer doors and he steps into the hospital. The fluorescent light of the room makes his complexion even more ghoulish, and after a moment I have to stop myself from staring at him.

Moreno steps in front of him and says, "Mr. Davis, I am Warden Moreno. Welcome to the Pantano State Hospital."

Moreno motions to me and adds, "This is Dr. Stephanie Fletcher, Lead Psychiatrist for the High-Security Ward."

"Good morning, Mr. Davis," I say.

His gaze is fixed upon the floor in front of him, but when I speak, his eyes crawl upward until they reach mine. He stares at me for several moments. *Through* me, really, as if there's something behind me that has seized his attention.

"We're not going to have any problems with you, are we?" asks Moreno.

Davis's eyes slowly trail over to the warden. "No, sir," he whispers. "No problems."

"Good," says Moreno.

Nunez and Clark lead Davis through the various stages of the intake as Moreno and I follow in their wake. Davis moves like a plastic bag in a gentle breeze. Floating purposelessly wherever the guards nudge him. He does not speak unless prompted, and even then his voice is quiet. It is almost as if he does not have a clue where he is or he simply does not care why he is here.

I can see that Warden Moreno is scrutinizing Davis's every move. He does not buy his impassivity, and if Davis snaps, he wants to be ready.

I am not as skeptical. If I had to guess, Davis's body is exhausted from the withdrawals and his mind is consumed by the fog of depression. Even so, I maintain my vigilance; impulsivity is about the only predictable thing in this place.

The physician gives Davis a brief physical examination, primarily to make sure that he is not smuggling contraband into the hospital or carrying head lice or obvious infections that could get other inmates sick. Davis has very prominent track marks on the insides of both of his arms, and I can't help but feel sympathetic toward him and what led to his addiction.

When the intake is complete, we escort Davis to the high-security ward. His compliance surprises us, but we are thankful for it all the same.

Stepping onto the ward, the monotony of the late morning is in full swing. A soap opera is blaring from the television in the day room with a number of patients staring blankly at it. There is a pair playing checkers in the corner. A couple more running mops along the linoleum floor as part of their work detail.

"You want to meet the other patients?" I ask Davis as we enter the ward.

He glances at me with confusion as if he is not sure what I asked.

"Mr. Davis?" I say.

"*Trent,*" he mutters, just loud enough so I can barely hear him.

"Trent," I say. "Do you want to meet the other patients?"

He glances around the ward slowly before answering, "I want to sleep."

"You're not hungry?" I ask. "Lunch will be in about thirty minutes. The food here is way better than in prison."

He shakes his head. "Just sleep, please."

"Okay," I say.

The guards and I escort him through the hallway until we reach a door halfway down.

"This is where you'll be staying," I tell him as I unlock the door.

I push the door open, but he does not enter. He just stands in the doorway with a blank gaze.

"Trent?" I say gently.

"No bars?" he asks.

"No bars," I answer. "Of course, this door here is reinforced with steel and will remain locked at all times. Understood?"

He nods.

"Good."

We guide him into the room and his attention drifts over to

the small concrete slab attached to the far wall that serves as a desk. There's a short stack of folded papers and envelopes on it.

"What are those?" he asks, motioning to the desk.

"Letters for you. We started receiving them shortly after your sentencing was announced."

"What do they say?"

"I don't know. We're not legally allowed to read your mail. We can only search the envelopes for contraband."

"Can I write back?"

"Yes. Just ask one of the guards for a pen and paper. The pens are those cheap, flexible ones, but they're good enough for writing short notes at least."

He nods again. "I like to keep up with my fans."

The thought of people admiring him sends a chill up my spine, but a commotion from the day room abruptly gets my attention.

"Why can't I meet him?" someone yells frantically. "I want to meet him!"

"You need to calm down, Mr. Schwartz," a guard orders.

"I want to meet him!" Mr. Schwartz howls back.

"Sit down. I am not going to tell you again," the guard retorts.

I hurry down the hallway toward the day room, leaving Trent with Nunez and Clark. When I get there, I see Mr. Schwartz standing toe-to-toe with one of our guards.

I thunder into the day room. "What is going on here? Mr. Schwartz, take a seat or be returned to your room."

"Dr. Fletcher," Schwartz pleads, practically in tears with hysteria. "Is it true he's here?"

"Who?" I ask.

"The Spawn!" he yells, his voice frantic. "Is he here among us?"

"Sit down," I reply, ignoring one of many pseudonyms given to Trent Davis over the years.

Mr. Schwartz seethes with excitement, but he takes heed and returns to his seat.

"Is it true?" he mutters to me. "Is he here?"

"Yes," I say flatly. "Mr. Davis just arrived."

Schwartz's body trembles until it reaches a fever pitch, yet he does not dare to move from his seat.

"When can I meet him?" he replies eagerly.

"Later," I say. "He's tired and needs to sleep. Do you understand?"

"The Duke of Darkness needs no sleep," responds Schwartz. "He may be *of* man, but *he* is not man. He is eternal. He is indestructible."

"Alright, Mr. Schwartz," I answer, realizing that he is quickly sliding down a slippery slope. "Why don't you go back to your room for a while so you can relax?"

"I don't want to!" he retorts, jumping from his chair and rushing out into the main corridor.

"Mr. Schwartz!" I yell, running after him. "Clark, grab him!"

Schwartz makes it halfway to Trent's room before he trips on his slippers and falls face-first onto the floor. Officer Clark rushes over to apprehend him before he can realize what has happened. He lifts Schwartz from the floor with his hands cuffed behind his back. All the while Schwartz sobs hysterically.

"Spawn!" he screams at Trent, who is standing at the doorway of his room. "Spawn!"

Trent stares blankly at Schwartz, and every nerve in my body tenses with anticipation to see what is going to happen next.

Slowly, Trent raises his shackled hands and places his index finger in front of his lips. Schwartz is immediately silenced by the gesture, his eyes locked on Trent with the utmost obedience.

"Be calm," Trent mutters, lowering his hands like a priest in prayer. "Emotions are for the weak, and hysterics for the power-less. If a man cannot maintain dominion over himself, then he certainly cannot expect dominion over others."

The corridor becomes eerily silent in the moments that follow. Trent is standing omnisciently with his shackled hands before him, and Schwartz is trembling in Officer Clark's grasp, as if he is the blind man who has just been healed by Christ.

Without another word, Trent turns toward his room and shuffles through the doorway.

Mr. Schwartz is quietly beside himself. His body trembles and tears stream down his cheeks, but he does not dare make a sound.

Warden Moreno and I stare dumbfoundedly at each other for a moment. I will not speak for him, but I know I am trying to figure out what the hell just happened.

Officer Clark is the first to break the silence, asking, "What do you want me to do with Schwartz, Dr. Fletcher?"

"Take him to his room," I answer. "Once he's composed himself, he can join the group again."

Officer Clark has to practically drag Mr. Schwartz across the linoleum to his room, his body stupefied by the experience.

Once they are out of earshot, Warden Moreno says to me, "So much for avoiding the circus."

"Yeah," I mutter ruminatively. "At least Davis behaved himself."

"For now..." says Moreno.

THREE

I see Trent waiting for me in one of the private counseling rooms the following morning. Through the glass of the door, his face looks puffy with exhaustion and his hair is disheveled as if he recently woke up.

I empathize with him. I haven't gotten a good night's sleep since Dr. Maynard died. Bags have started to form beneath my eyes and I feel much older than forty-six.

"How was he?" I ask the guard who is standing in post next to the door.

"He barely slept from what the night guards told me. The times he did fall asleep, he screamed himself awake."

"Screamed?" I replied.

"Night terrors," he says. "Or what we're assuming are night terrors, at least. Probably something for you to find out."

"Yup," I answer. "Keep a close eye on us, will you? Just in case. You never know with the new arrivals."

"Always," he says. "You never know with *any* of them."

I nod, taking a moment to harden my will before entering the room.

Trent glances up at me when I enter, his eyes red and sunken into his skull.

"Good morning, Trent," I say. "Do you remember who I am?"

"Yes," he mutters. "You're Dr. Fletcher."

"That's right," I say, taking a seat on the other side of the table from him.

Although his hands are shackled to the top of the table, he sits no more than four feet away from me and the proximity alone makes me anxious. I am always a little nervous in private sessions until I get to know the patients better. Despite the fact that it's my job to provide treatment for them, I never forget that they are extremely violent men who have done indescribable things.

"I apologize for the handcuffs," I add. "Standard procedure until we get to know each other a little better."

"Can't blame you," he answers. "If I were you, I wouldn't even be alone in this room with me, no less without handcuffs." His voice is so matter-of-fact it makes the comment that much more unnerving, as if violence is the only default he knows.

"Part of the job," I reply, trying to match the passivity in his tone to show that he does not terrify me.

I open a manila folder that contains all of the information that we have on him. Diagnostic results and notes from when he was evaluated prior to his competency hearing as well as background research I conducted on him beforehand.

"So how's this work?" he asks. "You going to pry me open like Dr. Pitt tried to do?"

"Not really," I answer. "I just want to talk to you. Get to know you better and see how I can best help you."

He smirks. "Pump me full of drugs so I am docile and easy to deal with, huh? I bet you got shit that'll send me into another dimension."

"No," I say. "Although I will try to see if we can get you something to control your symptoms."

"*Which* symptoms?" he asks.

"Well, it depends which ones you're experiencing. I know what Dr. Pitt noted when he first evaluated you, but that was almost a month ago."

"Nothing's changed," he replies. "If anything, it's gotten worse."

"What's that?" I ask. "The hallucinations?"

He nods dejectedly.

"Do you mind describing them for me?"

He shrugs. "There's not much to say. It's like this incessant monologue echoing in my brain all the time. Even now I can hear that little fucker whispering to me as if they're perched right on my shoulder."

"Larua?" I respond, assuming he's referring to the demon that he told Dr. Pitt possessed him at some point in his adolescence.

According to Dr. Pitt's evaluation, Larua is the primary symptom of Trent's condition. He told Pitt that Larua demanded he drink animal blood to nourish him, and that eventually progressed into drinking human blood. And that is what led to Trent's infamous crimes over the last three years. Supposedly.

"What are they saying?" I add.

Trent smirks. "That your blood must be delicious if you look as good as you do. Real... *rich*."

My skin crawls with how unnerved I am, but I do not dare reveal my discomfort to him. No matter what he says, no matter what he does, I have to prove to him that my skin is as thick as steel. Because if he thinks he can rattle me, he will burrow as deep as he can and tear me apart from the inside out.

"Do *you* enjoy that?" I manage to ask. "Drinking the blood, I mean."

He scoffs. "It doesn't matter what I enjoy. It's what Larua wants. It's what Larua needs."

"Do you know where Larua came from?" I ask. "Or why they chose you?"

"You think Moses knew why the burning bush spoke to him? Or that Muhammad knew why Gabriel came to him in Hira?"

My brow furrows slightly. "So you liken yourself to a prophet?"

"No," he says. "Prophets think they speak to God and I stopped believing in God a long time ago."

"But you believe in Larua?" I counter. "And you believe in the devil?"

"I hear Larua every minute of every day," he answers. "And I have seen the pupils of the devil's eyes and felt the touch of his claws. If you've seen what I have seen and heard what I have heard, you'd believe in them too."

Again, I show no reaction despite the fact that an icy chill runs the length of my spine.

"What do you mean that you've seen and felt the devil?" I ask.

He snickers. "That's for you to find out, isn't it? To crack my skull open and spill my brain out onto the table? Go ahead..." He tilts his head forward and leans over the table. "Dive on in."

I say nothing to him, holding my place in my seat despite my discomfort.

A grin smothers his face and he adds, "Are you afraid of me, Dr. Fletcher?"

I lock my gaze with his in an attempt to stand my ground and maintain some control over the conversation.

"What other symptoms have you been experiencing?" I ask.

He leans back in his chair as far as the chain connecting him to the table will allow. "Let's see..." he replies. "If memory serves me, I am supposed to be experiencing grandiosity, suspiciousness, hostility, emotional withdrawal, depression and mania, impulsivity, social avoidance, and disorientation. Is that right?"

"Those are some of the categories on the Syndrome Scale, yes."

He smirks. "Dr. Pitt believed I experienced them all, didn't he?"

"Do you?" I retort.

"Sure," he says with a shrug.

"Do you feel any of them currently?"

He sighs deeply. "How can you tell that someone is experiencing any of those? Emotional withdrawal? Impulse control? Avoidance? Those describe half the people in America."

"Yet you're the only one who ritualistically murdered six young women in your basement. Drank their blood and ate their major organs."

"So I have been told," he says. "Of course, nobody really knows what went on in that basement."

"Meaning what exactly?"

"Meaning that people only believe what they *want* to believe, and it's easier to accept a truth of their own creation than reality. Take God, for example. *God made man in his image.*" He scoffs, rolling his eyes. "What a farce. It was man who made God in his image, and God is nothing but a power-hungry, narcissistic piece of shit."

"All gods, or just the Christian God?" I ask, wondering where this fixation on religion comes from.

"Christians, Jews, Muslims, they all idolize what they see in the mirror, yet I am the bastard for calling them out on it."

"Maybe it's not what you say that ruffles people's feathers, but how you say it."

"If people didn't love how I say it, I wouldn't have had four records that went platinum."

Seeing an opening to redirect the conversation away from

his pseudo-prophetic pontification, I ask, "Can we talk about your music? I imagine it's a huge part of who you are, and I'd like to learn more."

"Would you now?" he replies with a grin. "And what would you like to know?"

"Anything, really. How you got started? What inspires you? Things like that."

His eyes narrow skeptically. "Have you ever even listened to my music?" he asks. "You strike me as a country fan."

"I admit, I am not real familiar with your songs," I say. "But I have heard a couple of them before."

"Which ones?" he asks, as if he's interrogating me. Testing my authenticity.

"'Left Hand of God' and 'Mud Vain' are the two that come to mind."

"Not 'Razor Blades'?" he replies deviously.

"Yes," I say. "That one too."

"Do you believe what everyone says?" he asks. "That 'Razor Blades' drove those people to kill themselves?"

I shake my head slowly. "It's not my place to say."

"You sound like a politician dodging a difficult question. How do you expect me to be honest with you if you're not open with me, Doc?"

"Okay..." I say, eyeing him as I consider my response. "I would guess those people already had suicidal ideation. The song just became the scapegoat for their families and a sensational story for the media."

Trent starts to chuckle, and after a moment, he mutters, "Of all the things for them to call me. The Vampire?" He scoffs. "That's smarmy even by their standards."

I ignore the comment, instead asking, "Why did you write 'Razor Blades'?"

"Why do you think?" he replies contemptuously.

"I don't know," I say. "That's why I am asking."

He shakes his head and rolls his eyes. "People hate talking about suicide despite the fact that most people consider it at some point in their lives. Thoughts of death are as much a part of human nature as greed and sexual perversion, yet we dare not say anything about it. You want to know what drives people to actually doing it? Stigmas and taboos. The more we try to bury something, the deeper the seed takes root."

"So you were trying to bring suicide into the spotlight?" I reply.

"You could say that," he answers. "Or you could say what everyone in the media says. That I *glorified* it and *romanticized* it." He rolls his eyes. "Ignorant..."

"Do you think of suicide often?" I ask.

He smirks, leaning over the table toward me. "As often as I think of killing," he mutters. He chuckles in my face and his breath smells acrid and rotten. He then shakes his hands against the chain that's pinning him to the table, adding, "You still want to be alone with me?"

FOUR

I sit in the dim light of my living room early that following morning. I did attempt to sleep for about an hour, but my mind just won't relax.

I wish I could talk to Dr. Maynard about Trent and pick her brain about his diagnosis. Schizoaffective disorder is such a complex combination of severe hallucinations, emotional withdrawal, and manic-depressive episodes that can only be observed over time. He certainly displays many of the symptoms, but the hallucinations in particular are so tricky to navigate. After all, I can't crawl into his brain and hear this demon for myself. I have to trust what he tells me about his experiences. But trust makes me extremely vulnerable. How do I know he is not lying through his teeth just to avoid prison?

Trent frightens me, and yet, there is this part of me that wants to know why he is the way he is. I cannot speak for other mental health professionals but, for me, mental illness is fascinating. How it manifests and presents itself in such unique and bizarre ways. It is not like physical medicine where there is often a distinct cause, like a tumor in the brain or an embolism in a vein. Something tangible and concrete that can be found using a diagnostic tool.

Mental illness often has no physical cause, so then my job becomes an archaeological expedition in which I must dig carefully to avoid disturbing the rest of the site or trigger a booby trap that was set specifically to keep me out.

With Trent, I can't help but feel that same sense of intrigue. Regardless if he is or is not psychotic, I know there is a root cause for why he is the way he is and I cannot allow one tough session to deter me from unearthing it.

What sticks with me the most are his comments about how people have drawn assumptions about him or his crimes without really knowing the background or without really seeking to understand. Then there was his explanation for his song "Razor Blades" and how the popular media distorted the purpose of the song altogether. It almost sounded like a writer who is frustrated by the fact that his critics missed the point of his novel or perverted its purpose to fit their own agenda, or a painter whose masterpiece is not seen for what it really is. I would in no way consider Trent's music artistic, but if *he* does, then his contempt makes some sense. After all, so many artists use their work as a means of feeling their way through the darkness that lingers in their minds. An assault on the art becomes an assault on the artist. Maybe that is the case for Trent Davis, I wonder? Maybe the key to his psyche lies within his music?

From what I know about his crimes, his most recent album was what caused investigators to suspect him in the first place. *Into the Maelstrom* was SOS's fourth album, released digitally about six months ago. The cover appeared to be some type of abstract artwork, but it was actually a close-up photograph of an emptied body cavity. What investigators later discovered was that it was a photo of Trent's sixth and final victim after he had removed and presumably consumed her major organs.

Into the Maelstrom was removed from Spotify and banned

from all commercial sites; it was available long enough, however, to sell more than one million copies, and the songs continue to live on in infamy in the darker recesses of the internet.

As if this is not disturbing enough, there is one more aspect of the album that is sinister beyond belief. Apparently Trent produced the album entirely by himself during the COVID-19 shutdowns in a house that was once the home of Stanley Palmer, known by most Californians as the Bakersfield Boogeyman. Back in the '90s, Palmer was a pedophile and serial rapist, abusing dozens of children in the basement of his home.

When investigators and prosecutors asked him why he chose Stanley's house as the recording studio for his album, Trent told them, "I wanted to explore all the messed-up edges of humanity. What better place to do that than here? Where the walls and floorboards will tell me all of their grisly secrets."

My curiosity getting the best of me, I grab my laptop and look through the lyrics of Trent's songs. Just the lyrics—no news stories, no commentary. Nothing other than Trent's own words. The echoes of his ominous brain.

I do a Google search for "SOS songs" and start working my way through the most-played list that appears.

"Razor Blades" is the first song listed, so I click on the second one: "Left Hand of God".

What intrigues me about this song is that it begins with lines from Psalm 118. For someone who loathes God and religion, Trent shows a relative familiarity with the Bible.

Then there is "Serpent Seed", a song that has created significant controversy and gotten Trent a whole lot of negative publicity over the years. From what I remember of Sunday school from my youth, the song resembles the temptation of Eve in the Garden of Eden. Although the way Trent writes it, it sounds like Satan rapes Eve and the first child she bears is his, not Adam's.

This song brings a number of questions to mind. Is Trent simply wanting to disrespect Christianity as his critics claim? Is it autobiographical, describing the sickness that wreaks havoc on his mind? Or is it cryptic for the sake of being misleading?

The last song I analyze is the title track of *Into the Maelstrom*, the lyrics of which were inspired by Edgar Allan Poe's short story, "A Descent into the Maelstrom".

I do not know much about Poe's story, but the lyrics convey someone's slow but inevitable slide into an enormous whirlpool. It feels eerily symbolic considering the circumstances revolving around the album's production and aftermath. Perhaps Trent's own descent into psychosis. What makes my heart ache for him is the powerlessness within the words. The desperation that he so obviously felt in the moments that he put the words to paper.

I access the audio track to hear him speak the words into existence, to feel his torment and despair intimately.

The song begins with white noise that fluctuates in volume. At first the changes are slow and controlled, ebbing and flowing with the tranquility of a meditation fountain. Then metallic percussion ripples through, distant at first but eventually dominating the chaos.

When the beginning stanzas come through, Trent barely whispers the words, as if an inner monologue has found a crack through which to escape his skull. But as the song progresses, the smooth rhythm becomes frantic. Fragmented into chaos and noise. The lyrics become louder too, as if feeding a hysteria to which Trent must submit.

By the end of the song, the background becomes complete pandemonium, forcing him to scream the final chorus as if the whirlpool is seconds from filling his lungs and drowning him.

And then, suddenly, nothing An auditory hollowness that makes the listener think—if only for a moment—that they themselves have lost their sense of hearing entirely. As if they are the ones who have been devoured by the maelstrom, their bodies suspended like an angel in the dark depths of the ocean.

I'm surprised to feel tears crawling down my cheeks by the conclusion of the song, and I have to force myself away from my computer.

Daylight eventually arrives and I take my time as I drive into work. My mind continues to wander, lulling me into a state of hypnosis. More than anything, the void in my soul aches, and the longer I think about Dr. Maynard's death, the larger that void becomes.

When I arrive at Pantano, the routine of the hospital absorbs me and forces me to repress my grief. I go through my morning checks with the staff and I briefly visit with each of my patients. How did you sleep? How are you feeling? The basic pleasantries to start the day.

When I get to Trent, he's sitting on the edge of his bed staring at the wall. I wait for a moment so as not to startle him, but he doesn't budge.

"Good morning, Trent. How are you feeling?"

He doesn't look at me. He just shrugs his shoulders ever so slightly, the tiniest hint of a response.

"Were you able to sleep?" I add.

He shakes his head. Again, no verbal answer.

"You sure you're doing alright?" I prod.

He nods, but he's catatonic otherwise.

I suspect that he's continuing to feel the pangs of withdrawal, but I also worry that he is spiraling deeper into a depressive state.

I go to the guard station and tell the day crew to keep a close eye on Trent. Let me know if they observe any changes in his behavior or affect.

As I'm talking to the guards, my cell phone rings and I see it's a call from the first-floor visitor's desk.

"Excuse me," I tell them, answering the call. "Yes, Angela?"

"I'm sorry to bother you, but I have someone here to see Trent Davis."

"He's not allowed any visitors at this time," I tell her. "Who is it?"

"His fiancée," she says. "Finley Keenan."

My stomach sinks a bit when I hear the name. "Tell her to wait there," I say. "I'll be down in a few minutes."

Usually if a patient is not allowed to have visitors, I just ask the desk staff to turn them away, but I have a feeling Ms. Keenan is not going to accept that with grace.

Finley Keenan has been adamant about Trent's innocence, although given the evidence against him, I do not know how that is possible. Nonetheless, she has been outspoken since Trent's arrest, not only creating a frenzy on social media but also protesting in front of the courthouse and county jail where he was being detained.

The last thing we need here is an unstable family member sparking hysteria, so I go downstairs to see if I can try to mitigate the situation and prevent a full-blown meltdown. I'm also undeniably curious.

When I arrive, I see a waifish young woman pacing in front of the receptionist's desk. Her pale skin, large ear gauges, and pixie-cut jet-black hair remind me of the title character of *The Girl with the Dragon Tattoo*, one of many movies I've streamed during my recent sleepless nights.

"Ms. Keenan?" I say as I approach her.

She faces me and I can see her pupils are so dilated that her irises are invisible. Clearly under the influence of something.

"I'm Dr. Fletcher," I add. "I am the lead psychiatrist of the high-security unit where Trent is staying."

"I want to see Trent," she replies frantically. "Where's Trent?"

"He's not allowed to have visitors yet," I tell her. "But if you don't mind, I was hoping you and I could speak?"

"What's wrong with him?" she responds, panic-stricken. "Did something happen to him?"

"No, no," I assure her. "Everything is fine. I just wanted to talk to you to learn more about him."

"Oh..." she says, her eyes darting around the waiting area. "You sure he's alright?"

"Yes. Do you want to follow me to the visiting area?"

"Umm..." she mutters. Her eyes continue to flicker as if she's expecting someone to ambush her at any moment. "Yeah. Sure... Fine."

I guide her through a door and down a short hallway to the visitation area. The room is a cavernous square with ten metal picnic tables bolted to the floor.

"Can I get you anything?" I ask as we take a seat. "Water, or coffee?"

She searches the visitation area, her hand scrubbing her arm anxiously.

"Ms. Keenan?" I say. "Can I get you anything?"

"Where's Trent?" she mutters. "I want to see Trent."

"He's not allowed to have visitors," I tell her as sympathetically as I can. "But I was hoping you and I could talk so I can help him. Is that alright?"

"Is he doing okay?" she asks.

"He's okay," I say.

"Why can't I see him then?"

"It's a policy of the hospital. Every new patient has to be evaluated before visitation is allowed."

"This is bullshit," she says. "He shouldn't be in here. He did not kill those people and he's not crazy. Everybody else is crazy."

"I know how hard it is to believe it, but in order to help him, we have to accept the truth."

"The truth?" she scoffs, scraping her arms more aggressively. "That's a joke. There is no truth. Just what everyone else *thinks* is true."

"I see," I say. "What do you make of Trent telling everyone that this demon made him do it?"

She snickers. "He was facing six first-degree murder charges. He would've told everyone he was Santa Claus if his lawyer said it would get him off the hook."

Her comment takes me aback slightly, the implication that Trent has been faking his condition this entire time.

"So you're saying his lawyer told him to say that he was possessed by a demon?"

"Nobody knows Trent as well as I do, and I *know* he's not crazy and I *know* he's not a murderer."

I notice she's avoided a direct answer, but I don't press her. She's obviously strung out, and I need to tread lightly so as to avoid her making a scene.

"How long have you known Trent?" I ask.

"Since I graduated from high school," she says. "So seven years now."

"How'd you meet?"

She smiles. "At one of his concerts," she says. "I convinced security to let me backstage, and we've been together ever since."

"That's nice," I say. "Did you stay with him at the Bakersfield house while he was working on *Into the Maelstrom*?"

"No," she answers. "When he works on an album, he has to immerse himself in it completely. No distractions. No outside influences. After *The Masquerade*, he was sick of people trying to tell him what to do. Producers and record labels ruining his art. He did not give a shit about the money or what people thought of his music. He just wanted to create. Music for music's sake."

"Did you ever get to see him or talk to him while he worked on the new album?"

"What do you think?" she snaps. "We were in the middle of a pandemic."

"I understand," I say, keeping my tone calm to try to de-escalate the situation. "That must've been hard to not have contact with him."

"It's the life we chose," she replies with intensity. "I love him and I'll do anything for him."

"I know you will," I say.

"So *when* will I be able to see him?" she asks, her tone becoming more ardent.

"That's up to him," I answer. "It depends on how he responds to treatment and if he proves he can be safe."

"What the fuck does *that* mean?" she retorts.

I hesitate for a moment because I really cannot tell her specifics about his suicidal ideation and psychotic episodes.

"It just means we have to make sure that everyone on the unit is getting along," I say.

She rolls her eyes and shakes her head. "You do not need to worry about him. He wouldn't hurt a fly."

There are six mutilated bodies to prove otherwise, I think, but I decide not to say it.

"Let's see how he's doing in a few weeks," I tell her. "In the meantime, you're welcome to write letters to him. That's how a lot of loved ones communicate with patients here."

"Fine," she replies dismissively.

Although she is acquiescing for the moment, I have a feeling she isn't going to stay silent forever. God help us if he is not ready for visitations soon.

FIVE

Trent is sitting on a bench bolted to the wall in the day room when I enter. His hands are cuffed in front of him and fixed to a chain that keeps him from moving more than a foot in any direction.

It is the first time we have allowed him to mingle with the rest of the patients since he arrived two days ago, but I walk around the room visiting the others so that I can keep a close eye on him.

When we first brought him out, the other patients were extremely interested in him, several of them trying to engage him in conversation. He did not answer any of them though, almost as if he could not hear a word they were saying.

He has been sitting there for an hour now, and for the majority of that time, he has kept his gaze fixed upon me.

I ignore him as I talk to the others, but I know as well as anyone else that he is watching my every move. As unnerving as it is, I believe that it is a display of dominance. His attempt to show me and everyone else that he is the alpha on the ward despite the fact that he is confined to a single square foot of space on the bench.

I prescribed him Paliperidone for some of his schizoaffective symptoms, and he received his first dose last night. The antipsychotic can take several weeks to really kick in, but I am hopeful that his behavior will become less erratic and more predictable as it does. Maybe once I get him regulated I will be able to understand the root cause of his condition better.

"I don't like the way the new guy's looking at you, Dr. Fletcher," whispers one of the patients, Edgar, to me as I make my way around the room.

"He's just getting used to things," I tell Edgar. "Don't worry about him."

"I don't know..." he mutters. "He's looking at you like you're a suckling pig. I don't like it."

"I appreciate you being protective of me," I say. "Just try to ignore him."

Edgar stares back at Trent for a moment, but Trent's gaze never breaks from me.

"They call him The Vampire, right?" Edgar asks me.

"Yes," I say. "But we're not going to call him that here."

"You think it's true though?"

"Do I think what is true?"

"You think he's a vampire?" he says.

"No," I answer. "Vampires aren't real, Edgar."

"I don't know..." he says, shaking his head. "He sure looks like a vampire."

"How do you know what a vampire looks like?" I ask with a laugh, trying to make light of the situation.

"I have seen the movies," he says.

"Like what?" I reply. "*Twilight*?"

Edgar laughs. "No—*Dracula*."

"Dracula isn't real," I say. "And neither are vampires."

Edgar shakes his head and mutters, "I don't know. Looks real to me."

From across the room, Schwartz calls out to Edgar, "He ain't a goddamn vampire. He's the Spawn of Sin!"

"What the hell does that even mean?" retorts Edgar.

Schwartz scoffs. "It means that he is not of this world. He is untouchable. Invincible. The second coming of the Morningstar."

Edgar glances at me and mutters, "And they say *I'm* crazy?"

"Death comes for non-believers in due time," interjects Schwartz. "You can deny him all you want, but eventually you'll see."

"Alright," I reply firmly. "We're done talking about this. New topic."

"You do not believe, Dr. Fletcher?" retorts Schwartz. "Even when he's right here before us?"

"Mr. Schwartz," I respond. "Do you need to return to your room?"

"I didn't start—"

"That's not what I asked," I cut him short. "Do you need to go back to your room for a while?"

"No..." he mutters, acquiescing.

I break my gaze from Schwartz, and my eye catches Trent again. His eyes are still fixed on me, but now a slight grin curls the edges of his mouth as if someone is whispering a dirty joke in his ear.

What the hell is going through your head right now, I wonder? Is Larua speaking to you, or is it your own inner monologue that entertains you? If only I could peer into his head and find out.

"Quit staring at her like that!" Edgar suddenly yells, startling me out of my thoughts.

Before I realize what is happening, Edgar storms across the day room and stands defiantly in front of Trent.

"Quit fucking looking—"

Trent launches from his seat, and if it wasn't for the

shackles trapping him to the bench, who knows what he would have done to Edgar.

Edgar yelps in terror, falling backward on his rear end and cowering in Trent's hunched shadow.

Everyone in the day room freezes for a moment, our eyes locked on Trent's motionless form as he glowers at Edgar.

After several seconds, Trent mutters to him, "Bow before me, minion. I am worse than any nightmare you could possibly imagine. You live because I allow you to live, and when you die, rest assured it's because I killed you."

Edgar whimpers, and slowly, Trent returns to his seat with his eyes locked on him.

Another moment of blood-curdling silence passes before Trent looks up at me and says, "Take me back to my room."

I glance over at Officer Nunez, who is just as stupefied as everyone else. I tell him, "Take Mr. Davis back to his room now."

As Nunez carefully unshackles Trent from the bench, I grab Edgar and guide him back to his seat across the day room. His whole body trembles, and he mutters incantations that take me a second to make out.

"*Libera nos a malo*," he breathes over and over and over as if his very life depends on it.

"Don't move," I tell Edgar once he is seated.

I get another guard to watch the day room for me, then I hurry down the hallway to where Nunez is waiting for me with Trent in front of his room. I unlock the door and Nunez nudges him inside.

"Don't take the cuffs off just yet," I say to Nunez.

He nods, keeping his hands on Trent's arms and watching him intently.

"You mind telling me what that was all about?" I say to Trent.

"Yes," he answers serenely. "I do mind."

"Let me rephrase then. What the hell was that all about?"

Trent glances up at the ceiling, breathing deeply through his nose for a moment. "Oh, nothing," he replies. "Just putting a dissident in his rightful place is all."

"This may be a psychiatric hospital, but I will see to it that you never leave this room if you cannot control yourself. Is that understood?"

His eyes trail down to me. "*Control myself?*" he responds. "*I* am the paragon of control, Doctor. It is *you* who is not in control. Despite the power you think you wield in this place, it is nothing more than a guise. A false sense of security that will leave you in ruin."

"Duly noted," I say to him, brushing his prophecy aside like a stray hair in my face. To Officer Nunez, I say, "Take his cuffs off. He's not to leave this room until further notice."

Nunez removes Trent's cuffs and steps out of the room.

"By the way," I say to Trent. "When I learn that you're faking your condition, I will personally make sure that you end up on the Condemned Unit at San Quentin."

Trent glowers at me in silence for a moment before replying, "It is life, not death, that terrifies me."

I shut the door and Nunez locks him inside.

"Fucking lunatic," grumbles Nunez. "You really think he's faking it?"

"I don't know," I say, shaking my head. "Too early to tell."

"If *that* isn't insanity, I don't know what is."

We start walking down the hallway toward the day room when Nunez adds, "What was Edgar mumbling to you when you picked him up off the ground?"

"*Libera nos a malo,*" I say.

He looks at me quizzically. "What does that mean?"

"It's Latin. It means 'deliver us from evil'."

SIX

I should have guessed that Trent's fiancée, Finley, was going to show up again sooner rather than later.

It is early on the following Monday morning when my phone rings and it is Angela from the visitor's desk.

"Hi, Dr. Fletcher," she says. "The fiancée is back to see Trent. I see he's still on restriction. Should I have security escort her out?"

I sigh, not wanting to deal with this first thing in the morning. "No, she'll throw a fit," I tell her. "Let me come down and try to talk to her first."

"Okay," says Angela. She sounds relieved and I can't blame her. I have a feeling Trent's fiancée will not leave as willingly as she did the previous week.

I make my way down to the first floor, thinking about the lack of progress that Trent has made. We have not allowed him to mingle with the other patients since the incident with Edgar the previous week, and unless I start seeing signs of improvement in my sessions with him, he will be spending most of the foreseeable future locked in his room.

When I reach the visitors waiting area, I see Finley pacing frantically in front of the receptionist's desk.

I enter the room and say, "Ms. Keenan?"

Finley turns abruptly. "Where's Trent? You said I'd be able to see him today."

"I said it would be at least a week before visitors are allowed," I answer. "And unfortunately, he will need to remain on restriction for a few more weeks."

"A few more weeks?" she replies. "But you promised—"

"I promised nothing," I interject. "Visitation is a privilege that he has neither earned nor is therapeutically ready for."

"What does that even mean?" she demands.

"His treatment is going to take time," I tell her. "I am happy to explain more but I need you to calm down first."

"No!" she retorts. "Let me see him now!"

"Ms. Keenan, you need to calm down or I will have security remove you."

She begins to pace around the room. "This is bullshit!" she growls. "You don't think I know what's going on here? I know what you people are doing!"

I quickly turn to Angela and tell her to call security before putting my attention back on Finley. "Ms. Keenan, this is your last warning. If you do not calm down, you will be removed from the hospital."

Given how slight Finley is, I am not too worried that she poses an immediate safety threat. However, I cannot have her creating such a disturbance.

She continues to throw a tantrum though, stomping her feet and clawing at her arms until several guards show up. As soon as she sees them, she crumbles to the floor and sobs in a heap. "I just want to see him!" she howls hysterically. "Just let me see him, goddammit!"

The guards grab her by the arms and she becomes

completely limp in their grasp as if she has lost all control of her body.

"Let's go, miss," one of them says.

She continues to sob, making no effort to stand or walk on her own. The guards look at me for guidance, waiting for me to give the final order to drag her out of the hospital.

"Hold on a second," I say, kneeling in front of her as they hold her arms. "I could use your help with Trent, Finley. But I need you to be calm so we can talk, understand? Can you do that for him?"

Tears continue to stream down her cheeks, but her sobs slowly begin to abate and her breathing becomes less frantic.

I add, "I'm going to have the guards help you up and take you back to the visitation area, okay?"

She nods, her eyes bloodshot and teary.

"Alright," I say, motioning to the guards to help her up.

As they lift her off the ground, her legs wobble beneath her and it takes her several moments before she can stand on her own.

When she is ready, the guards lead her back to the visitation area and we take a seat at one of the tables.

"You want some water?" I ask her.

She shakes her head slowly. "You really think I can help him?" she asks me.

"I do."

"I don't know how," she mutters dejectedly. "Nothing I have done so far has worked."

"Maybe it's not something you can *do* that will help him," I say. "Maybe it's something you *know* instead."

She looks at me quizzically. "Something I *know*? Like what?"

"Well," I answer, "I am curious if you know anything about his song, 'Into the Maelstrom'? Like, what inspired him to write it, or what it means?"

Skepticism comes over her expression, and she asks, "How is that going to help?"

"I need to understand him better to see what might be causing his symptoms. But because of his condition, it's very hard to get him to open up. I am wondering if his songs have those secrets buried inside of them."

She does not respond for several moments, eyeing me as if trying to determine how genuine I am being.

Finally, she shrugs and answers, "Your guess is as good as anyone's. He's very private about his music. Protective of it. He never said much to me about it no matter how badly I wanted to know."

"Why do you think he chose to record the album in the Stanley Palmer house?" I ask.

"I don't know," she says. "In one of his earlier songs, he says, *I am the nudge that shoves you*, and I think that is the goal with a lot of things that he does: make people uncomfortable and get a rise out of them."

"So you think he did it for the publicity?" I ask.

"No," she says, shaking her head. "I think he did it to get as far under people's skin as he could. To let people know that no matter what they did to cancel him, he wasn't going to disappear. He would always be there no matter how hard they tried to keep him out."

"Why do you think he's like that?" I ask.

"His childhood wasn't exactly the American dream," she answers sardonically. "His mom was a lunatic Jesus freak and he got bullied all the time for it. He didn't belong anywhere and he knew that. Same for a lot of the people who love his music. The ones who actually listen to the lyrics, at least. He is our voice. He speaks our stories out of the shadows and into existence."

"I never thought of it like that," I say, recalling the despair that was so visceral in some of the lyrics that I read. "What do you make of this most recent album?"

She looks firmly into my eyes. "I think it's his masterpiece."

"Why is that?" I ask, trying not to sound too skeptical or judgmental.

"It's so much more than an album. It's a collage made of pieces of his soul. Is there anything more masterful than that?"

I feel like I am hearing Trent when she says this, and it makes me reconsider my assumptions about their relationship. I figured she was more or less a glorified groupie, but hearing her now puts a different gloss on it.

"You make it sound like Picasso's *Guernica*," I say.

She replies, "Great art only comes from great suffering, right?"

This makes me pause in thought for a moment, particularly the part about great suffering. Dr. Pitt hypothesized in his initial evaluation of Trent that he suffered from PTSD, and although he did not unearth anything specifically, it makes me wonder what Finley knows.

"What do you know about Trent's childhood?" I ask. "You mentioned that his mom was a little crazy and that he got bullied at school?"

"Yeah," she says. "His mom got knocked up out of wedlock, but because she was a devout Catholic, she couldn't get him aborted. I guess she told him she tried ways to miscarry, but God was determined to punish her for what she'd done. She always told Trent that he was the curse for her sins." She shakes her head slowly. "What kind of monster says that about her own kid?"

"That's awful," I mutter, storing every detail in my memory as best I can.

"When he was little, she'd drag him to church all the time as if it was going to fix him, and then when it did not and he got older, she'd make him whip himself like some medieval monk. I thought he was lying at first when he told me, but then he showed me his bare back and the whole thing was just covered in scars... Looked like a wild animal had tried to claw him to death..."

She pauses to prevent the tears from overcoming her again. As I wait, my mind goes to the lyrics of Trent's songs that criticize religion and it suddenly makes so much sense why he hates God and Christianity.

Finley soon adds, "I don't know too many details about the bullying when he was in school, but I know he got harassed constantly and got the shit kicked out of him a bunch of times."

"Was he a good student?" I ask, considering the poetic nature of his song lyrics. "It seems like he would've done well in English at least."

"No," she answers. "People like him do not fit into school. He can't sit still, for one thing. He's got what he calls the monkey brain. Says ideas swarm his mind like hornets. He got in trouble all the time because of that and his teachers hated him for it. He eventually just stopped going to school altogether."

"I see..." I reply, pausing so that she can continue.

Her eyes lock with mine, and tears begin to gather as she asks, "You're really going to try to help him?"

"I am certainly going to do my best," I say. "I can't guarantee anything, but I have had a lot of patients show significant improvement over the years."

"Good," she says, the faintest hint of a smile coming to her expression. "Then maybe he can get out of here and we can go on with our lives."

I feel a hollowness come over the room after she says this, and with hesitation, I reply, "Ms. Keenan... I have to tell you that no matter how much better he gets, it's very unlikely that he'll be able to come home."

Her faint smile disappears. "Why is that?" she asks.

"The things he's done," I say. "They can't just be... *forgiven*."

She stares at me with confusion as if she does not have the slightest clue what I am talking about.

"The murders?" I add.

Her expression slowly hardens and she replies, "How many times do I have to tell you? He did not kill those people."

I try to say, "I understand how difficult it must be to—"

"No!" she interjects. She rises from the chair, and the despair in her eyes transforms into savagery. "He didn't do it!" she screams.

"Ms. Keenan—" I say, trying to calm her down.

"You tricked me, you bitch. You don't want to help him. You just want to keep framing him."

The guards immediately come over to her and restrain her arms.

"Get off of me!" she growls, struggling against their bulk. "They're raping me! They're raping me!"

Despite how much smaller she is than the guards, her strength is deceptive and she flails about wildly, kicking and clawing at them like a rabid animal.

"Get off me!"

The guards continue to struggle against her, but within a matter of moments they drag her out of the visitation room.

SEVEN

Trent stares at me from across one of the tables in the empty visitation area. His hands and ankles are both cuffed to his seat so he can barely move.

"Why are we meeting in here?" he asks me flatly.

"Because, after what you did in the day room last week, I do not particularly trust you."

His expression shows no reaction. "Is that why the guards are in here too?"

"Yes," I say, glancing at the two men standing at the nearest wall ready to pounce at a moment's notice if need be.

"What about patient-therapist confidentiality?" he asks.

"They know not to listen," I tell him. "Besides, this isn't the first session they've had to monitor."

Trent snickers ever so slightly. "You wise up quickly, don't you?"

"About what?" I ask.

"About me," he says. "It didn't take you long to realize that you can't trust me."

"Maybe in time I will."

"*I* wouldn't," he replies.

"What about Finley?" I counter. "She seems to trust you an awful lot."

He rolls his eyes. "She's even crazier than I am. Telling everyone that I'm innocent? That I had nothing to do with those murders?" He shakes his head ruminatively. "With all the evidence in that house, who else could it have been?"

"Maybe she just loves you too much to accept the truth. She wouldn't be the first person to fall into that trap."

"Like I said—crazy."

"Loving you is insane?" I ask.

He scoffs, "Love in general. It's just something humans made up to make themselves feel better."

"But you're engaged to her," I say. "That must mean something."

He shrugs.

"How would you describe your relationship with her?"

"Infatuation," he says with intensity. "Unreciprocated infatuation."

"You don't care about her?"

"I don't care about anyone," he replies apathetically.

"I don't understand. Why stay engaged to her then?"

"She's the only one who's been willing to stick around despite knowing what I am."

My brow furrows slightly. "What do you mean?"

"I'm like a fatal car crash. Everyone's curiosity draws them to the scene, but as soon as they see blood, they turn away. But not Finley. She wants to see the blood and the bodies. The more she learned about my demons, the closer she drew toward me. She is the moth and I am the flame."

Hearing him talk like this makes me wonder what kind of darkness lies within him. What secrets hide within his psyche?

I add, "If that's the case, then why didn't she live in the Bakersfield house with you?"

"I work best when I'm alone," he answers. "I needed a space where I could fully submerge myself in isolation."

"That makes sense. Did you choose that house for any particular reason?"

He grins slightly. "Of course I did. I wanted to be somewhere that I could shed my skin and see what lay beneath."

I glance at him quizzically. "What do you mean by that?"

"Read between the lines," he says, taunting me.

"It sounds like self-analysis to me, but I am not trying to put words in your mouth."

"Why not?" he retorts. "Everyone else does."

"Because I want to get to know you," I answer.

"You want to get to know me?" he says skeptically. "Listen to my music. Everything you want to know is there."

"I must admit, I am fascinated by the most recent album," I tell him. "The title track in particular. I know it's an allusion to the Poe story, but I can't help but feel like you're pouring yourself out for everyone to see all of the rawness within. It hits me profoundly, yet I do not fully understand why."

"Because the song isn't about me," he says. "The song is a looking glass back onto the listener. What you think you see in me is actually what you see in yourself."

"I suppose so," I say, although truth be told, I think he is deflecting and projecting here. A classic defense mechanism.

"Do you feel safer believing the song is about me?" he asks.

"What do you mean by *safer*?"

"It's one thing to be caught in a downward spiral," he answers. "But it's a whole other level to submit yourself to the power of the current and not fight against the inevitable. People would rather choke to death on a lie than digest the truth."

"Do *you* live by that?" I counter. "Do you digest the truth?"

"I don't claim to be perfect, but I at least see what's in front of me."

Silence falls between us again, so I bring the subject back to where I started. "So how did the Bakersfield house specifically help you *shed your skin*, as you said? You could've isolated yourself anywhere. Why there?"

His eyes narrow. "You mean, why Stanley Palmer?"

"I guess," I say, hesitant.

He smirks again. "You are a curious one, aren't you?"

"Curious about *you*—yes."

He leans forward as far as the shackles will allow him to go before whispering, "You gotta watch out for curiosity. You might not like what you find out."

I ignore the eeriness of his comment and reply, "Is that what happened to *you*? Is that why you wanted to be in that house? Curiosity?"

He leans back again and a smile grows over his expression.

"No..." he mutters. "*That* was Larua's doing. He brought me to that house. I was just going along for the ride."

"Why did Larua bring you to the house?" I'm curious if he will use Larua as a way of dissociating himself from his experiences.

He grins. "Larua works in mysterious ways. He is my guide through the darkness. He knows where he's taking me. '*Theirs not to reason why. Theirs but to do and die'.*"

I sense that he's drifting into psychotic elusiveness, so I try to bring him back to reality. "How are the hallucinations anyway?" I ask.

"Not any worse than they were," he answers with a shrug. "Is that the kind of progress you're looking for?"

"It'll take some time for the Paliperidone to kick in," I tell him. "When it does, the hallucinations should improve."

"*Improve?*" he remarks. "It's just kicking dirt over the top of what's there. Hiding it from view. That's all any drug does—masks reality."

"Is that what the meth did for you?" I retort.

He shrugs, dismissing the question.

"That's where I come in," I add. "These sessions will hopefully get us to the root of your condition."

He starts to laugh softly, but the sound still echoes in the vacant visitation area.

"Why are you laughing?" I ask, my tone flat and unassuming.

"Your confidence," he answers. "'*I'll get to the root of your condition*'. The roots of what is going on with me are so deep and entangled that you're only going to get caught in the snare yourself. Let me give you some advice: send me to San Quentin and have them lock me up in the darkest hole they can find because no good is going to come from what you're doing."

I allow silence to fall between us for a moment, if for no other reason than to show I won't respond to this.

Finally, I say, "Tell me more about why Larua brought you to the Stanley Palmer house."

His eyes narrow and his smile disappears. "Why does it matter?" he asks.

"Because I was under the assumption that Larua appeared after you started living in the house, not before."

"I have been living with Larua for as long as I can remember," he says.

"What age do you think that was?"

He shrugs, answering, "Seven... maybe eight."

"Who were you living with at that time?" I ask. I assume he was living with his mom, but my hope is that it will open up a conversation about their relationship. Knowing that Trent's hallucinations began at such an early age makes me wonder if he experienced some type of trauma or abuse around that time. From what Finley told me, the abuse may have been at the hands of his mother.

Spitefully, Trent replies, "That bitch who gave birth to me."

"I take it you didn't get along with your mother?"

"You *are* insightful," he retorts. "No, we didn't get along."

"Do you want to tell me more about that?" I ask, hesitant because I do not want to trigger his already volatile temperament.

"What do you want to know?"

"Start with whatever comes to mind."

"Well, she hated the air I breathed. How's *that* for a start?"

"That's good," I reply, my tone sympathetic. "Why did she hate you?"

His expression hardens. "She had me out of wedlock but was a Catholic zealot. The way she saw it, I was the embodiment of her sins. Why *wouldn't* she hate me?"

"Did she ever say that to you directly?"

He scoffs, "Every goddamn day."

"Did she do anything to you because of that?" I ask.

"You mean, did she beat me?" he retorts with contempt. "She never put her hands on me, if that's what you're asking."

"What did she do?"

"Dragged me to church and made me kneel on pebbles until my knees bled. Made me whip myself with my own fucking belt and beg her false deity for mercy and forgiveness. Forced me to scrub my wounds with steel wool and bleach as part of the purification process afterward."

"That's horrible," I mutter, allowing my sympathies through.

"Yeah, well, that's fucking life, isn't it? A chain of miserable moments."

"And you were just a kid when she did that?" I ask.

He nods. "I sure as shit did not let her do that when I was big enough. I must have been twelve or thirteen when I took that belt and beat *her* to within an inch of her life. Doused her in a jug of Clorox so she could feel what I had felt my whole life. Goddamn psycho... She's lucky I didn't fucking kill her."

One would think that Trent's body would be seething with

anger by this point, but to my unease, he is completely calm, almost as if he is in a meditative state.

"What happened after that?" I ask.

"Family services took me away," he says. "At first the cops wanted to press charges against *me* and send me to juvie, but when they saw the scars on my back, they realized what she had been forcing me to do to myself and charged her instead."

"Where did you end up?"

"Out of the pan and into the goddamn fire," he answers. "You know how many people are foster parents simply so they can collect the checks? It's a fucking scam. I ran away so many times that when I turned sixteen they just stopped looking for me. Probably thought I was dead in a ditch somewhere. I bet those people couldn't believe their goddamn eyes when they started seeing my face in the media for my music. Like a corpse rose out of the ground."

"That's unbelievable..." I tell him. "And Larua was with you that whole time?"

Trent smiles and answers, "Every step of the way."

"It sounds like he helped you through a lot of that then?"

"In some ways," he says.

"But not in others?" I probe.

His eyes quickly lock with mine, and he looks at me in the same way he was staring at me in the day room last week.

"We're not talking about Larua," he replies with an iciness that curdles my blood. "You got that?"

EIGHT

Sleep continues to elude me, so much so that I don't even bother laying in bed to try.

Trent consumes my brain. The more I speak with him and the more he opens up to me about his childhood, the more I see behind his ghoulish facade. Trent Davis was not born into this world as the curse his mother made him out to be; he was transformed into it the same way that a dog is abused into savagery.

As for Trent's elusiveness regarding Larua, my guess is that the demonic voice is the manifestation of his abusive childhood and is therefore highly sensitive. I want to delve into this further, but I doubt he is in a place to confront those traumas yet, no less tell me about them.

Rarely do I feel true sympathies for my patients, but Trent's history strikes a nerve within me that I cannot help but feel deep in my core. I, too, am the victim of childhood abuse, and as bizarre as it may be to have empathy for a man like Trent Davis, I do.

Something he told me is sticking with me though: *everything I want to know about him is buried in his music.* Maybe he is leading me by the nose with this, but there is a chance that the dark secrets of his psyche are in plain view just waiting to be seen.

Sitting in my dark living room, I stare at my laptop screen and comb back through his music, analyzing the lyrics of the deep cuts of his albums.

From "R.I.P. (Rest in Pain)", part of the chorus is *"If the purpose of life is to feel, then I'll take the pain"*. "Stones or Sticks?" has a similar theme. The song tells the story of a boy whose abuser makes him choose to be beaten by stones or sticks, but by the end of the song, the boy grows up and bludgeons his abuser to death with a rock. An obvious allusion to Trent's mother now that I know the story behind it.

Another reference to his mother's abuse is "Tabasco" which contains the refrain *"Mix Tabasco in my tea to burn my curse out"* and finishes with *"Mother? I am going to kill you, and then I am going to fuck you!"* I'm a fan of The Doors myself, so I believe the latter part was inspired by Jim Morrison's drug-induced ranting from "The End".

The last song I look at is from *Into the Maelstrom* entitled "Mr. McFeely". It is a play on several songs from *Mister Rogers' Neighborhood*, using lines like *"Won't you be?"* and *"It's such a good feeling"*, but the gist of the song is anything but innocent or inspirational. In a fragmented, stream-of-consciousness style, it depicts the thoughts and feelings of a man luring and then molesting a child.

A flood of memories rises out of the deepest chasms of my own soul, and I almost can't bring myself to read the lyrics when I realize what they are about. Yet, I find myself reading them over and over again.

At first, I wonder if the lyrics are an admission of guilt on Trent's part? That perhaps they describe what he did to his victims before he murdered and cannibalized them. The more I read though, the more I consider where Trent was when he created the song: the home of Stanley Palmer, the Bakersfield

Boogeyman. Several lines directly connect to the infamous serial pedophile, such as *"My tie is your noose"* a reference to how Stanley Palmer used neckties to asphyxiate his victims, as well as *"That's what you get. A speedy delivery"*, a twisted catch-phrase that he said to his victims when he was finished abusing them.

I feel disturbed to my core as I wonder why Trent would write such a demented song. As I consider this though, what he said to me in our most recent conversation surfaces in my mind: "Larua brought me to that house. I was just going along for the ride."

What did he mean by that, I think? Why did he feel that was the best place to "shed his skin and see what lay beneath"?

This latter statement lingers in my psyche for a moment before it hits me: if Larua is the manifestation of his childhood trauma, then why would Larua bring him to the Stanley Palmer house? Why wouldn't he be drawn to something connected to his mother since she seemed to be the source of his trauma?

"Holy shit..." I breathe to myself as the realization strikes me.

Knowing that Trent was born in 1982 and Stanley Palmer committed his crimes between 1987 and 1992, I immediately go to Trent's file to see if he ever lived in or near Bakersfield during his childhood. As bad as the abuse from his mother was, I do not think this is what caused Larua to appear. I cannot help but wonder if Trent was one of Stanley Palmer's victims, the trauma of which was so sinister that it forced him to compart-mentalize it as a figment of his imagination?

What I discover only partially confirms my theory. Trent did, in fact, live in Bakersfield as a kid, but only from 1985 to 1986. I then go to the internet to search for a list of Stanley Palmer's victims, but Trent's name isn't on the list. Either my hypothesis is wrong, or Stanley Palmer was abusing children for a longer period of time than investigators realized.

I grab my telephone and dial the number for Dr. Pitt, the forensic psychiatrist who initially evaluated and diagnosed Trent.

"Hey, Dr. Fletcher," he answers cheerfully. "How are you?"

"I was hoping to discuss Trent Davis," I tell him.

"Oh..." he mutters, his tone hardening. "How has he been for you guys?"

"As good as can be expected, I suppose. Although I feel like I am chasing a ghost when it comes to treating him."

"I do not know if a man like him is *treatable* in the traditional sense of the word. Perhaps *manageable*, but *treatable* is a whole other realm. Of course, I only spent a few days with him."

"That's partly what I was hoping to talk to you about," I say. "I know that you suspected he suffered from post-traumatic stress, but you did not note anything specific as a source of trauma. I am just curious as to what made you think PTSD was at play?"

"It was a hunch for sure, but I did not believe the demonic possession was a mere symptom of his schizophrenia. Based on what I have seen in other patients, I think it's a manifestation of something far more sinister than that."

"Do you have any guesses as to what kind of trauma he experienced?"

"Definitely physical abuse of some kind, given the barbaric nature of his crimes."

"What about sexual abuse?" I ask.

"Possibly," he answers. "Although Trent swore he did nothing sexual with his victims before or after he killed them, so it's unlikely that he himself experienced sexual abuse."

"Do you believe that?" I reply. "That he did not do anything sexual with his victims?"

"Yes and no..." he says with hesitation. "In my opinion, power was Trent's primary objective; however, the intimacy of cannibalism could have provided him with sexual gratification of some kind. Similar to what it did for Jeffrey Dahmer. Of course, Trent was actively withdrawing from meth and barbiturates at the time of my evaluation, so it wasn't easy to get a straight answer out of him."

"Did he ever say anything about why he chose the Stanley Palmer house?"

"No," he answers. "Given how publicly controversial he was as a musician, I would guess he did it for sensationalism."

"So you don't think he had a personal connection to Stanley Palmer in some way?"

Dr. Pitt is silent for a moment before answering, "Do *you*?"

"I don't know," I reply. "At this point, all I have are theories based on the lyrics of his songs. I was able to get him to tell me about the abuse he experienced from his mother, but it doesn't explain why he isolated himself in *that* particular house."

"Does it need to?" Dr. Pitt asks. "Given his condition, it wouldn't surprise me if most of what he did had irrational motives."

"I suppose..." I say, trailing off with doubt.

"Or maybe he was just obsessed with Stanley Palmer," suggests Dr. Pitt. "It wouldn't be the first time someone was infatuated with a criminal."

"I hadn't considered that," I say. "If that's the case though, doesn't it seem like he would have committed similar crimes? Aside from the house, there really aren't any other connection points between his crimes and Stanley Palmer's."

"That is true," he says. "Have you tried asking him directly?"

"Of course," I say, "and every time he gives me some enigmatic answer. '*I wanted to shed my skin and see what lay beneath*'. What does *that* mean?"

"Your guess is as good as mine," Dr. Pitt says. "One thing you can't overlook with a man like Trent Davis is the impact of his psychosis. He'll speak in riddles that have no answers, and those who are naive enough to try to solve them will end up down a rabbit hole to nowhere."

I am silent for a moment, my memory replaying several of the enigmatic statements that Trent has fed me, namely *Listen to my music. Everything you want to know is there.* Was he giving me a key to his soul or simply coaxing me into a wild-goose chase? How many of his songs are nothing more than wolf traps?

"Dr. Fletcher?" adds Dr. Pitt, shaking me out of my rumination.

"Yes. Sorry."

"Do you understand what I am saying?" he asks.

"Yes, of course," I reply. "I appreciate your thoughts."

"Do not hesitate to reach out," he tells me. "I know how exhausting it is to work with guys like him."

"Thanks," I say and hang up the phone.

NINE

I feel conflicted for several days after my conversation with Dr. Pitt. Is Trent being truthful about his childhood traumas and, if he is, was he an unknown victim of Stanley Palmer, or is Trent's psychosis scattering breadcrumbs to lead me down a path to nowhere? I cannot simply ask Trent if he is being honest with me, so I will have to find some other way of confirming my suspicions.

I begin with the California Department of Social Services, asking them to send over all information pertaining to Trent's case starting with when he was first removed from his mother's custody through his time in the foster care system.

The file is dense with several hundred pages of forms and reports. There are also dozens of photographs documenting the physical abuse he endured, most notably the scarring on his back from the self-flagellation that his mother forced him to do. I almost can't believe what I see in the photos. His back is a mosaic of abuse; some of the wounds are still fresh while others have scarred over from years earlier.

Combing through the initial reports, I find that his mother was evaluated by a psychiatrist shortly after she was arrested

and they diagnosed her with paranoid schizophrenia. Schizophrenia is extremely heritable, so this only confirms Dr. Pitt's
initial diagnosis of Trent as well as my ongoing observations of
his symptomatology. I make a note to myself to look into where
his mother is now so that I can try to interview her if possible. I
figure if I can understand her better, maybe I can understand
him as well.

After Trent was taken by social services, he was placed in a
residential treatment facility on the fringes of Los Angeles. He
remained there for three months until he began his journey
through the foster care system. He lived in homes throughout
the southern California area, never staying longer than a few
months at each. Most of the time he ran away; however, there
were two instances in which his foster parents had him removed
from their homes. His last documented residence was in 1998
when he was sixteen years old. After that, his caseworker at the
time marked him as a runaway and his file became inactive.

Trent's earliest music was not discovered on YouTube until
2009, so it is anybody's guess as to where he went or what he
was doing for the decade that followed. In truth, it is a miracle
that he wasn't found dead in an alley somewhere. He somehow
managed to keep his life together enough to spark a successful
music career and maintain it for as long as he did.

What I learn about Trent certainly does not excuse what he
has done, but it at least helps to explain why and how it
happened. In addition to the schizoaffective disorder and the
PTSD, he clearly suffers from deep-seated abandonment and
attachment issues, factors that only exacerbate his complex
condition.

I finally feel like I am getting somewhere with him. One of
the toughest parts of treating a condition like his is unearthing
the root cause, and I get the sense I am on the right track.

Despite my encouragement, I have to stay patient.
Exploring the black hole in his history is going to take time.

Only he can tell me about his life in those years, and pulling intelligible information out of him has proven to be a painstaking task.

I seclude myself in my office at the hospital and search for his mother to see if she is still alive and within the Los Angeles area. I know it's a long shot, but speaking to her may reveal more of what lurks in Trent's mind.

After some digging, I learn that his mother currently lives at the Romero House, a Franciscan convent on the southern edge of the Santa Lucia Wilderness. I doubt she'll agree to speak to me, especially about Trent, so instead of calling the convent, I decide to drive the two hours to try to meet with her in person.

My motives are slightly selfish, I will admit. As stressful as things have been recently, I could use some time away from the hospital, especially a peaceful drive along the coastline. Dr. Maynard frequently talked about the importance of maintaining a work-life balance, so I try to keep her advice in mind.

Despite the fact that Pantano is only twenty miles away from the nearest beach, I haven't seen the ocean in months. There is something about the infinite expanse of the Pacific that calms and restores me. Maybe it is simply the fact that it allows me to forget about my professional duties for a few hours, or maybe it's more existential than that. Seeing the mass of water pushing to the horizon and beyond makes me realize just how small and insignificant humans are in this world. How powerless we truly are in the grand scheme of everything. The perspective is comforting.

The Romero House is tucked up into the foothills of Big Sur, and it makes perfect sense why the original founders chose this particular area for a convent. If God does in fact exist, then this is the place you would most likely catch a glimpse of Him.

The buildings that make up the complex are simple. There is a small administration building, a chapel, and living quarters that border a forested courtyard at the center of the campus.

What strikes me most is the silence. An absence of sound found only in places of the utmost reverence.

Pantano State Hospital is quite the opposite. Noise rises out of the floor the way mist rises from a lake's surface at dawn. As if the building is purging itself of the madness contained within.

When I walk into the main building, a young nun greets me.

"Welcome to the Romero House," she says. "How can I help you?"

"I was hoping to meet with an old friend of mine," I tell her. "Sister Catherine Davis?"

"Oh?" she replies. "Is she expecting you?"

"No. I was on my way up to San Jose and figured I'd stop by."

"I see," she says. "Let me see if she's available."

The young nun hurries down a corridor and appears shortly after with a much older nun in her wake. Her wrinkled face is tightly framed by her habit, and her expression is austere and authoritative.

"Good afternoon," she says to me. "I am Mother Alberta, the abbess here. Sister Naomi tells me you'd like to see Sister Catherine?"

"Yes," I say. "If it's not too much trouble, of course."

"No trouble at all," Mother Alberta replies. "It's just that Sister Catherine doesn't have many visitors. How do you know her?"

I hesitate briefly. I can't tell her my real reason, so I quickly throw something together.

"Oh, she's an old family friend," I say. "She and my mom were friends back when I was a kid."

"I see," Mother Alberta replies, although I am not sure if she buys my story. She turns to Sister Naomi and adds, "Why don't you see if Sister Catherine is available to have a visitor."

The young nun nods and hurries off again.

Mother Alberta remains with me, her face expressionless within the rigid confines of her habit.

I stand there awkwardly as regret rises within me. I'm not religious in any way, but lying to a nun—an abbess, no less—feels inappropriate if not immoral. Worst of all, I get the feeling that she knows I am lying about my association with Catherine Davis.

Mother Alberta says nothing to me about it. She simply waits, silent judgment radiating off her.

Several minutes pass before Sister Naomi returns with who I am assuming is Sister Catherine. At first glance, she looks like any other stranger I have encountered, but when she gets closer, I see her nose is deformed, likely from not getting it treated properly after Trent nearly beat her to death all those years ago. Then I notice the wrinkles of old scars on her cheekbones and brow, and it makes me wonder if Mother Alberta and the other nuns know the secrets of her past.

"Who are you?" Catherine says to me gruffly.

"Stephanie Fletcher?" I answer with hesitation. "You and my mom were friends when I was a kid?"

Catherine looks at me skeptically for several moments and asks, "What was your mama's name?"

"Roxanne?" I say, my regret rising even more.

Catherine's eyes narrow, and I can't tell if she is genuinely trying to rack her memory for my mother's name or if she is simply toying with me.

Finally, a smile comes to her hardened expression, and it is then that I really see the hereditary connection between her and Trent. The way her mouth curls and her cheekbones shift is exactly how he looks when he grins at me.

"Of course I remember her!" she replies with joy. "How is she these days? It's been so long."

Her response catches me off guard and I fumble for my words. "Oh, she... uh... she's hanging in there."

"Good," Catherine says, her smile growing. "Why don't we go for a walk and you can catch me up?"

"Sure..." I say, wondering if she actually thinks we knew each other at some point in our lives.

Mother Alberta and Sister Naomi say nothing as Catherine leads me out of the main building and into the courtyard. Once we are a good distance away from the main building, she stops and faces me.

"I am so happy to hear that your mother is doing alright," she says to me. "And you seem to be doing pretty well yourself."

"I am really sorry," I reply ashamedly, "but you don't know me or my mom. I lied back there so that I could talk to you alone."

Catherine grins. "Of course I don't know you," she says frankly. "Even Sister Naomi could tell you were lying. But you sought me out and came all this way to talk to me about something, so I figured I'd play along just to see what you wanted."

"Oh..." I mutter, immediately feeling foolish and saying nothing else in response.

"So, what is it then?" she prods. "Why did you come find me?"

"It's a long story," I say with a sigh, "and I am not entirely sure where to start."

"Anywhere is fine," she says assuredly.

"I am a psychiatrist at the Pantano State Hospital," I begin. "One of my patients is your son, Trent."

Her brow furrows slightly. "I don't have a son," she says.

I remain silent for a moment, reading her expression to see if she really doesn't remember Trent. Her reaction seems genuine.

"You do," I reply slowly. "Although I can understand why you would want to believe you do not."

"You've mistaken me with someone else," she says with a

slight laugh. "I am pretty sure I, of all people, would know if I had a son or not."

"Ms. Davis—"

"*Sister Catherine*," she corrects me.

"Sorry... Sister Catherine, I realize how bizarre this is, but I could really use your help."

"I do not know how I could help you," she replies, her jovial tone becoming firm. "I do not know anyone named Trent, and I certainly don't have a son with that name."

"I know you want to believe that," I tell her, "but what I am telling you is the truth. You had a son in 1982 at the Kern County Hospital—"

"Shut your mouth," she hisses, her voice hushed so only I can hear. "It's true that I gave birth to a child all those years ago, but let me make something clear: he was never my son. Do you understand me?"

I nod, but say nothing.

"Is that why you came all the way out here?" she adds. "To ask me about him?"

"Yes," I mutter.

"Well, he stopped being my problem a long time ago," she replies. "So whatever he's gotten himself into is between him and God."

Hesitantly, I say, "So... you don't know what happened? What he did?"

"No," she answers. "In case you haven't noticed, this is a convent; we intentionally remove ourselves from the sins of society so that we may be free of the burden of distraction and strengthen our connection with God."

I say nothing in response, my mind racing as I figure out how to proceed.

Apathetically she adds, "What happened to him anyway? He hurt or something?" There is a sense of hope in her tone when she asks this, and I cannot help but feel sickened by it.

"Goodness, no," I answer.

"Then what?" she adds. "Someone kill him?" Again, her tone is eerily sanguine.

"No," I say. "He's not dead."

"Pity," she replies. "There's too much sin floating around this world already."

"Ms. Davis—"

"*Sister Catherine*," she corrects again.

"Trent murdered six people," I blurt before I can think of a more subtle way of phrasing it.

That reverent silence falls over us like a heavy fog, and Catherine stares blankly at me. I cannot tell if it is out of shock, horror, or complete apathy.

Her expression wrinkles and she whispers, "He did *what*?"

"Last year..." I tell her, "during the pandemic..."

She stares at me again, her head shaking ever so slowly back and forth. "I..." she tries to say. "How..."

"You don't want to know the details," I answer. "Trust me."

"Oh... Lord..." she breathes, lifting her head toward the sky and falling to her knees.

"Sister Catherine—" I say, quickly kneeling beside her in case she faints.

Eyes closed, she keeps her face cast upward and locks her hands out in front of her. "*Ave Maria*," she mutters rapidly, "*gratia plena, Dominus tecum. Benedicta—*"

"Sister Catherine—" I try to interrupt her, but she continues to rattle off the Latin prayer as if it is the only thing keeping God from striking her down on this very spot.

She repeats the prayer two more times, each incantation faster and more panicked than the previous one. When she is finished, she remains on the ground with her hands clenched so hard together that her fingers have turned bright red.

"Sister Catherine?" I breathe.

"This is the curse for my sins," she mutters ruminatively.

"No matter how much I repent, no matter how hard I pray, the Lord cannot forgive me. He is omnipotent, and yet, even He is powerless to forgive me for what I have brought into this world. I knew it the moment I laid eyes on him that he was the beast of the number six-hundred and sixty-six. I tried to do as God had instructed Abraham, but He wouldn't allow it. I tried to purge him of the evil within, but he is not of God. He is the spawn of Satan. The incarnation of sin. And just as the Holy Virgin bore the Saviour, so also have I borne the antichrist."

Sister Catherine begins to sob, and like a feeble dam trying to hold back a raging flood, her body quivers and heaves.

I place my hand gently on her back to try to calm her, but her hysteria only grows, so much so that I doubt she even notices I am still here.

By this point, the commotion that we have caused gets the attention of several other nuns, and they hurry over to us when they see Catherine's distress.

"Get Mother Alberta," one says to another. "Tell her that Sister Catherine is having one of her fits."

"I'm sorry. This is my fault, I upset her," I tell them as they kneel beside her and comfort her.

"It's not your fault," one of them says. "This happens quite often, actually."

"She'll be okay in an hour or so," says the other. "She just needs time to calm down."

I rise and take several steps back, watching the two nuns soothe Catherine as if she is a child in the midst of a crisis.

This is going to sound terrible to say, but as I watch them console her, I feel no pity or sympathy for her. Despite the torment taking hold of her, all I see is a wolf in sheep's clothing.

TEN

"Who are you really?" Mother Alberta asks me from the dank confines of her quarters.

Behind her desk hangs a single portrait of the Sacred Heart of Jesus. It feels like his gaze is locked directly on me as if he is the judge glancing down at me from his courtroom bench.

"My name is Dr. Stephanie Fletcher," I tell her. "I am a psychiatrist at the Pantano State Hospital."

"What brought you here?" she replies. "Why did you wish to speak to Sister Catherine?"

"I cannot tell you," I say.

Alberta stares at me flatly. "*Cannot* or *will not*?" she retorts.

"Both..." I answer. "It's confidential and deeply personal to Catherine."

"I see," Alberta says. "You're not by chance Catholic, are you?"

"No," I say.

"So I am assuming you're not familiar with the Franciscan Missionaries then?"

I shake my head.

"Well," she adds in a passively condescending way, "when a

child of God chooses to join an order such as ours, she surrenders herself completely to our Lord, His Son, and the Holy Mother Church. That includes anything that is, what you call, deeply personal or confidential to her."

Trying not to sound confrontational, I reply, "If that's true, then I imagine you already know."

Alberta's gaze does not budge or waver, as if she is incapable of expression. "I imagine we do," she says frankly. "We confess our sins openly and often here, and Sister Catherine bears a particularly heavy cross."

"She does," I say.

Alberta interrogates me with her gaze briefly before adding, "So why did you come here?"

"To learn as much as I can about *her cross*, as you put it."

Alberta nods with thought. "Her son..." she says.

"Yes."

"I do not know how much you're going to get out of her," Alberta adds. "Most days, she pretends that he never exists. The days that she does acknowledge him... well... you witnessed firsthand what can happen to her."

"She has a very serious psychiatric condition," I say. "Until she receives proper treatment, she will never be able to cope with what has happened in her life."

"She has Christ for that," replies Alberta with a threatening firmness. "That being said, we are not as archaic here as the modern world may believe. Sister Catherine does receive psychiatric treatment. It's been a stipulation of her membership for as long as she has lived here, in fact. Believe it or not, she has improved dramatically in the time that she has been with us."

"I see..." I say, staring at her blankly as the silence settles over us.

Alberta adds, "So what were you hoping to ask her about?"

"I have some theories about why her son is the way he is, and I was hoping she might be able to shed some light on those."

"That may prove to be too difficult for her," she says. "I imagine I know most of what she remembers about that time of her life anyway. Ask me what you were planning on asking her."

"Okay..." I answer, unsure that she will be able to provide the information that I am looking for. "Is it true that she forced Trent to whip himself when he was a child?"

"Yes," Alberta says, her expression as flat as if I asked her what she had for breakfast that morning.

"And is it true that he nearly beat her to death when he was twelve?"

"Yes," she replies.

"Did *she* ever lay a hand on him?" I ask.

"No," Alberta answers.

"She never beat him herself? Abused him sexually?"

"Is he claiming she did?" she asks skeptically.

"No, but given his symptoms, I have reason to believe he was abused by someone. Physically or sexually."

Alberta's brow furrows slightly. "She never abused him... Not like *that* anyway."

"Do you know who did?" I ask.

She shakes her head slowly. "I do not," she replies. "I do know that he was a pathological liar though."

"How do you know that?" I ask with skepticism.

She sneers slightly, the first semblance of human expression that I have seen from her. "From what Sister Catherine has told me, Trent accused a lot of people of a lot of things when he was a child. He accused priests and congregants of their church of trying to molest him. He accused his teachers of beating and berating him. He even accused other children of trying to kill him. Not a single accusation bore any truth."

"I see," I reply, although in my mind I dismiss her hypothesis that he was doing it simply to get attention. It is probably true that most of his accusations were false, but I wonder if they were in fact his subconscious mind crying out for help. I add, "Has Catherine ever mentioned the name Stanley Palmer to you?"

"Yes..." Alberta says with hesitation. "Apparently Trent accused him of assault as well. *After* the allegations against Mr. Palmer started to emerge, of course. But they weren't even living in Bakersfield at that time."

"They were before," I say. "Isn't there a chance that Trent was one of his first victims?"

"I suppose... But given Trent's track record, it's more likely that he lied about it to get attention. It's very common in children like that."

"Children like what?" I reply, trying to squelch my resentment at her phrasing. "Children who are grossly neglected by a mother with untreated schizophrenia?"

Alberta nods. "To put it bluntly... yes."

"Blunt or not, it's reality."

Alberta stares at me firmly for a moment before replying, "I know it's easy to judge someone like Sister Catherine, but her sins are between her and God. All *we* can do is love her and support her in her repentance."

"What about Trent?" I counter. "Are his sins between him and God too?"

"Sins?" she mutters with disgust. "What he has done is far beyond mortal sin. No child of God, no matter how adrift he may be, could do what he did to those poor girls. The secular world says that he is possessed by a demon as if it's the punchline of a joke, but as far as I am concerned, it is anything but a joke. He *is* the devil incarnate. Look into the eyes of a man like that and you will see a blackness that is not of our divine world. It's a blackness that is darker than the deepest pits of hell."

"So you don't think that a man like Trent Davis can be saved?" I reply.

"No," she says firmly. "Evil like that is beyond conversion.

You can mask it or pretend it isn't there, but you cannot rectify it."

I say nothing in response to this, my mind mulling over Alberta's words. As a clinician, I believe that no person is beyond repair. All people, no matter how broken they may be, have the right to rehabilitation. The right to hope. But Alberta's faith gives her a luxury that I do not have; she has a scapegoat in her superstitions. Beliefs driven by fear and folly that for thousands of years have allowed society to treat the insane as if they were savages.

Luckily, science has proven otherwise in the last century. Psychological abnormality is not beyond our understanding or our control. In fact, its cause is often at our own hands.

Yet, it is easier for people to believe in archaic demonology because it gives them that false sense of security that men like Trent Davis were born evil, not molded into it.

ELEVEN

For the first time since Trent has arrived at the hospital, he is showing signs of normalcy. Even in the sterile fluorescent light of the visitation area, the pallor in his face is fading, and his skin no longer looks like tissue paper stretched across the edges of his skull. Even the hollows of his eyes are beginning to brighten, revealing the chocolate-brown hue of his irises.

"How are you feeling?" I ask him from across the table.

"Better," he says. "Much better, actually."

"You look better. Like you're finally getting some sleep."

He nods. "I never realized how little I was sleeping before. Even with the barbs."

"You're sleeping through most of the night then?"

"Yeah."

"No night terrors?"

He shakes his head. "That shit you've got me on must be some powerful stuff. Better than any other drug I have had before."

"Well, the Paliperidone is made for your condition. Meth and amobarbital are not."

He shrugs and his shackles rustle beneath the table. "Gotta work with what you've got."

"How are your other symptoms?" I ask. "The hallucinations and the suicidal thoughts?"

He answers with a grin, "Haven't heard that little fucker in over a week. Same with the suicidal thoughts." He pauses and glances down into his lap. He looks relieved, as if he is Sisyphus being told he no longer has to roll the boulder uphill for eternity.

"That's good," I say. "I'm pleased you're feeling better mentally. It means you can actually start the healing process."

"How am I going to do that?" he asks.

"By confronting the things that have shaped who you are and what you've done. Digging deep into your psyche and getting rid of everything that's been building up in there."

"Head shrinking?" he scoffs in jest. "Yeah, no thanks."

"I know you don't *want* to do it, but you *need* to if you want to get better long-term."

"Better for what?" he retorts. "It's not like I'm going to leave this place if I do, right?"

It's a question I've been asked before by other inmates with long sentences. "Quality of life for one thing," I answer. "The better you are, the more privileges you can have and the more enjoyable your time here will be."

He replies sardonically, "You mean, I can sit in the day room without being chained to my chair? What a privilege..."

"You know I am talking about more than that. Besides, if you show real progress over the long term, you may be able to get transferred to a low-security hospital at some point. Those facilities are like country clubs in comparison to this place."

He glowers at me skeptically. "I murdered six people. What judge is going to allow me to be transferred to a low-security hospital?"

"You'd be surprised," I say. "I have had a number of patients who have received transfers."

"Any of them do what I did?"

"Murder?" I reply.

"No," he says, his tone becoming harsher. "Cannibalism."

"No..." I answer. "You're the first to do that."

"That's what I thought," he mutters, pausing for a moment. "You know I only drank their blood, right? That bullshit about me eating their organs was all for the media."

"What'd you do with them then?" I ask, surprised that he is willingly telling me any of this.

He answers flatly, "Burned them in the fireplace."

"Why?"

"*I will go into thy house with burnt offerings,*" he says. "*I will pay thee my vows.*"

"I beg your pardon?" I say.

"*Then shalt thou be pleased with the sacrifices of right-eousness, with burnt offerings,*" he adds.

My brow furrows quizzically. "You burned them as sacrifices?"

He smirks. "*Thus sayeth the Lord.*"

"I'm confused. You said you didn't believe in God yet you killed those people for Him?"

"No," he scoffs. "I just find it amusing how hypocritical the Bible is."

"So why'd you burn them then?" I ask. "Why'd you kill the people in the first place?"

"For Larua. Everything was for Larua."

"And Larua brought you to the Stanley Palmer house?"

He nods.

"Why do you suppose they did that? I mean, of all the houses in California, why that one?"

Trent eyes me carefully. "Why do *you* think they picked it?"

"I don't know," I say. "That's why I am asking."

"You're full of shit," he replies with a grin. "I think you have a very particular theory for how we ended up there."

I hesitate, wondering if this is the right time to directly ask him if he was abused by Stanley Palmer.

"Go on, Dr. Fletcher," he says. "Dazzle me with your psychoanalysis. Why did Larua draw me to that house?"

"Well," I say, "I have been wondering if you crossed paths with Stanley Palmer at some point."

"Crossed paths?" he replies tauntingly. "You're going to have to be more specific than that."

"Did you ever meet him or know him?" I ask, trying to gently coax him into talking about it, and watching his expression for any sign of emotion or reaction.

He only smirks. "Still not specific enough, I'm afraid. What do you really want to ask me?"

"Were you abused by him when you were a kid?" I reply, steeling myself for his answer.

Trent bursts into laughter. A loud, mocking laughter that echoes throughout the visitation area like a series of gunfire.

"And there it is!" he exclaims. "Shrinks must be sexually deprived because they always find a way to bring issues back to sex. Do you think that's why Freud was so obsessed with it? Because he wasn't getting enough action in the bedroom? Or maybe he was molested by his mother, and thus the birth of the Oedipus complex? Do you suppose *that* is what is going on with me? Some deep-seated sexual desire for my mother that cannot be imagined?"

As he talks, my own traumas crawl out of the depths of my psyche and rise to the surface of my consciousness. The face of my abuser. The things that were done to me and what I was forced to do.

I suppress any reaction to the memories though, focusing as much as I can on the present moment.

"Your song 'Tabasco' certainly hints at that," I answer,

hoping that a little bit of verbal sparring will get Trent out of his current thought trench.

"*Touché*," he replies playfully. "Of course, the particular lines you're talking about are just homage to the Lizard King. An old tip of the cap from one poet to another."

"Did she really make you drink tea mixed with Tabasco?" I ask, the other lyrics of the song coming to mind.

"Yes," he says. "She was a fucking lunatic."

I don't respond to Trent as I consider my recent interaction with his mother.

A grin emerges on his face and he adds, "I guess the apple didn't fall far from the tree."

TWELVE

I still remember my abuse as if it happened yesterday. I was eight years old. My parents went out for the evening and my babysitter was a teenage girl from our neighborhood, Michelle Fischer. She had watched me a couple of times before so I was familiar with her. She played dolls with me which surprised me because she was a high schooler and had grown out of childish things like that. I figured she was just being nice, but it made me feel good all the same. I liked her, and as far as I could tell, she liked me.

She let me watch movies that my parents never would have let me watch. *The Shining. Poltergeist. Friday the 13th. Halloween.* R-rated movies that I only half understood. Like seeing clips of war without knowing what "war" actually is. She told me I had to keep this a secret or else we would both get into big trouble.

Michelle liked the violent and sexual parts of the movies, so she would rewind those and watch them again and again. The part where Jack Nicholson slams the ax blade into Scatman's chest. When Kevin Bacon's throat is lethally pierced with an arrow from beneath the mattress he is laying on. Any scene that showed a bare-chested young woman, or a man and a woman being intimate with each other. She liked the latter in particular. She would freeze the television on those parts and watch them for several minutes. Sometimes she would just watch, but other times she touched herself in her private areas. She told me that was what women did—touched themselves like that—and that one day I would become a woman too. I didn't know what she meant by that, but I knew that I wanted to grow up and become a woman.

Then she started touching me. I remember feeling intensely uncomfortable with it, but she told me that was natural for a girl becoming a woman to feel that way. That womanhood was a mix of discomfort and pleasure. She told me to relax and let her help me become a woman.

She wanted me to keep all of this a secret too, like watching the movies themselves. We could *really* get into trouble, she said, and if I valued our friendship as much as she did, I would be sure to not tell anyone.

At the time, I did not know there were names for what she was doing to me.

Abuse.

Molestation.

Rape.

These words were not part of my vocabulary, so I certainly didn't realize how wrong her behavior was. All I knew was that she liked me, and if letting her do those things to me meant that she would like me more, then I wouldn't complain or tattle on her.

She was my babysitter and abuser for two years.

When she finally left, I never told my parents what she did to me. Instead, I repressed every memory about her. I pretended that those years of my life simply did not exist. Like I had been in a coma that whole time. Or temporarily dead.

I was a shy girl to begin with, but I receded into myself even more once the abuse started. No matter how much I tried to forget what happened, the imprint it left on me could not be swept away. I was a pane of broken glass, but still intact in the window frame. Still keeping the breeze from entering the home but marred with dozens of hairline fractures, waiting to crumble at a moment's notice.

The pane finally shattered when I was sixteen.

I don't remember feeling depressed at the time. Just extremely confused. I was confused about why Michelle had chosen to do those things to me. Why she had betrayed our friendship like that and lied to me. I had not become a woman like she said I would. Other girls my age were boy crazy, while I was attracted to nobody. Boys, girls, it didn't matter. I was skeptical of everyone and terrified of what they could do to me. My classmates thought I was either gay or autistic or some combination of both because of how I acted, and for a while, I wondered the same thing too. Prayed for it even. At least if I was a lesbian I had a chance to love and trust another person the way I was supposed to. If I was autistic, then at least I had an explanation for why I was the way I was. I might not like it, but I could understand myself and who I was.

Deep down though I knew that neither of these things was the case. I was simply broken. A plaything that couldn't even be handed down to someone less fortunate.

That was when I started cutting myself. Not because I wanted to die, but because I wanted to feel. The pain when the blade cut across my skin. Immediate. Intense. Completely in my control. I could stop at any moment or push myself beyond my limits. Whatever I wanted. Whatever I needed. There is no feeling more intense and intoxicating than pain.

That's the thing about abuse: it robs you of control. So much of victims' behavior is an attempt to regain that. It's why some women who have been sexually abused are promiscuous; they perceive a sense of choice in their actions. Power even. A woman can make a man dance like a marionette with the power of a single string if it is connected correctly.

I went in the opposite direction. I feared a repeat of the abuse, so I avoided any situation that could get me in the vicinity of that path. It extends far beyond physical intimacy. When you have been raped, it isn't just your body that was violated; it's your entire psyche, as if your abuser's hands groped your very soul.

I was pretty good about keeping my arms and legs covered, and the cutting a secret, but my P.E. teacher happened to notice the scars on my forearms one day and told the school counselor. Although I did not realize it at the time, that afternoon saved my life. My parents had no clue why I was cutting, but they knew I needed professional help. That's how I met Dr. Maynard.

Dr. Maynard was incredibly soft-spoken and unassuming. The type of person who was incapable of being judgmental in any way. I remember the first time she met with me, she hardly spoke a word, and when she did speak, it was usually a question of some kind. When I answered, I could tell she was not just hearing what I was saying; she was truly listening. Absorbing my words and feeling every emotion within them. Not trying to correct what I was feeling or how I was perceiving it. Just acknowledging them for what they were. Seeing me for who I actually was.

The walls of my psyche eventually broke with her. All of the memories that I had locked away suddenly burst forth as if I was confessing my sins on my deathbed.

Throughout all of this, she listened intently. When I cried, she gave me tissues. When I screamed, she did not tell me to calm down. She allowed me to feel every emotion that I needed to feel in those moments. The grief. The hatred. The self-loathing. The guilt. She understood that all of these were trapped inside of me, and the only way for me to get better was to purge them from my system. To push them out the way our skin pushes out a splinter as it heals.

Because of this vulnerability, I felt transference toward her several times, my deep-seated emotions toward Michelle being unconsciously redirected toward Dr. Maynard. Not once did she shy away from it or allow herself to be ensnared by it. She recognized transference as a therapeutic leverage point and used it to draw my infections out. I do not know how she did it so skillfully. Handled well, it can help someone overcome the worst trauma; handled poorly and it will destroy everyone who comes in contact with it.

When it was time for me to go to college and pick a career field to pursue, mental health was the obvious choice. I wanted to understand myself better, but I also wanted to help others who had experienced trauma. The more I learned, the more fascinated I became with the human mind. The enigmatic inter-action between our biology and our experiences. The opaque bridge that connected the physical world with the incorporeal.

How I ended up in correctional psychiatry was a happy accident. I did several internships at juvenile centers around Sacramento because it was a requirement for graduation, and as weird as this sounds, I was immediately drawn to corrections and criminology. In so many ways, criminal behavior is only a surface-level problem. When I work with criminals, it's more important to address the driving force deep in their mind. If we can repair the damage there, we have a hope of correcting their behavior in the future.

I suppose that is why I feel so passionately about corrections as rehabilitation rather than punishment. If our justice system only punishes people, then we are no better or more evolved than the ancient Babylonians. People are more motivated by reward than punishment, and our current thirty-five percent success rate further supports that. Criminality is corrected through treatment, not punishment.

It's not a quick or easy process. The more severe the crime and the more complex the dysfunction, the more challenging the rehabilitation. Working with patients like Trent Davis, it takes years to see significant improvement. Decades even.

But I have hope.

Dr. Maynard firmly believed that everyone had the potential to achieve mental health, and that the key to treatment was finding and purging the sources of dysfunction.

This mindset certainly worked for me, and as long as I stay patient with Trent, I believe it can work for him too.

THIRTEEN

I was worried that Trent was going to be triggered by my last session with him. Between asking him about Stanley Palmer and talking about his mother, I had touched on what I believe are two of the darkest spots of his psyche.

To my surprise, however, Trent shows no signs of reaction or regression over the next two weeks. His moods continue to become more predictable and his behavior less erratic. He even gets to the point where he asks me if he can have his fiancée, Finley, visit him.

"Are you sure?" I ask, hesitant about his request. "Can I ask why?"

"I want to end things with her," he answers.

"Oh..." I respond, slightly taken aback. "You do?"

"Yes," he says. "I need to move past this shit, and if I am ever going to do that, I can't have her lingering behind me like my goddamn shadow. She sends me several letters a day, constantly bringing up all this shit about my innocence and trying to convince me to appeal my sentencing. It's insane and I don't have the energy to deal with it anymore."

"Okay," I respond, considering how Finley is going to react

to the news and the impact it might have on the hospital to deal with it. "Do you want to do it in person or over the phone?"

"In person," he says.

"What about Finley? Can she handle it? I don't want her to have a meltdown and have to involve the guards. This place is volatile enough without openly inviting what we know will be a hysterical mess."

He eyes me skeptically. "How many murderers and rapists do you have here? I'm pretty sure you can handle a frail little junkie like her."

I watch him carefully. I get an odd sense from him, almost as if he's not telling me everything.

"Is that the only reason you want to meet with her?" I ask.

He nods, but his gaze is still fixated elsewhere as if he is staring into an invisible portal in the air between us.

"Okay," I say, hoping that I won't regret my decision.

We take a day to get everything set up on our end for him to have a visit. We block out the entire visitation area for them so that they can have some level of privacy. We will also have three guards, Warden Moreno, and myself waiting on the periphery in the event that Finley doesn't take the break-up well.

Moreno and the guards wait in the visitation area while I retrieve Finley from the visitor's desk. As soon as I see her, I feel bad for her. She dressed herself up as if she and Trent are going out for a night on the town.

"Hi, Dr. Fletcher!" she says, hurrying over to me.

I force a smile. "Hello, Finley. You ready?"

"Of course!" She can hardly contain her excitement, and I wonder if she is high on something.

As I escort her back to the visitation area, I go through the general rules with her. No physical contact of any kind. No passing anything to him. Etcetera, etcetera.

I doubt she hears much of what I'm telling her.

When we enter the visitation area, Trent is waiting at one of the tables with Moreno and the three guards standing on the fringes.

"Baby!" she screeches, hurrying over to him. "I can't believe it's you!"

One of the guards moves to intercept her and guides her to her seat.

Trent hardly blinks, no less show any form of emotion.

"I'm so excited to see you," Finley says, bouncing in her chair like a little kid. "How are you doing? Are they treating you alright?"

She tries to reach across the table to touch him, but the guards quickly reprimand her and she pulls her hand back.

"I'm doing fine," he says flatly. "Getting better."

"Have you been getting my letters? I write to you every day."

"Yes."

"I miss you so much," she adds, her voice cracking with emotion. "I feel like my heart's been ripped out of my chest and crushed with a hammer over and over."

"I know..." he mutters without the slightest hint of feeling.

"Do you miss *me*?" she asks, her voice begging for him to return her affections.

Trent disregards her question. "We need to talk. This isn't going to work—you and me."

"What?" she mutters, confused. "We're engaged. What do you mean, this isn't going to work?"

"I can't be with you," he says. "Not when I am locked up in here—"

"Yes, you can," she interjects desperately. "We'll beat this—I know we will—it's just going to take some time. Keep fighting, baby, you have to keep fighting."

His eyes narrow and his expression becomes impatient. "What the fuck are you talking about?" he counters coldly. "There's nothing to fight. *Nothing*."

"The *sentence*," she says. "They can't lock you up like this for something you didn't even do."

"Are you high? Of course I did it. Every piece of evidence that they have proves it."

"Stop it," she hisses. "The more you say that, the more you'll actually believe it."

"It's the truth! Let this shit go already, Fin, for Christ's sake."

"No no no no no no," she mutters nonsensically. "You're innocent, baby. I know you are. They're brainwashing you in here. Don't you see that? They've convinced you that you're guilty when you're not." Emotion chokes her voice as she adds, "Now you want to break up with me? I'll bet *they* told you to do that, didn't they?"

"No, goddammit. They didn't tell me to do shit."

Finley turns toward me and snaps, "It was *you*, wasn't it? You told him to do this."

"Dr. Fletcher didn't tell me to do anything," Trent counters.

She turns her attention back to Trent. "They know that I am the only one who believes you're innocent, and if they can cut me off, then there's nothing else to stop them from controlling you completely. Don't do this, baby, *please*, don't do this."

She tries to reach across the table again, but Trent shrinks away as much as the shackles will allow.

"Fin, you're strung out," he says. "How many times have I told you that the gak is making you lose your mind? Do yourself a favor; get off the pipe and clean your life up."

"Stop saying that!" she exclaims. "I. Am. *Not*. Crazy!"

Warden Moreno intervenes. "Alright, we're done. Guards, please escort Ms. Keenan out of the hospital."

Two of the guards step forward. "It's time to go," one of them says.

"Fuck you, I'm not going anywhere!" she snaps.

"Ma'am—"

"Look at yourself right now," Trent interjects. "If this isn't crazy, I don't know what is."

"Fuck you," she barks again, leaping from her seat.

The guards immediately put their hands on her shoulders.

She shrugs them off, backing away from the table. "You want to just quit and rot away in this shit hole?" she says to Trent. "That's your choice. But I know better. I'm not going to stop fighting no matter what you say."

"For fuck's sake. Get clean so you can see reality for what it is."

"*Reality?*" she blurts. "What sense of reality do *you* possibly have? Schizophrenic and addicted to every drug known to humankind? The only reality you know is what this bitch is telling you."

"Finley—" I try to interject.

But her outburst only magnifies, deafening her to our voices.

"I bet you want to fuck her," she hisses at Trent. "Is that it? You want to fuck her the way you wanted to fuck your own mother, you sick ass?"

"Shut up," Trent retorts, his tone becoming angered for the first time in the conversation.

"That *is* it," Finley prods, her desperation replaced with a perverse joy. She glances at me slyly, then returns her attention to him. "She *does* kind of look like her, doesn't she? You want her to strip you down and whip you, Trent? Choke you and sodomize you? Have her do what you made me do to you, you sick fuck?"

"Shut your goddamn mouth!" he barks, straining against the shackles and shaking the table as much as he can.

"Get her out of here!" commands Moreno.

The guards grab her by the arms and she flails about wildly.

"Rape!" she bellows. "Rape!"

The guards drag her toward the door, her fists flying through the air in all directions.

I look over at Trent, and his face is lifted toward the ceiling. "*Ave Satana*," he mutters over and over again, adding a macabre resonance to the pandemonium within the room.

"I won't give up, Trent!" Finley screams as the guards remove her from the visitation area. "I will die for you!"

The door slams shut and Finley's shrieks become muted whispers.

I return my attention to Trent, who has remained in his semi-hypnotic state, chanting, "*Ave Satana, Ave Satana.*"

"Get him back to his room," Moreno tells the guard.

The guard disconnects the chain that holds Trent to the table and lifts him up from his seat. Trent does not resist, continuing the chant as he shuffles out of the visitation area.

When they're gone, the room becomes painfully silent, and I can barely bring myself to look at Moreno. I want to break the silence, but I don't even know what to say.

After several moments, Moreno finally says, "You think *that* was the closure he was looking for?"

I don't respond. I don't know if Moreno is being facetious or if he's trying to filter his exasperation.

He adds, "I want him on full restriction until further notice. Is that understood?"

"Yes," I answer. "Listen, if I knew—"

"Don't go there," he retorts. "What's done is done."

"I know, but I should have had better judgment."

"Yes, you should have, but so should I. I knew this was a bad idea, but I allowed it. All we can do now is learn from it, alright?"

I nod.

He pauses for a moment before adding, "You think what she said was true?"

I hesitate. "Who knows? Considering how he reacted, there's probably some truth to it. Especially the masochism."

"What a creep..." he mutters with disgust. "What about being attracted to you? He ever make advances toward you before?"

"God, no," I quickly reply. "He's been hostile at times, but never sexual."

"No transference?" Moreno adds.

"No," I say. "I've never gotten the feeling that he's projecting his hatred of his mother onto me."

"We can always reassign him to someone else," he says. "Maybe even transfer him to Santa Ana or Coalinga."

"No," I counter firmly. "We'll lose any ground we've gained with him so far."

"Based on what just happened, it's hard to believe we're gaining ground."

"I hate what happened as much as you do, but this could very well be the therapeutic breakthrough I have been looking for. My suspicions about sexual abuse seem to be spot-on."

Moreno doesn't respond for a few moments as he thinks.

Soon, he shakes his head slowly and says, "This damn place... just when you thought you knew how screwed up the world is, you're quickly reminded that you don't have a damn clue."

I nod ruminatively, and as my mind processes everything, the lyrics of "Tabasco" find their way into my ears...

Mother? I am going to kill you, and then I am going to fuck you!

"How are you holding up?" Moreno asks, interrupting my thoughts.

"With Trent?" I answer.

"No. With..." He pauses awkwardly as if searching for the appropriate phrasing. "With things outside of work."

"Fine," I reply dismissively.

"You sure?"

"It's nothing that concerns you."

"Okay," he answers. "I'm not trying to pry, but you should know that I'm worried about you."

"I'm fine," I insist. "I only told you to get approval for the day off, not to get your sympathy or pity."

"I know. I just wonder if you're in a head space to deal with someone like Davis is all. If you need to take some time off, I understand."

I try not to take offense at the suggestion that I'm too weak to fulfill the duties of my job in the midst of grieving. I can't help it though. He has no right to put his nose where it doesn't belong, and I'm angry that I had to tell him about Dr. Maynard's death in the first place. My private life is my private life.

I squelch my agitation, however. "I appreciate the concern. If anything changes, I'll let you know."

FOURTEEN

Interstate 5 is blindly dark in the dead of night.

My headlights pierce the blackness.

The dashed white line to my left. The solid white line to my right.

I travel through the void.

My skin crawls. Aches. With Him. For Him.

He sees through my eyes. Feels through my skin. His blood courses through my veins.

He is Trent. He is Larua. He is the Underworldly Lord.

He is my virus. My plague. My sickness.

I hunt the way He hunted. Searching the shoulder of the interstate for my prey. Someone hopeless enough to wander the fringes of the night.

His work will become my work.

I will honor and glorify Him.

I can do all things through Him who strengthens me.

Time ceases to exist.

I live inside a dream.

The only things that tell me I haven't entered another

dimension are the green mile markers on the shoulder. The signs for the upcoming exits. The speed limits.

I may as well be traveling into the depths of hell.

She appears out of nothingness. Young. Frail. A perfect sacrifice.

She shuffles along the shoulder as if her mind is anywhere but here. Maybe she prays that death will come for her. End her misery.

Allow me to be your salvation then. Grant you passage into the underworld.

I pull the car over just as I pass her. I turn my flashers on and roll down my window.

I poke my head out and call to her, "You want a ride?"

She hurries over to me, her form bathed in the dim crimson from the taillights.

"Thanks so much," she says. "You're a lifesaver."

FIFTEEN

My cell phone rings early that following morning, startling me out of a dream. As soon as I see that the call is from Pantano, a surge of adrenaline hits me. Only under extreme circumstances does the hospital call me after hours, so I know that whatever this is must be an emergency.

"What's going on?" I answer, nearly falling out of bed to get dressed.

"It's Davis," a guard says, his voice obviously flustered. "Son of a bitch tried to bleed himself to death."

"What!" I reply, nearly dropping my phone with shock. "How the hell did he do that?"

"It looks like he gnawed the shit out of his arm," the guard responds. "Had to have hit the artery with how badly he was bleeding. He's lucky one of us heard him fall on the floor, otherwise we wouldn't have found him until morning check."

"Holy shit," I say. "Where is he now?"

"They rushed him to the emergency ward to get him sewn back up."

"I'm heading over there now," I tell him.

"Dr. Fletcher—" he interjects just as I am about to hang the phone up. "There's one more thing. He left a suicide note... sort of. He wrote something on the wall with his blood. *On this spit I will roast...*"

"On this spit I will roast?" I mutter.

"Yeah... Does that mean anything to you?"

"No," I say, perplexed. "Leave the room as is for now, understand? Do not clean or touch anything."

"You got it," he answers.

I hang up the phone and jump into a random pair of pants and a shirt.

Despite it being four o'clock in the morning, there are a number of vehicles on the roadway and I dodge and weave between them as I race toward the hospital.

When I arrive at Pantano and get down to the emergency ward, the doctor is still in the process of sewing Trent's arm back up, so I return to the high-security ward to check out his room.

The ward is eerily quiet and calm despite what has happened earlier. All the other patients are asleep in their locked rooms, and the night guards slowly walk up and down the dim corridors in their typical fashion. The light in Trent's room is still on, casting a pale yellow beam of sterile light into the hallway.

When I reach his room, the scene is unreal. I am immediately reminded of the scenes from *The Shining* in which blood pours from the elevator shaft in a torrential flood. Blood covers every surface imaginable, as if Trent was in a brutal fight. The bed linens, the floor, the walls. Their bone-white color stained in various shades of red.

Then I notice the writing on the wall. Trent's suicide note...

ON THIS SPIT I WILL ЯOAST

The blood has streaked down from every letter, making it

seem like the message is wriggling like a cluster of maggots on the wall. The other thing I notice is how he made the "R" in "Roast" backward, exactly how Danny writes "*RED𝑅UM*" in *The Shining*.

Flashbacks of Michelle flood my brain. I hear Danny screaming, "Redrum! Redrum!" on the television as Michelle touches me. My thigh. My groin. I am mortified and nauseous. The more her hand explores me, the more paralyzed I become.

I shake the memory from my vision, focusing on the enigmatic note on the wall.

I feel like I have seen or heard this sentence before, and I rack my brain for one of Trent's thousands of song lyrics that I have analyzed. Nothing strikes a chord in my memory, so I take several pictures with my smartphone for later reference.

I return to the emergency ward shortly thereafter, and by that time Trent is out of the procedure room and in the small recovery area. They only gave him a nerve block, so he is still conscious with his wrists cuffed to either side of the gurney and a guard standing watch at the foot of the bed. I expected him to look haggard, if not completely demoralized, but instead, he is wide-eyed and beaming as if he recently downed several energy drinks.

"You're here early," he says to me in a joking manner.

"Yes," I reply firmly. "When a patient tries to bleed himself to death in his room, I don't take that lightly."

"Bleed to death?" he scoffs. "Who told you I was trying to kill myself?"

"The blood that's all over your room," I say.

Trent snickers. "Inspiration can look like that sometimes. I heard when Van Gogh painted *The Starry Night* that his asylum room was drenched in blue paint."

"Inspiration?" I reply curiously. "Inspiration for what?"

"To create," he answers, his eyes widening with excitement.

"Okay..." I respond, trying to figure out what he is talking about. I turn to the guard and ask, "You mind giving us a minute?"

He nods and leaves the area.

When the guard is out of earshot, I return my attention to Trent.

"So the message on the wall?" I say.

He smiles. "The chorus of my new song. Part of it anyway. Still working out the melody, but I got a good feeling about it."

I have never seen him so excited; if I didn't know the circumstances, I would think he was showing further signs of progress and mental stability. But the goriness of his room tells me otherwise.

"Why did you try to hurt yourself then?" I ask.

"Hurt myself?" he retorts confusedly. "You mean my arm? Those flimsy little pens they give me run out of ink so fast. And I had to write with *something*, so I improvised."

"You tore your arm to pieces so you could use your blood as ink?" I reply.

"Yes," he says as if it is the only logical conclusion one can draw. "Did you guys really think I was trying to kill myself?" he adds with a smirk.

"Yes. You do realize you almost died, right?"

"You're overreacting. Larua wouldn't let me die even if I wanted to."

"I beg your pardon?" I say.

"Larua won't let me die," he answers. "A tapeworm knows better."

I don't know what to say to this. Trent is clearly not thinking straight and I fear that he is slipping into a state of regression.

"Tell me about this song," I finally say. "What's it about? What inspired you to write it?"

"It just came to me. I was laying in bed and the chorus slithered into my head out of the silence." He begins to sing the lyrics in a soft, eerie chant: *"Buried inside me; You hurt so good; Stuck little piglet; Scream and cry not; Your flesh is so pretty; Just take it to the top; I feel so dirty; My God saw you watch; Stuck little piglet; On this spit I will roast..."*

This final line hovers in the air for several moments, and the implications of the lyrics leave me feeling disturbed.

"What do you think?" he asks, his gaze locking onto me as if he has just sung an impassioned ode.

"It's interesting," I answer. "What's it about?"

"Just someone I used to know... A special friend."

"Who was your special friend?"

"Pooh Bear," he says. "That's what I would call him at least. He would call me Piglet."

"*He?*" I reply with surprise, thinking that the reference in the song was about Trent's mother abusing him.

"Yeah," he answers. "Most people knew him as Mr. Stan, but he wanted me to call him Pooh Bear."

"Mr. Stan?" I say wearily. "As in Stanley?"

"Yup," Trent replies. "That's him."

The weight of an anvil settles into my stomach and the realization hits me with such force there is no way I can stop it. I was right; Trent was abused by Stanley Palmer, and now the truth has finally trickled out of his psyche through this new song.

My face must show my surprise, because Trent asks me, "Is something wrong?"

"No," I say. "I just need to get some water. Can I get you anything?"

"I'm good," he replies, apparently not realizing the deep-seated secret he has revealed.

As I leave his room, a painful sense of empathy overcomes me. The imagery. The metaphor. It all strikes me so profoundly that I am completely overwhelmed.

I need someplace to be alone for a moment to gather my

thoughts, so I hurry down the hallway and find the nearest bathroom. Once I am by myself, emotion rises from deep within me and leaves me quivering and breathless.

I know what is happening to me even though I desperately want to deny it. It's not countertransference in the traditional sense, yet it is just as dangerous. The traumas of a patient mirroring those of the clinician. Memories that are so dormant—so seemingly benign—that only a single ember glows in the depths of the psyche. But an ember can be stoked back to life, creating an inferno that consumes everything in its path.

I'm not the first clinician who carries psychological baggage. Up to eighty percent of therapists and psychiatrists experience acute mental health symptoms at some point. Freud himself suffered from a psychosomatic condition later in his life. The key is confronting it quickly. Acknowledging the distress and taking the necessary steps to address it.

I am still in control here.

SIXTEEN

Once Trent is released from the emergency ward, I tell him that I want him to write the song lyrics that have been coming to him lately. The ones for the song he started writing on his wall as well as any others that he has thought of. My theory is that it might be the way he can start tackling his childhood trauma, unlocking all of those memories he has repressed. I remember him saying that writing songs is a compulsion for him, and I wonder if his mind subconsciously wants to purge his memories.

He is skeptical at first, but after some thought, he agrees and I provide him with another flexible pen and extra sheets of paper.

He fills the papers until the pen runs completely dry. When I bring him another and more sheets of paper, he takes them with the fervor of a child and fills those pages within a couple of days too.

When I ask him if I can read some of his work, he hesitates, saying, "They're not ready yet."

"That's okay," I tell him. "I'd like to see the progress."

His eyes narrow. "I've never let anyone see my work before it's ready."

"I don't want to interrupt your creative flow," I reply. "But I am curious about your process. How the songs evolve from the first word to the final product."

He looks at me firmly as if he is examining my genuineness. "Can I trust you?" he asks.

I wonder if he means this specifically about the songs or more generally about himself.

"Of course you can," I tell him sympathetically. "Patient-therapist confidentiality applies to this as well."

He nods and hands me the stack of written pages. "Let me know if you have any suggestions," he says.

"I am not a poet," I reply with a self-deprecating laugh. "I don't think you want my suggestions."

He smiles, but not in his usually creepy, unnerving way.

He lets me take the song lyrics to my office, and I spend the morning reading the fragmented pieces that he has written down.

His words are raw; more so than the previous music he's released. Less symbolic and enigmatic too. As if to completely uncensor his experiences.

Several of his songs explicitly target his mother and the things she made him do to himself. Others graphically describe what Stanley Palmer did to him. Molestation. Sodomy. Rape. How he lured Trent and manipulated him. How Trent tried to tell his mother about what was happening and how his mother ignored him.

At times, I have to stop reading and step away from his words so that my own memories do not surface too much. The line between empathy and countertransference is razor thin, when the therapist's feelings are projected back onto her patient. But I am acutely aware of that tightrope. My balance will not falter.

Although I am pleased that my initial instincts about Trent were accurate, I am deeply disturbed by what he endured as a child. Even my own experiences pale in comparison to his, and while it does not excuse the atrocious things he has done, it at least helps me understand them better.

The other part that encourages me is the fact that he's finally opening up and releasing his traumatic memories. Having gone through the process myself, this is the point at which true healing occurs. I just need to keep him writing. Keep him purging those demons that have been trapped inside so long.

I find myself channeling Dr. Maynard. Doing what she would have done. Keeping her spirit alive through my work. Honoring the gifts she gave to me.

SEVENTEEN

She wasn't the one.

Not the *right* one, at least.

Not for my first.

My first has to be perfect.

For myself and for Him.

I took her up to Stockton like she asked. Dropped her off at a truck stop outside of town and came back.

Not on Interstate 5.

Not through our sacred hunting grounds.

Through Big Sur.

Through the coastal wilderness.

If I am lucky, I will see Him in the darkness.

He will tempt me. He will infect me with a disease that bears a beautiful symptom.

My soul will be His and we will be one.

Make me one with You, my Underworldly Lord.

EIGHTEEN

"Dr. Fletcher?" I hear on my voicemail two weeks later. *"This is Mother Alberta from the Romero House. I need to speak with you regarding Sister Catherine. It's urgent. Please call me back as soon as you can."*

Her voice sounds worried, drastically different from the controlled firmness that I remember of her.

I can't imagine why Sister Alberta would need to speak to me urgently, but I return her call.

When Alberta answers, she sounds perturbed and distracted.

"Sister Catherine has run away," she tells me. "I was hoping you might know where she went."

"I am sorry to hear that," I say, trying to be as sympathetic as I can. "But why would *I* know where she went?"

"I didn't know if she mentioned anyplace to you when you last spoke with her," she says.

"No. She didn't even say anything about leaving the convent."

"She was very upset after your visit," Alberta says. "More so than usual."

"I apologize for that. I wasn't trying to upset her. I was just trying to learn what I could to help her son."

She stifles a scoff. "A monster... and at the expense of a fragile woman."

"That was not my intent—"

"Intent is only as good as the deed that follows," she interjects. "And I am afraid your visit did more harm than good."

"Not for Trent," I counter. "He has made significant progress because of what I learned from you and his mother."

"In your eyes maybe," she replies. "But not in the eyes of God."

"I suppose you're right," I answer, hoping a sign of yielding will get her to back off. "How long has she been missing?"

"Twelve hours, roughly," she says. "Nobody has seen her since evening prayer last night."

"Maybe she went for a walk and got lost?" I suggest. "That's a pretty remote area you're in."

"We keep close track of Catherine's whereabouts," she replies. "For reasons that you witnessed yourself. She doesn't go anywhere without someone knowing about it, so she must have disappeared in the middle of the night."

"Has she been acting out of the ordinary lately?" I ask. "Behaving in any unusual way?"

"*Much* of what she does is unusual," Alberta responds. "That being said, she *has* been praying more. She kneels in the adoration chapel for hours on end until she can hardly stand up. I am shocked her rosary has not broken with how often she handles it."

"Is she sleeping?"

"Why does that matter?" she retorts impatiently.

"It matters because I am wondering if she stopped taking her medication. Paranoid schizophrenics can be very impulsive and illogical when they are not medicated. Who knows what's going through her mind right now."

"She takes her medication," Alberta insists. "We make sure of that."

"You would be surprised," I counter. "Patients can be incredibly creative when it comes to not taking their pills. Even if you watch them take it, it doesn't mean they've actually swallowed it."

"I am well aware," she says. "We learned the hard way with her, so we only give her injections now. So yes—I know for a fact that she is taking her medication."

"Have you filed a missing persons report?" I ask, hoping that I can end the conversation soon. It is not that I am not worried about Catherine, but I have a feeling that Alberta did not actually want my help and only wanted to blame me for her disappearance.

"Of course," she says defensively. "As soon as we discovered she was missing this morning."

"Let the authorities do their job then," I tell her with finality. "As remote as the convent is, there are only so many places she could have wandered off to. My guess is she got lost in the surrounding wilderness no more than a few miles away."

The line goes silent and I get the impression there is something that she is not saying or asking me.

Soon, she adds, "Can you ask *him* if he knows what happened to her?"

"*Him?*" I reply, confused. "Him who?"

"Trent," she says. "Ask him where she is."

"He's not going to have a clue where she went," I answer, trying not to sound condescending. "I'm not even sure he knows she's alive."

"Satan knows," she answers with the utmost gravity. "He always knows, and if he knows, then Trent knows as well. The devil has power far beyond human understanding."

It takes all of my will to not scoff at the absurdity of this. Satan and hell and demons and everything else do not exist, I want to tell her. Beliefs are one thing, but what she is talking about is as fanciful as *Alice's Adventures in Wonderland.*

"I am not going to justify his own delusions by telling him that," I answer. "He has enough difficulty distinguishing fantasy from reality as it is."

"Fantasy?" she replies, taking offense to my implication. "Are you suggesting that evil is just a figment of our imagination?"

"No," I say, considering my own past experiences. "Evil as an abstract most certainly exists. But personified in some deity? That is a scare tactic used to get people to go to church."

The line goes silent again, and I fear that I have gone too far with sharing my thoughts on the matter.

After a moment, she replies hollowly, "In your eyes maybe..."

"How about this," I say, trying to rectify the offense I've caused. "I will ask Trent if he has any idea where she might have gone, okay?"

"Sure," she says.

"Will you let me know if you find Catherine in the meantime?"

"Yes," she answers curtly, and I realize that I have offended her beyond repair.

"Until then..." I say, mainly because I do not know what else to say.

"I'll be praying for you," she tells me just before the line goes dead.

The call leaves me perplexed, primarily because I do feel a little responsible for Catherine's disappearance. It is possible that my conversation with her roused up toxic memories that sent her into a state of psychosis. Even if they administered her medication with fidelity, it does not make her immune to psychological breakdown.

I had to do it though, I tell myself. If for no other reason than my professional obligations to Trent.

As for Mother Alberta's superstitions regarding demonology, I have to simply shake my head and dismiss them. It continues to baffle me how we can be so scientifically advanced as a society, yet there is still a significant portion of the population that believes in the supernatural and the mythological. God and the devil and Christ and demons and heaven and hell—these are all delusions created thousands of years ago to explain earthly phenomena we did not understand, and now they are being used as leverage points to expand and maintain the power that religions have in our societies.

I am biased though. If God is all-loving and all-powerful, then He should not have allowed an eight-year-old girl to be abused and raped for two straight years. Stanley Palmer and Catherine Davis should not have been allowed to do the things that they did, and Trent Davis should not be what he is. The evil in our world is not the result of the works of the devil, nor is it the byproduct of God's indifference or powerlessness. Evil is simply the consequence of human fragility when put under the pressure of extreme circumstances. Nothing more. Nothing less.

NINETEEN

The breaking news alert hit my smartphone early this morning. The headline alone forces my heart to race, the type of autonomic reaction that makes you break into a cold sweat.

Body Found Along Interstate 5: Grisly Similarities to Vampire Murders

I can barely bring myself to open the article and read it. At the top of the feed is a photo of Soledad County Sheriff's deputies securing the crime scene on a nondescript shoulder of the interstate southwest of Fresno.

The article reads:

The body of a woman was found on the shoulder of Interstate 5 early this morning. According to the Soledad County Sheriff's Office, the body was found on the northbound shoulder near Exit 36. Detectives with the Sheriff's Office noted grisly trauma to the victim's abdomen and discovered that all of the major organs had been removed. The Sheriff's Office offered no comment when

asked if they suspected a copycat of the Bakersfield Vampire,
Trent Davis.

My disbelief only grows as I read. The implications of a
copycat are what unnerve me initially, but then the more
cynical parts of my mind consider the coincidence of Trent's
mother going missing a few days prior and I wonder if she might
actually be the unfortunate victim. Although Romero House is
over two hundred miles away from the crime scene, there is the
possibility—albeit unlikely—that she was abducted and
murdered.

I don't mention the news to Trent during my session with
him that afternoon. I need him to stay focused on his treatment.
Continue to purge the demons that haunt him.

But my mind is distracted. Is this actually a copycat? Or is
the media sensationalizing the story for views?

Several days pass before my wild hypothesis about
Catherine is finally put to rest. Another article is posted with
the results of the medical examiner's report. Although the
victim has yet to be identified, her age is estimated as early thirties, so there is no way that Catherine is the victim. That being
said, the medical examiner did confirm the similarities with
Trent's crimes. He determined that the cause of death was
blood loss via a large wound to the throat and that the organs
were removed post-mortem. The exact same *modus operandi* as
Trent.

The article also mentions that neither the murder weapon
nor the victim's organs have been found, indicating that the
crime itself was committed elsewhere.

The day only becomes more coincidental from that point
when I receive a call from the Soledad County Sheriff's Office
later that afternoon.

"This is Detective James Navarro," the caller tells me. "I'm investigating the homicide of the young woman on Interstate 5. Perhaps you're familiar with the case?"

"I have seen a couple of news articles online," I answer. "Stuff about similarities to the Bakersfield Vampire murders?"

"That's correct," he says. "That's why I am calling you, actually... sort of an unusual request."

"Okay..." I reply hesitantly. "What is it?"

"You're the psychiatrist currently working with Trent Davis, right?"

"Yes."

"I was wondering if I could pick your brain about him? I imagine you've learned quite a bit about what makes him tick, and you might be able to give me some insight into this new killer."

"I don't know. I can't give you specifics as it relates to Trent's treatment or his condition. Patient-therapist confidentiality applies to criminals as stringently as it does to civilians."

"I understand," he answers. "I'm not asking you to break confidentiality. I was just hoping you could review the casefile and give me your thoughts on the psychological profile of this new killer."

"Of course," I tell him. "Although, I'm a clinician, not a profiler. You may be better off talking to the California Bureau of Investigation. After all, they're the ones who investigated the original Vampire murders and found Trent."

"CBI doesn't play well in the sandbox with others, if you know what I mean."

"I do," I say, recalling my own frustrations with the inter-agency politics of the Department of Corrections. "Why don't you send me a copy of the casefile to review and then we can meet virtually later? Are you free this evening?"

"Absolutely," he answers.

We schedule the meeting for seven o'clock, and he emails me a copy of the casefile shortly thereafter.

The casefile is relatively thin at this point. The full medical examiner's report is included along with a few police reports and a statement from the trucker who discovered the body and called 911. The medical examiner's report includes photographs of the victim's body, and I immediately get flashbacks of the photos of Trent's victims. The wounds inflicted upon this woman are nearly identical to Trent's, so much so that you could easily mistake her for one of his victims.

The photos of the wounds don't bother me for some reason. Even the ones showing the victim's exposed abdominal cavity. Maybe it's because of my time in medical school where we dissected and examined so many human cadavers that you almost forgot they were once people as well.

Only when I get to the photos that show the victim's face do I have to look away several times to collect myself. Despite being in her early thirties, the rifts in the victim's complexion reveal a long, difficult life. Skin pockmarked and teeth showing significant signs of decay. An addict of some sort, for sure. Probably meth or crack if I had to guess. Something that buried its hooks in her and became her master. Forced her into a transient life that she couldn't even imagine when she was a child.

Realizing this makes my heart ache for her. It makes me want to know her story and how things ended up the way that they did.

The medical examiner's report shows no sign of sexual assault, similarly to Trent's crimes. It makes me wonder about the motive for the killing. Anger? Power? Or psychosis, as was the case for Trent? It's difficult to say based on the physical evidence alone. I remember when Trent's crimes were being investigated, there were hundreds of theories floating around the internet and none of them ended up being accurate.

I am a little nervous when I log into the meeting with Detective Navarro. I have few hypotheses regarding the crime, and I am not sure what insights I will be able to provide to the investigation.

Detective Navarro appears on my computer monitor and gives me an awkward virtual wave. He appears to be around my age with thick black hair showing the first signs of aging in scattered wisps. He is wearing a suit jacket, with the knot of his tie pulled down slightly.

"Good evening, Dr. Fletcher," he says. He smiles, revealing a friendliness I do not expect from a cop.

"Hi there," I say, returning the wave.

"Thanks for doing this for me. I know how busy you must be."

"Happy to do it," I say. "This type of stuff fascinates me, so no trouble at all."

"Did you have a chance to look at the casefile?"

"I did," I say. "Although I don't know if I got anything that you don't already know."

"Well, let me ask you this: do you think we're right in suspecting a copycat?"

"It's hard to deny the similarities to the Vampire murders," I reply. "The cause of death. The M.O. The location of the body. It certainly seems like a tip of the cap to Trent."

"That's what I was afraid of..." he says ominously. "I was hoping you were going to tell me that I'm crazy and that the possibility of a copycat is absurd."

"Do you know anything about the victim?" I ask. "Who she is or where she comes from?"

He nods slowly. "They just identified her this afternoon. Her name is Sonja Wagner. Thirty-two years old. Came to California from Washington when she was seventeen. Arrested a dozen times for possession and prostitution. Served two stints at Frontera."

"Geez..." I respond, my heart breaking that much more for her. "So she's spent most of her time in the L.A. area?"

"Based on her arrest records, yes. Doesn't exactly narrow down a suspect pool for me."

"No," I say. "I would imagine there's a laundry list of people she knew who are capable of doing this—"

"But," he interjects. "How many of those people have connections to Trent Davis?"

"What do you mean, *connections*?" I ask. "You make it sound like the copycat knows Trent."

"Maybe he does," he answers.

"That seems like a total shot in the dark," I say skeptically. "Lots of copycats are nothing more than obsessed fans. Eddie Seda and the Zodiac. Derek Brown and Jack the Ripper."

"What about Veronica Compton?" he counters. "Tried to copy the Hillside Strangler to make it look like someone besides Kenneth Bianchi did it."

"True," I say. "But I would consider that more an outlier than the norm. Don't forget that Bianchi manipulated her into doing it after he was imprisoned."

Navarro does not reply to this; he simply nods slowly as if a profound point has been made.

"What?" I add, eyeing him skeptically.

"Does Davis receive fan mail?" he asks.

"Yes," I say. "Dozens of letters every day as a matter of fact."

"Maybe his copycat corresponds with him," he suggests. "That's how Veronica Compton's relationship with Bianchi started."

"It's possible... Of course, we're not legally allowed to read patient mail. We can only scan and search it for contraband."

Navarro doesn't respond for a moment as he thinks. "What if you ask Davis about who writes to him? See if anyone mentions the copycat murder or tries to brag about it."

I stifle a grin so as not to appear condescending. "I don't think so."

"Why not?" he counters, more defensively than I expect.

"For one thing, the chances of the copycat doing that are extremely unlikely. But even if he did, Trent isn't going to willingly tell me about it. I have to practically use a crowbar to get any ounce of truth out of him. Besides, it's blurring the line of patient-therapist confidentiality if I pass information that I've learned from those sessions on to you."

Navarro is silent, but judging by the flicker of his eyes, I can tell he is trying to choose his words carefully. Finally, he responds, "With all due respect, I don't think patient-therapist confidentiality should take precedence over a murder investigation that he might be able to help us with."

"For what it's worth, I don't either, but unless there's evidence that indicates he's involved or knows something, there's not much I can do."

Navarro sighs with frustration. "What if I talk to him then? Do you think he would agree to meet with me?"

"I doubt it," I answer, shaking my head. "You're welcome to contact his lawyer to see, but I don't think you'll get very far with that. Trent has nothing to gain from helping you."

"Yeah, you're probably right..." he mutters ruminatively.

"Do you have any evidence that supports the idea he's corresponding with this new killer? Something that you could use to get a warrant?"

"Unfortunately, no. Just the similarities in the MO and my own suspicions." He trails off briefly before adding, "My fear is that this murder isn't going to be a one-off. There's going to be others."

"All the more reason to not waste time shaking trees that are barren," I say. "I'm no expert in murder investigations, but in my own work, I know that aimlessly wandering down rabbit holes is a pointless endeavor. There has to be evidence that leads you there."

"That's the problem though. Aside from the body itself,

there really isn't any evidence. No fingerprints. No blood. Nothing except for traces of bleach."

I don't say anything for a moment, racking my brain for possibilities. "What about Trent's fiancée?" I add, recalling Navarro's earlier comment about Kenneth Bianchi and Veronica Compton. "*Ex*-fiancée, I should say."

"Ex?" he replies confusedly.

"Yeah, Trent broke up with her a few weeks ago. It got pretty ugly and the guards had to drag her out of the hospital. She told him that she wouldn't give up on him and that she would die for him."

Navarro eyes me skeptically. "You're talking about Finley Keenan, right? She couldn't weigh more than a hundred pounds. You really think she's capable of murdering someone?"

"She gave two of our guards a run for their money," I answer, thinking about how she thrashed in their arms like a wild animal.

"I don't know... I suppose it's possible, but what would her motive be? Mimic his crimes to make it look like the real Vampire is still out there and exonerate him?"

"Maybe. Or maybe she thinks it'll win him back."

"Jesus..." he breathes, shaking his head slowly. "You think she's that crazy?"

"She fell in love with him, right? I don't know if you can call that certifiably insane, but I wouldn't put anything past someone with that kind of obsession."

TWENTY

"We have a situation in the mailroom," Warden Moreno tells me hurriedly over the phone a few days after my meeting with Detective Navarro. "A courier just dropped off a package for Trent Davis."

"A package?" I'm confused.

"Yeah," he says. "One that's about the size of a milk crate."

"Huh? Who's it from?"

"There's no name on the return address. Just the initials *S.W.* with the address *712, W. 13th Street, Bakersfield, California.*"

"What?" I answer with surprise. "That can't be right; that's the address for the Stanley Palmer house."

"You gotta be kidding me," he grumbles.

"That's really bizarre. Did you try to open it?"

"No. For all we know, it could be a goddamn bomb."

"Christ," I mutter, my confusion transforming into nervousness. "You really think someone would do that?"

He scoffs. "Some lunatic trying to blow the hospital up because Davis is here instead of San Quentin? I sure as hell wouldn't put it past them."

"Do I need to evacuate the unit?"

"Not yet. I called the Chorro County Sheriff and he's sending the bomb squad over. Just keep everyone calm until you hear from me. We may need to evacuate, but I am going to avoid that if at all possible."

"Okay," I answer.

Moreno hangs up the phone and I immediately go out to the guard station to tell the staff what is going on.

People are understandably worried by the news, but this isn't the first time that the hospital has received some type of threat before. Victims or their family members who are angry because the perpetrator isn't suffering in a traditional prison. Political vigilantes who want to take justice into their own hands.

Most threats are nothing more than scare tactics, but they're still unnerving.

I assure the team that Moreno is just being cautious and that we need to conduct ourselves in front of the patients as if nothing out of the ordinary is going on until we hear otherwise. Maintain our routines and the semblance of normalcy.

Despite what I tell the team, I'm worried. What could be inside that package, and who would send it to Trent directly?

The unit feels quietly tense as I await the call from Moreno. Most of the patients are in their rooms while a couple who have work detail are mopping floors. The more time that passes, the more anxious I get. If it's a bomb, then why haven't I received a call to evacuate the unit? If it isn't a bomb, then what on earth could it possibly be, and why did the sender put the Stanley Palmer house as the return address?

Nearly an hour passes before I finally hear back from Moreno.

"I need you to get down here now," he says hurriedly. "It's not a bomb, but you need to see what's inside this thing."

"What is it?" I reply, trying to rush down the hallway without startling everyone and making a scene.

"Just get down here," he says and hangs up the phone abruptly.

My mind races with adrenaline as I run to the elevator and go down to the mailroom.

When I get there, the bomb squad officers are packing up their equipment while Moreno and the sheriff are huddled beside a table with the package opened in front of them. Both are wearing nitrile gloves, carefully inspecting the contents within.

"What's going on?" I say, to get their attention.

Moreno turns and I can see that much of the color has run out of his face. The sheriff doesn't look as mortified, but he's somber nevertheless.

"You're not squeamish, are you?" asks the sheriff.

"No..."

He hands me a pair of nitrile gloves and they step aside for me to look in the box.

When I peek in, my mind hardly registers what I'm seeing.

The box appears to be stuffed with ziplock bags each containing a dark maroon liquid of some kind. Hesitantly, I lift one of the bags out to get a closer look. I can see there's some type of object about the size of my fist submerged in the liquid. Almost like a cut of beef soaking in its own juices.

"It looks like..." I mutter, but I can't bring myself to say what I think it is.

"Organs," says the sheriff gravely.

Shaking my head, I return the bag to the box and step back from the table. "That can't be..." I breathe. "They've gotta be from an animal... Some kind of prank..."

The sheriff removes a different bag and holds it up to the light.

"I'm no coroner, but it looks like a human heart to me," he

says. He grabs another bag that is twice the size and adds, "And this is a stomach."

"Christ..." Moreno replies, motioning for the sheriff to stop. He grabs an unfolded piece of paper from the table and hands it to me, adding, "This letter was tucked in there, too."

I take the letter and read:

My Underworldly Lord,

The sacrifice has been completed and the requested offerings are contained within. A heart, a stomach, a liver, a spleen, and a womb for the five vertices of man. Send Larua my regards with this glass of claret.

Your humble servant

I read the letter several times to try to chisel away at my disbelief, but each pass through the note only leaves me more perplexed and horrified.

The sheriff interrupts my thoughts, showing me a sealed specimen cup full of blood. "We think this is the glass of claret that he's referring to—"

"What the hell..." I reply, dumbfounded.

He adds, "I am going to send everything over to the lab for processing ASAP. I am hoping that the organs and blood are from an animal and this is all just some fucked-up prank, but I don't think we'll be that lucky."

"You think they'll match that woman they found on Interstate 5?" I ask.

The sheriff shrugs dejectedly. "Maybe we should hope they do. Because if they're human but they don't match her, then we've got a second victim out there." He pauses and motions to the letter in my hand. "If I'm reading that note right, it sounds like Davis directed this copycat to continue his work. Has he ever mentioned anything like that before to you? A fan who showed interest in his crimes, or something like that?"

"Not to me," I answer. "But I know that Trent receives fan mail almost daily."

"Does he write back to them?"

"Some of them. But he never talks about it with me."

"Can we find out who he's writing to?" he asks. "You guys keep a log of that, right?"

"Yes," Moreno says.

"I'd also like to have our detectives interview Davis about this. It's a long shot, but maybe he'll slip up and tell us something we can use to find this guy."

I glance at Moreno and he briefly sees my hesitation.

"That will be more of a challenge, I am afraid," he answers. "You'll have to get permission from his lawyer or a warrant to do that."

"Fine," the sheriff replies. "All I ask is that you two cooperate with the investigation when the time comes."

"Of course," says Moreno.

I on the other hand say nothing in response. There's something about the sheriff's inflated sense of authority that just rubs me the wrong way. Pantano may geographically be in his jurisdiction, but his authority within the hospital is not as limitless as he seems to think.

"Dr. Fletcher?" the sheriff asks.

"As long as it doesn't violate my ethical obligations," I say.

My answer clearly doesn't please the sheriff, but whatever snide remark comes to his mind, he keeps it to himself.

Moreno soon dismisses me, and I have a feeling that he and I will be discussing inter-agency relations in the very near future. I don't particularly care. My duty isn't to bureaucrats or even the Department of Corrections; it's to my patients, regardless of the horrible things they've been convicted of.

That being said, the package makes me wonder if Detective

Navarro is right about Trent corresponding with the copycat somehow. The wording in the letter, *as requested*, is particularly suspicious. As high and mighty as I have been about patient-therapist confidentiality, I can't help but wonder if Trent will tell me what he knows. If he does, in fact, know something and it poses a threat to someone, then legally, I am allowed to break confidentiality and tell the authorities.

When I return to the unit, the staff are all very interested in what the fuss was about, but I dismiss them as diplomatically as I can and tell them it was nothing more than a false alarm.

As soon as their curiosity is satisfied, I head down the hallway to Trent's room. The door is locked, and through the window I can see he is sitting on his bed vigorously writing on a sheet of paper.

I knock to let him know I am there before I unlock and open his door.

"Can I bug you for a minute?" I say, peeking my head in.

"Yes," he mutters, but he doesn't look up from the paper.

I step inside of his room, but I keep the door propped with my foot. "Have you heard anything about a young woman being found dead on Interstate 5 last week?"

"There was something on the news," he says dismissively. "But I didn't pay much attention to it."

"They think it's someone copying your crimes, Trent. That didn't catch your attention?"

"A lot of people have tried to copy my music," he answers. "It doesn't surprise me that someone's trying to copy my crimes, too. People think that imitation is the greatest form of flattery, when in reality it is nothing more than the gallows of novelty."

"I'm sorry?"

He stops writing and looks up at me abruptly. His eyes are wide and his gaze fixates on me. "Have you ever seen *The Starry Night*?" he asks.

"By Van Gogh? Of course."

"The *original*," he specifies impatiently. "Not a photocopy."

"No," I answer. "I haven't seen the original."

He returns his gaze to the page in his lap. "Figures... Even those who see it in person do not really see it."

"What are you getting at?" I ask.

"A copy only captures a fragment of the whole," he tells me. "And it only captures what is obvious and superficial. You see the cypress, the town, the celestial bodies, but you do not feel the energy that the work holds. The topography that the brush-strokes created. The way changing light dances on the ridges in the cured oil and brings the twilight to life. It's not a master-piece because of what it is at face value. It's a masterpiece because it immortalized part of the artist's soul."

"Okay," I say curtly. "So you're not happy that someone is copying you?"

He shrugs. "I'm indifferent to it. I can't control how people are inspired by my work. My only job is to put it out there and let people interpret it for themselves."

"But you agree that someone is copying you?"

"It certainly seems like they are."

"Do you know who it is?"

He glances at me slyly. "Maybe I do and maybe I don't."

"Don't be cryptic with me," I urge. "Do you know who your copycat is?"

He sighs and glances upward. "You see, this is what I hate about the majority of people. They can't solve a riddle on their own or read between the lines of a lyric. They want the meaning to be poured into their heads without expelling a single ounce of energy. No thought. No creativity. That's what our society has been reduced to. A bunch of mindless voids that cannot think for themselves or do something original. You want to know who the copycat is? Step into the labyrinth and find out for yourself."

TWENTY-ONE

She was a gorgeous sacrifice.

Her heart for Jupiter.

Her liver for Mercury.

Her spleen for Mars.

Her stomach for Ouranos.

Her womb for Venus.

Her blood binds us. We are united in her death.

But the glory is fleeting.

The ecstasy temporary.

She was the perfect drug that I cannot stop craving. My veins itch. My skin thirsts.

I need another dose.

What are you waiting for? Push me another dose.

I am an empty shell of myself. Larua occupies me. Trent speaks through me.

But it's not so easy. This fix to find.

She can't be bought behind a liquor store. Not found in the shadows of an alley.

I must slither on the pavement. The desert is my salvation.

Patient.

Quiet.

Waiting.

No abrupt movements or sounds. She must not see the danger until it's staring her in the face and carving out her insides.

Anticipation builds the pleasure. I savor its sting.

Out of the darkness, she appears. My prey. Unsuspecting.

The itch overcomes me. To feel her pulse. To taste her blood.

Just as He commands me.

Deja vu strikes me as I pull over and roll my window down.

"You want a ride?" I ask.

She stops and stares. More hesitant than my first.

"Where you headed?" I add.

"L.A.," she says. Exhausted. Scared.

"I can take you as far as Bakersfield."

She steps forward, but pauses.

Does she know she shouldn't? Can she smell my lust?

"Everything alright?" I ask.

She hovers. Thinking. Debating. Looking around as if the darkness will make her a better offer.

She steels herself and replies, "Sorry. Yeah. I'm good."

She hurries over to the side of the car. Opens the door. Slides into the seat.

Her musk strikes me. Filthy and sour. Soiled.

Her existence alone could stain the interior.

When did you fall, my angel?

When did God forsake you?

When did He invite you to hell?

TWENTY-TWO

Several days after the package was sent to the hospital, I get a call from Detective Navarro.

"I heard Trent Davis received quite the package the other day," he says. "The lab just confirmed that the organs and blood belong to the copycat victim, Sonja Wagner."

"Shit..." I mutter dejectedly. "I was hoping it was someone playing a prank with pig organs or something."

"I am afraid not," he replies. "Of course, the copycat's screwing with us all the same. I am sure you noticed that the return address was where Davis committed all of his crimes?"

"I considered it, yes. And the sender's initials just happen to be those of the victim, too."

"Right."

"What do you make of that, if you don't mind my asking?"

"If I had to guess, he wants us to know what's inspiring him. And that this is only the beginning."

Silence settles over the phone, and I have a feeling that Navarro has an ulterior motive for calling me. "I can't imagine you only wanted to notify me that the organs were identified," I add.

"No," he says hesitantly. "I was hoping you would reconsider my request to speak with Davis."

"Between you and me, I asked him about the murder the other day and he almost seemed offended that someone would try to imitate him. Practically likened himself to Van Gogh, if you can believe that."

"Wow..." Navarro stifles a snicker. "If that's not narcissism, I don't know what is."

"I am not so sure," I retort. "I think he truly sees himself as some visionary artist. Both in his music and in his crimes."

"And you don't call that arrogance?" he replies skeptically.

"No. Trent genuinely doesn't care how other people see his work. They can love it or hate it and he's completely indifferent to them. If anything, he tries to shirk positive attention."

"What makes you say that?" Navarro asks, his tone intrigued.

I pause for a moment, debating if I should disclose any more information.

"I am not asking for anything that is confidential, of course," he quickly adds, likely sensing my hesitation.

"Well, he cut ties with the one person who believes he is innocent."

"The fiancée?"

"Yes. If Trent was a narcissist, then it seems like he would do everything he could to maintain her adoration. He, on the other hand, completely shoved her away."

"Hmm..." Navarro mutters, falling silent.

"Have you had a chance to look into her yet?"

"No, not really. I've been trying to track down Sonja Wagner's last known whereabouts, but I haven't gotten much. It still amazes me that in this day and age people can be so invisible."

"She's a shadow," I say. "Someone who exists on the fringes of society."

"Yeah... She's certainly an ideal target for the killer. Much like the fiancée, actually. She's more likely to be a victim than the copycat, in my opinion."

"Maybe she hired someone to do it?" I suggest. "Like you said, mimic his crimes to make it look like someone else committed the Vampire murders instead of him. As obsessed and strung out as she is, I wouldn't put anything past her to try to prove his innocence. She herself may not be physically capable of doing it, but she might know someone who is."

"It's certainly a possibility," he says.

"It doesn't hurt to try to talk to her. Especially if you imply that Trent is involved and could face additional charges as an accomplice, she might tell you something to protect him."

"That's not a bad idea," he replies, pausing briefly and sighing. "I don't know... I still think Davis could be a big help. Especially now that the copycat has tried to make contact with him, and in such a dramatic way. I just can't believe this is his first attempt to communicate with him."

"Like I told the Chorro County Sheriff, you'll have to get permission from Trent's lawyer or a warrant showing probable cause if you want to speak to him."

"I know," he says, disappointed but accepting of the reality.

We speak for a little while longer, but as soon as the call ends, I feel guilty about not being more helpful. Despite my resistance to letting people speak to Trent, I too cannot shake the suspicion that he knows something that might lead Navarro to the copycat.

The guilt weighs on me throughout the day and I take it with me into my next session with Trent that afternoon.

I have gotten to the point with him where we can speak in one of the therapy rooms again. He's still restrained to the table, but at least it's more private than the visitation area.

"How's the songwriting going?" I ask him.

He breathes deeply and grins. "The muse smiles on me," he

answers. "For now, anyways... The words just pour out of my head without even thinking about it."

"And the hallucinations?" I add.

"Silence," he says. "Even if Larua wanted to speak, I couldn't hear him over the melodies that come to me. Speaking of which, can I get some studio time? I want to take advantage of the inspiration while I still have it, you know?"

I hesitate. "You know we can't do that, Trent."

"I don't need much," he adds. "Even just a computer and a decent microphone. I do all the sampling and mixing myself."

"Still, though..." I tell him. "Those are privileges that we might be able to work up to at some point, but not right now."

"Hmm..." he grumbles dejectedly, leaning back in his chair in silence. He remains this way for several moments until he adds, "What if I gave you something of value? Would you give me some recording equipment then?"

I eye him skeptically, wondering what game he's trying to play. "No," I answer firmly. "Privileges aren't negotiated."

"You haven't even heard what I am willing to offer." He says this teasingly, not confrontationally.

"Because it doesn't matter," I retort.

"On the contrary, I think it matters greatly to you and to the police."

Does he know that Navarro has been consulting me, I wonder? And if so, how?

"What is it then?" I reply, curt.

A smirk emerges on his face. "What if I told you I know who the copycat is?"

I watch him intently for several moments, scrutinizing his honesty. Do you actually know, I wonder? Or are you bluffing to get something you want?

"Do not waste my time," I tell him. "You told me the other day that you don't know who it is."

"I said I *might not* know," he corrects.

"Okay. Then who is it?"

He scoffs. "That is no way to negotiate."

"I already told you I am not negotiating with you."

"Then maybe the police will. My understanding is that they're very interested in speaking to me."

"That's your choice to make, not mine."

He smiles and his eyes narrow. "Why do you like to be so difficult with me?"

"Excuse me?" I reply, his question catching me off guard.

"These periodic bouts of defiance," he adds. "One minute you're compassionate toward me and the next you're harsh. Tell me why."

"I mold to the situation," I say, unsure of where he's going with this. "Sometimes patients need compassion; other times they need detachment."

He eyes me skeptically. "That's awfully manipulative, don't you think?"

"How so?"

"Well, you pull me close and then you shove me away. It makes me wonder how you really feel about me."

"It doesn't matter how I feel about you. You're my patient."

"But if I wasn't," he retorts. "If you did not have your professional obligations, what then? Would you want to throw me in the stocks, or have me chain you to the bed?"

I rise from my chair and prepare to leave the room. "I am going to wait outside," I tell him. "When you're ready to have appropriate conversation again, you let me know."

As I approach the door, he says, "Tell me this then. What do you think my copycat is trying to accomplish? Is he trying to mimic me, or is he trying to show me that he can do it better?"

I stop just before I open the door.

He continues, "Most of the people who write to me either want to fuck me or crucify me, but not this one. This one wants to learn. To be my disciple. Even when I deny him, he doesn't stop seeking guidance."

I turn to face him. "Who?"

He shrugs. "He's never given me a name. He just signs the letters with *Your humble servant*."

"How many times has he written to you?"

"Four or five, I guess."

"And have you ever written back?"

He glares at me skeptically and says, "I'm not telling you that. Not until I get some recording equipment."

"I see," I tell him, sensing that he's going to use this as a point of leverage and manipulation. "Perhaps that's something you can work out with the police then."

TWENTY-THREE

I stand in the corner of the therapy room, with Trent shackled to the table next to his lawyer and Detective Navarro sitting across from them.

Trent's lawyer begins, "Before we start, I want to make sure we're clear about the terms of our agreement. My client will share whatever information and insights he can as it relates to this investigation with the explicit understanding that he is not admitting complicity in this crime."

"Understood," Navarro replies with a nod.

"Furthermore, my client requests access to the following recording equipment." Trent's lawyer removes a handwritten list from his jacket pocket and places it on the table in front of Navarro.

Navarro glances at the list for several moments before responding, "There's almost twenty thousand dollars' worth of equipment here. The only way I am going to pay for that is if his cooperation leads to an arrest."

"That's not what we agreed on—" his lawyer retorts, but Trent nudges him and speaks into his ear for several moments.

I watch Trent skeptically. Although I am eager to hear what

he knows, I question how honest he is going to be. Does he actually have information regarding the copycat, or is he just going to make it up so he can get what he wants?

Trent pulls away from his lawyer and sits back in his chair. He's demure, seemingly unfazed by the negotiation.

"The top three items now," his lawyer says. "The rest after the suspect has been apprehended."

Navarro looks at Trent. Patient, but intent. Sizing him up, I imagine. Asking himself if this will be worth his time or not.

After several moments, Navarro answers, "Fine."

Trent shows no reaction, and silence quickly settles over the room.

Navarro waits a few seconds before adding, "Well? Are you going to tell me what you know or not?"

Trent shakes his head slowly and mutters, "Patience is bitter, but its fruit is sweet."

"I beg your pardon?" replies Navarro.

"Patience is bitter," Trent says more clearly. "But its fruit is sweet."

"Seriously?" Navarro retorts. "I don't have time for your bullshit. Either tell me what you know, or I'm out of here."

"Alright, alright," Trent replies coolly. "No need to be uptight, Detective."

"Do you know who your copycat is or not?" Navarro presses.

"Yes and no," Trent responds. "By name? Not in the traditional sense. But the way he talks is memorable. I'm sure I have met him before."

"When?"

"I don't remember exactly," Trent answers. "An effect of the drugs, I suppose. He's a long-time fan who called himself Pazuzu. I think he took the name from the demon in the movie *The Exorcist*."

My ears prick as soon as he says this. Yesterday, he told me that he didn't know the name of his copycat, so he was either lying to me then or he's lying to Navarro now.

I keep my mouth shut. I don't want him knowing I'm on to his game.

Navarro adds, "Do you know where we can find him?"

Trent shrugs. "In California, I'd imagine."

"You know what I mean," Navarro retorts firmly.

"He didn't give me his home address," Trent responds snidely. "But I can ask him, if you would like?"

"Never mind," Navarro says, his patience already wearing thin. "When did he first contact you?"

"He's always written fan mail to me."

"I mean, after you were sent to Pantano. How long before he reached out to you?"

Trent thinks for a moment. "Maybe a week? I don't really recall."

"And how many times has he written to you since?"

"A dozen, I'd say. Couple of times a week, at least."

When I hear Trent say this, my skepticism rises. The day before, he told me that the copycat had only written to him four or five times, so either he lied to me then or he's lying to Navarro now.

I remain quiet, waiting to hear what other lies Trent plans to weave.

"What does he talk about?" asks Navarro.

Trent rolls his eyes and says, "What *doesn't* he talk about? The guy's a raving lunatic and tries to use me as his therapist."

"How so?"

"He always talks about killing himself. Says his mind seethes when he's alone and he can't stand to hear himself think. I have told him several times over the years to just do it already, but he never does. If you ask me, he doesn't actually want to die; he just wants the attention. Like a neglected, pathetic child."

"What makes you think he's your copycat?" Navarro asks. "Suicidal doesn't make him homicidal."

"Sure it does," answers Trent. "Only when you're comfortable with the idea of taking your own life can you even consider taking someone else's."

"Was that the case for you?" replies Navarro.

"Don't answer that," interjects Trent's lawyer before he can say anything. To Navarro, he adds, "He's only agreed to talk about this new case, Detective. Keep your questions relevant."

"My mistake," Navarro says. "Tell me more about why you think he's your copycat."

Trent answers, "After I was arrested, he started asking a lot of questions about my crimes. Why I did them. How I did them. He wanted very specific details, as if he was writing a training manual on my techniques."

"Did you ever write him back?"

"Not until a month ago," Trent says. "He was being insistent and I didn't want to be rude."

Navarro looks at him quizzically. "Where did you send your responses if you don't have his address?"

"He gave me a P.O. box."

Navarro retorts, "You just told me that he did not give you his address."

Trent stifles a grin. "A P.O. box isn't a home address, is it?"

"Don't be a smart ass. Where's this P.O. box?"

"Dyer, Nevada."

"Nevada?" replies Navarro skeptically. "That's a long way from where we found the body."

Trent shrugs. "I'm just telling you what I know. How he gets the bodies out there is for you to figure out."

"*Bodies*?" Navarro asks. "What makes you think there's more than one?"

"If there isn't already, there will be," Trent answers, his eyes lighting up with joy. "Pazuzu is eager to please, and now that his first is out of the way, he won't take so long next time around."

Navarro eyes Trent, trying to mask his distaste for him, I would imagine.

"This is your chance to redeem yourself," Navarro says to Trent, an attempt to appeal to his better nature, I suppose. "To prove to the world that you're not the monster they think you are."

"Hmm," Trent mutters, leaning forward intently. "See, that's where your logic is faulty. I *want* the world to know what a monster I am because I am a mirror of the world. What people see in me, they will hopefully see in themselves."

I see Navarro's expression flicker in that moment, and although it happens in the blink of an eye, I can tell that he realizes just what he's up against with Trent.

"You think you can appeal to some sense of conscience with me?" Trent adds mockingly. "You're going to have to be more creative than that if you want to manipulate me."

Navarro says nothing to this, and for several moments, the room is deafeningly silent.

Trent sneers at him. "That's all that I have for you now. If I think of anything else, I'll be sure to let you know." He leans back in his chair dismissively as if to finalize the end of the meeting.

Navarro stares at him, stifling whatever reaction or emotion is boiling within him.

"That's it?" he finally replies, annoyed. "A nickname and some bullshit P.O. box?"

Trent shrugs. "You haven't proven yourself worthy of more information yet."

Navarro retorts, "I don't care if you think I am worthy or not. Our deal is information leading to an arrest or you get nothing on this list." He crumples the piece of paper and tosses it on the ground.

Trent only snickers.

"There are no breadcrumbs down this rabbit hole, Detective. You'll have to claw your own way through the darkness."

Navarro rises from his chair briskly. To Trent's lawyer, he says, "I want a word with you outside."

Trent's lawyer stands and follows Navarro out of the room.

I watch Trent from my place against the far wall, trying to figure out what he wanted to accomplish with this meeting.

Trent mutters, "Cops make themselves such easy targets, don't they?" His gaze wanders the vacant air above him, but I know he's talking to me.

"Why did you do that?" I ask him. "You could've told him anything and gotten what you wanted."

Trent glances over at me. The slightest hint of a smile curls his mouth. "I couldn't help myself," he says. "As badly as I want to make music, fucking with him was just too tempting."

"So is any of what you said true? The P.O. box or this crazed fan, Pazuzu?"

"Truth is so relative," he tells me. "You can't have truth in the absence of lies just as you can't have good without evil."

"Trent," I urge. "Was that the truth or not?"

"In its own way, yes."

"Meaning what, exactly?"

"Meaning that I *do* have a fan who calls himself Pazuzu, and my copycat *has* sent me letters from a P.O. box in Nevada."

"But is Pazuzu the copycat?" I reply.

Trent shrugs dismissively. "It isn't beyond the realm of possibility."

"But you don't know for sure?"

He grins. "How can we be sure of anything? Copernicus was declared a madman for suggesting that the earth was not the center of the universe, but now we hold that to be an undeniable truth. A lunatic in his era and a genius in ours. If you ask me, reality is only that which enough people agree upon at any given time. Imagine what insanity will look like in a hundred years."

"So you liken yourself to Copernicus now?" I reply, not hiding my incredulity.

Silence settles over the room, and a tension rises in its wake. Despite knowing that this is part of the chess match Trent likes to play, I hate it when he gets like this. I used to think it was a symptom of his schizoaffective disorder, but now I realize it is simply part of who he is at his core.

But I try my best to change the subject. "Hearing you talk to Detective Navarro made it sound like you're proud of this copy-cat, but didn't you tell me yesterday that imitation destroys novelty?"

"*Addito salis grano*," he answers. "You can't believe everything you hear."

"So you were lying to him?"

"Maybe," he says with a shrug. "Or maybe I was lying to you. Maybe I have been lying to you ever since I got here."

TWENTY-FOUR

"You think he was telling the truth?" Detective Navarro asks me in my office after the meeting with Trent.

"Partially," I say with hesitation. "I do think he's been corresponding with the copycat, but I don't think he actually knows who it is."

Navarro shakes his head. "I want to know how he's communicating with him. I have looked through the logs of his outgoing mail and I can't find any P.O. boxes or addresses in Dyer, Nevada."

"What about addresses that he frequently sends mail to in general?"

"There are several dozen," he says. "The guy must spend half of his day writing to his fans."

"Yeah. The other half he spends writing songs."

Navarro sighs with frustration. "I think he's toying with us."

"He definitely is," I say. "But with all due respect, you're allowing him to toy with you. As soon as you tried to get his help, you made yourself vulnerable to him."

"I know," Navarro mutters ruminatively. "The problem is that he's our only decent lead so far."

"What about forensic evidence?" I ask. "Either from the crime scene or the package?"

"Both were clean," he answers. "And because the victim was transient, we have no idea when or where she was last seen alive. No friends or relatives to help us figure out where she might've been abducted from. No way to cross-reference that location with known offenders or persons of interest."

"It seems like the outgoing mail log is your best shot then," I say.

Navarro removes a packet from the casefile and places it on my desk. "You mind taking a look at it? See if any of the names or addresses jump out at you?"

"Sure," I tell him, curious to know if any of the names will jump at me.

As I look at the list, none of the addresses look familiar; however, two names catch my attention.

Finley Keenan and Catherine Davis.

The first is no surprise to me, but the second causes me to hesitate. Initially, I think my eyes are playing tricks on me, but when I see the address for the Romero House, I have to agree it's no mistake. I didn't realize he knew she was alive no less where she lives. Plus, the date on the letter was only a few days before she went missing, so then I start to wonder if the coincidence is no coincidence at all. Did he have something to do with her disappearance, and does it have some connection with the copycat?

"What's wrong?" Navarro asks, jarring me out of my rumination.

"Sorry," I say, holding the log out to him and pointing to Finley's name. "When Trent first arrived at the hospital, he sent multiple letters to his fiancée every week, each to an address in a suburb of Bakersfield. The letters continued until he broke up with her a month ago. What's weird is that Trent has sent six more letters to that address since then, but he's changed the recipient's name to Parker Barrow."

"Who's Parker Barrow?" asks Navarro.

"I have no clue. I've never heard Trent mention that name before, and this is the only place that the name shows up."

Navarro glances at the log briefly before replying, "You think he's still writing to the fiancée?"

"I don't know why he would," I say skeptically. "Like I told you before, the break-up got ugly real quick. Besides, he seemed adamant about ending things with her."

"Maybe they got back together after the fact?"

I shrug. "It's possible, I guess. But I feel like he trusts me enough to have brought that up during one of our sessions. Plus, if they legitimately got back together, why would he use the pseudonym instead of her real name? What is he trying to hide?"

Navarro is silent for several moments as he considers this. "The only thing that makes sense is he's working with the copycat."

"You think the fiancée is the copycat?" I reply.

"I don't know," he says, hesitant.

"She's certainly got potential motives," I add. "Maybe she thinks she can create reasonable doubt if the murders continue even after he's locked up? Or maybe the break-up caused her to try something desperate to win his affections back?"

"Maybe," he replies. "I think she's mentally unstable enough, but I still don't know if she's physically capable of mimicking his crimes. Not as flawlessly as it was done, at least."

"People can surprise you," I retort.

Silence falls between us and my mind continues to consider Finley as a suspect. As I think about it, it dawns on me that nobody at the hospital has heard from her since they broke up. It seems extremely unlikely that she would accept Trent's rejection so quietly, and now I wonder if the break-up wasn't legitimate at all. Maybe it was just part of a ploy to help divert suspicion away from her.

"What if she's working with someone?" I suggest to Navarro. "Maybe she convinced one of their junkie friends to help her out?"

"It's worth looking into," he says. "I'm still going to try to hunt down this Pazuzu guy that Davis mentioned, but I am curious to find out what the fiancée has been up to. In the meantime, do you mind seeing if you can convince Davis to cooperate with us?"

"I can try. But I've got to be honest with you, I'm really starting to doubt the rapport I thought I had with him."

Navarro eyes me briefly before asking, "What's your endgame with him, anyways? I know it's probably none of my business, but it sure seems like trying to rehabilitate someone like him is a lost cause."

I shake my head ruminatively, debating how much I want to share about myself.

"It's hard to explain, but I feel this weird kinship with patients like him. The things he went through as a kid? I feel for him. It doesn't by any means excuse what he's done, but I don't think he was always the monster he is now. I think he was born as innocent as we all are, but what happened to him as a child completely shattered him. Having gone through my own mess of shit as a kid, I easily could have ended up down a path like him. But I got lucky. Someone saved me. So the least I can do now is try to pay that forward."

"That's admirable," he replies, his tone sympathetic.

I'm sure my vagueness makes him curious about my history, but he doesn't pry. I guess he figures if I want to tell him about it, I will.

The silence soon feels awkward, and he must sense my discomfort, because he soon changes the subject.

"Did anything else in the log jump out at you?" he asks.

I consider telling him about the letter that Trent sent to his mother before her disappearance, but I decide against it. There's no way she could be the copycat, and it feels irrelevant to point it out to him.

I shake my head and answer, "No."

Navarro and I discuss the case for a little while longer before he leaves my office and I escort him out of the hospital.

For the rest of the day, my mind wanders and I feel an uneasiness settling on top of me. Not only do I wonder about how Trent knew where and how to contact his mother, but I also feel like he has been manipulating me. Have I allowed a trauma bond to form between us that he somehow sensed and exploited? Was the break-up with Finley a decoy to deflect suspicion? Is he more involved with the copycat murder than we think?

My thoughts eat at me until the late afternoon when I see Trent out in the day room with the other patients. We no longer shackle him to the side bench, but he sits by himself as he writes vigorously on a piece of paper.

I pull up a folding chair near him and take a seat.

"Can we talk?" I ask.

He ignores me, his hand continuing to sweep across the page.

"Trent?" I add more forcefully.

"I heard you the first time," he responds apathetically.

"Can I talk to you?"

"About what?" he replies. "You going to lecture me again about the meeting this morning?"

"No," I tell him. "It has nothing to do with the copycat, actually."

"Then what?"

"Who do you know that lives at the Romero House?"

His hand stops in the middle of the page and he gives me a side glance. "Why do you want to know?"

"Curiosity more than anything. Especially knowing your attitude toward religion, it seems odd that you would send a letter to a Catholic convent."

He returns his attention to the piece of paper in his lap. "I just wanted to get reacquainted with an old friend."

"Who?" I press.

"If you saw the address, then you saw who I wrote the letter to."

"Catherine Davis," I mutter. "Your mother."

"My mother," he scoffs with disdain. "She was nothing more than the host I was forced to occupy for nine months."

"How did you find out where she was?"

"Like I've told you before, I have my sources."

"Was it Finley?"

He rolls his eyes and shakes his head.

"Was it Parker Barrow?"

He glances at me. "You've been putting your nose where it doesn't belong, Doctor."

"Who is Parker Barrow?"

"Nobody. Parker Barrow is a ghost."

"Is it actually Finley? Is *she* your copycat?"

Trent bursts into laughter and his voice thunders throughout the day room.

"You have quite the imagination," he replies between gasps. "Finley is nothing more than a junkie whore."

"Who is he then?"

"He is a mirage. A red herring for anyone stupid enough to try to chase him."

"So you've been sending letters to no one?"

He smiles, but remains silent.

I can feel the frustration rising within me, so I turn the conversation back to Catherine.

"Do you know your mother went missing shortly after you sent the letter? She fell into a psychotic fit and ran away from the convent."

He snickers. "I hadn't heard that. What a tragedy. Have they found her yet?"

"Not that I know. Is your letter the reason she had a breakdown?"

"Your guess is as good as mine."

"What'd you say to her?"

He answers deviously, "That I was happy to hear that she was alive and doing so well."

I glower at him with skepticism.

His sheepish grin grows and he adds, "I also told her that Larua is eager to taste her blood."

"For Christ's sake. Why did you do that?"

He shrugs. "I just wanted her to know that I'm thinking of her."

I shake my head with disapproval.

"I didn't know it would cause her to lose her shit," he says with a laugh. "But it does make it that much better."

"You shouldn't have done that," I reply. "I don't care how much you hate her."

He eyes me incredulously. "You have no grounds for an opinion on this. She deserves everything that's coming to her. The world corrects itself in due time, and vengeance will be brought on her sevenfold."

"How?" I ask. "What do you mean, *everything that's coming to her*?"

"You'll get your answer soon enough. Of course, they'll have to find her first."

His tone is so calm and so sinister that it causes me to hesitate for several moments.

Finally, I respond, "She didn't run away... did she?"

He breathes deeply, a look of perverse satisfaction overcoming him. "That detective thinks he's stumped right now?" he mutters. "He's not seen anything yet."

"What happened to her, Trent? Where is she?"

Sardonically, he answers, "With God, of course."

TWENTY-FIVE

The threatening nature of Trent's comments makes me uneasy. Did he coordinate his mother's abduction and murder, I wonder?

Patient-doctor confidentiality aside, I know I can't keep this information to myself.

I call Navarro shortly after my session with Trent to tell him that Catherine Davis might be the next copycat victim.

"His own mother?" he replies. "What makes you think that?"

"The way he was talking about her disappearance made it sound like he knows what happened to her. Like he orchestrated it somehow."

Navarro is silent for a moment before he replies, "Do you believe him?"

"About this? Yes. The hatred he has for her is indescribable."

"Why didn't he kill her when he was committing the other murders then? Why wait until he was locked up and couldn't do it on his own?"

"I don't think he knew where she was."

"I don't know... I mean, which scenario is more likely: she had a psychological breakdown and ran away, or Davis had his copycat abduct and murder her?"

"I hear you, but if she simply ran away, don't you think someone would have found her by now?"

"In Big Sur?" he replies, doubtful. "There's a lot of remote wilderness out there, and God help her if she got lost. The elements would have gotten to her long before someone could find her."

"All the more reason to send a search party out there," I say, my sympathies overriding the fact that what she did to Trent when he was a child was unforgivable.

"I can try to make a call up to the Monterey County Sheriff's Office," he tells me. "But I don't know how many resources they're able to dedicate to a search."

"It's worth a try," I reply. "How's the rest of the investigation going? Have you had any luck with Finley?"

"We haven't found her yet," he answers. "She wasn't at her apartment, so we'll search drug houses in the area to see if she's shacked up somewhere."

"Have you looked at her social media?" I suggest. "Maybe she's posted something that could hint at where she's been."

"Her accounts have been inactive for weeks."

"For someone who used to post daily, that seems suspicious."

"I agree," he says. "All the more reason to find her."

"How about the Pazuzu guy? Any thoughts as to who he is or where you can find him?"

"We've got a couple of hits from national crime databases," he answers. "One guy from Las Vegas. Another from Sacramento. And the last one is in Portland."

"None of those are remotely close to the crime scene," I reply dejectedly.

"Unless he drove the body all the way out here, but I agree

with you. It seems unlikely. The fiancée is definitely the strongest suspect so far. Did Davis say anything about her this last time you spoke to him?"

"Yeah. He laughed in my face when I asked if it was her."

"Damn. What about Parker Barrow?"

I scoff. "You don't even want to know what he said. He gave me a line of shit about how Parker Barrow is a fake name and he sent blank letters simply as a red herring for you to waste your time on."

"That can't be his only purpose. It's got to be a diversion from something, but what?"

"Your guess is as good as mine. I couldn't get anything out of him."

Navarro sighs. "We're missing something. I just don't know what."

"I'll keep working on Trent. Sooner or later he's going to slip up and tell me something. Will you keep me in the loop if you learn anything new on your end?"

"Of course," he says.

After the call, I remain in the silence of my office and try to consider everything that's snowballing in front of me. What really happened to Catherine? To what extent is Trent connected to the copycat? Why is he sending letters to Finley's address, and who is Parker Barrow? Is Finley the copycat or is it someone else?

My ruminations cyclone onto themselves, and I find myself digging one empty hole after another without any semblance of an answer.

As frustrating as the investigation is, it has given me a good distraction from Dr. Maynard's death and my grief. I know I am only postponing working through the pain, but I am not in a head space to tackle that yet. After all, it's only been two months since she passed.

I miss her deeply. If only I could pick her brain about Trent and the copycat.

As my mind spirals in thought, I happen to see the file folder with all of the song lyrics that Trent has written over the last few weeks. Like a muse, I hear his voice in my mind saying, *Listen to my music. Everything you want to know is there.*

If Trent uses his songs to process his deepest, darkest secrets, then wouldn't he have written about the copycat somewhere?

I dive into the folder and comb the lyrics for any references to Pazuzu, Parker Barrow, Finley, or imitation in general. The first dozen are only about the traumas he endured at the hands of Stanley Palmer and his mother, but then I find a song entitled "Cuckoo Bird". The lyrics describe a bird with spectacular plumage that tries to mimic the omnipotent narrator, yet in its attempt to do so, it transforms into a mangled cuckoo.

I am immediately reminded of what Trent told me when I first asked him about the copycat. How imitation is the gallows of novelty. That this new crime is a cheap duplicate of his originals. It makes me wonder if the bird in the song is his copycat, and its metamorphosis reveals his disapproval of the attempt to flatter?

If that's the case, then Navarro's theories about Trent aiding the copycat are false. It also means that what Trent is telling us about the copycat may not be accurate either. Maybe he is using it to toy with me and Navarro? Maybe he is corresponding with the copycat, but instead of encouraging him, he's trying to stop him?

The possibilities feel endless, and my hope that I can unravel the enigma morphs into doubt.

I continue searching through the songs until I find one that makes my heart leap out of my chest as soon as I see it. It is called "Head Shrinker".

The lyrics are extremely stream-of-consciousness, but they

more or less describe a parasite crawling into someone's head and ravaging their brain. Instantly my palms start to sweat and my heart beats a mile a minute. He wrote this for me, I think. He had to have. He knew I would find it. He *wanted* me to find it. Yet another attempt to crawl into *my* head and pull on the strings. He isn't the first patient to attempt this, but he's certainly the most cunning.

The more I read it, the more my panic and fear are replaced with anger. He's rubbing my face in this charade he's been playing. The improvement I thought I was seeing in him has been nothing but a ruse. Larua was never eradicated, only hidden from view. A diabolical wolf dressed in sheep's clothing.

TWENTY-SIX

I pluck a hair off her lifeless head and mutter, "He loves me."

I pluck another.

"He loves me not."

Then a third.

"He loves me."

Followed by a fourth.

"He loves me not."

How many strands of hair are on the average human's head, do you think?

A thousand?

A million?

Will I stand here for eternity, plucking her scalp bare until I can find out?

"He loves me— He loves me not."

What do I want from Him anyways?

Acknowledgment?

Acceptance?

Affection?

None of these things He offers me.

He fuels me, yet He scorns me.

He drives me, yet He dismisses me.

We do not share this work.

I am merely a cheap imitation. A tin-stamped copy of the original. A counterfeit.

In His eyes.

I am not the low-budget sequel despite what he says. I carry the torch. I have taken up the mantle.

His work is not my work.

My work is my own.

I am the new virtuoso. The creative genius. The visionary.

The student is now the prodigy.

The disciple the deity.

No. We do not share this work.

Mine will be infinitely better.

TWENTY-SEVEN

I'm staring sleeplessly into the darkness of my living room early that next morning when my cell phone rings. Immediately, I think that something terrible has happened at the hospital. Looking at the caller ID, I see that it's Detective Navarro, and my heart leaps with the thought that they've discovered another copycat victim.

"Yes?" I answer with uncertainty.

"They found her," he tells me, his voice exasperated. "Catherine Davis. She was..." He trails off, unable to finish his sentence.

"She was what?" I ask anxiously. "What happened?"

"S-she w-was..." he stutters. "She was crucified."

"*Crucified?*" I retort, thinking I had to have misheard him. "What are you talking about?"

"I have never seen anything like it..." he says. "They found her in the Los Padres wilderness late last night. Steph... her hands were nailed into a plank that was fixed to the trunk of a tree about six feet off the ground, then her feet were nailed to the lower part of the trunk."

"What?" I reply, my mind spinning in a thousand directions. "Are you sure it's her?"

"The abbess from her convent just identified her," he says. "We're at the coroner's office waiting for the M.E. to determine the cause of death."

"Oh my God..." I mutter, the disbelief stunning me into silence.

Navarro is quiet for a few moments as well. "That bastard knew about it. *Orchestrated* it even. You said it yourself that he took responsibility for her disappearance. He dangled it right in front of our goddamn faces."

"I didn't truly think it was possible though. Not with him locked up in Pantano."

"I didn't think so either..." He trails off again, his bewilderment taking the words from him. "There's no way the fiancée did this. Not on her own, at least. She's got to be working with someone else."

I don't respond as the shock wears off and my mind clears. If this is the work of the copycat, I wonder, then why was the M.O. so different? Certainly crucifixion is barbaric in its own right, but aside from the victim being Trent's own mother, there is no connection to him or his original crimes.

"I am not so sure this is the copycat," I finally say. "In fact, I don't think this has any connection to the Sonja Wagner murder at all."

"What makes you think that?"

"If the victim was some random elderly woman, would you suspect a link to the copycat?"

"Probably not. I would think we had some new lunatic among us. That being said, Davis admitted to being involved in this."

"I don't doubt that he had something to do with his mother's death," I say. "But the guy who murdered Catherine is not the one who murdered Sonja."

Navarro is silent as he considers what I have said. He soon sighs and grumbles, "What the hell... You're thinking there are *two* psychopaths out there, now?"

"Maybe," I answer. "I'll talk to Trent first thing this morning to see what I can get out of him. You just find out what you can from the crime scene."

"What are you even going to say to him?" he asks hesitantly.

"I am going to tell him that the police found his mother alive and well and see how he reacts."

"Alright," he replies, his tone bearing doubt.

I hang up the phone and get dressed as quickly as I can. I do not feel somber. I feel angry. I feel as though Trent has gotten the best of me and Navarro and everyone else. I play my interactions with him in my mind, searching for the moments that I exposed my vulnerabilities to him and allowed him to manipulate me. Was I too compassionate or empathetic with his past? Did I allow my idealism to cloud my judgment? Have I been too arrogant in believing that I could treat him? At what point did I allow the wool to be pulled over my eyes?

I call the hospital and tell the night shift guard to wake Trent up and bring him to a therapy room so I can meet with him.

As I drive to Pantano, I imagine what I'll say to Trent as well as all the ways he will try to stump me. Whatever happens, I tell myself, I cannot allow him to burrow under my skin anymore. Despite what he wrote in his song, he has not shrunk my head. I must shrink his.

When I arrive at the hospital, I hurry up to the unit where Trent is waiting for me.

He looks extremely alert, as if he has been waiting for this exact moment. He smiles when I open the door and step inside.

"This is a pleasant surprise," he says. "To what do I owe the pleasure?"

"I wanted to be the first one to tell you," I answer gravely, taking a seat at the table across from him. "They found your mother lost in the woods of Los Padres. She's delirious, but she's alive at least."

Trent eyes me skeptically. "You got here early just to tell me that?" He snickers, adding, "You're a terrible liar, you know that?"

"How am I lying?" I reply, keeping my voice flat and composed.

"You didn't come all the way down here just for that," he replies. "What do you really want to talk to me about?"

"You said you had something to do with her disappearance, right?"

He shrugs derisively. "Maybe."

"How were you involved? Because right now, they're thinking she left the convent on her own, wandered into the woods in a state of psychosis and got lost. I am failing to see how you were involved in that."

"Larua wanted to see her again," he answers. "Larua drew her out. I just set up the reunion."

"What was Larua supposed to do with her?" I reply, thinking that he's using the name in reference to the actual killer.

"Only Larua knows his entire plan. I simply serve him in whatever way I can."

"Was he supposed to murder her?" I retort, ignoring his prophetic rambling. "Because if he was, he failed miserably. Couldn't even get rid of a crazy old woman."

Trent's gaze hardens, and he mutters, "Larua never fails."

"He did this time," I counter.

Trent snickers at me. "You really are a terrible liar. I have already told you that she's with her god. Larua told me."

"Tell me how he killed her then."

"In a way fit for a sheep. The same way her shepherd was executed for his blasphemy."

I stare at him in silence as I mull over his cryptic confession. He knows about the crucifixion. Navarro was right; Trent knows who killed her. The question is: who is it and where can we find him?

"Is Larua inspiring your copycat too?" I ask.

"Larua works in mysterious ways," he says.

"But you don't know for sure?"

"I do not want to tell you everything," he answers. "As I have said before: that takes all the fun out of it."

"Fine," I retort. "Did Larua have your copycat murder your mother?"

"*Murder?*" he scoffs. "A virus like her is not murdered; it is eradicated. Purged from this earth like Sodom and Gomorrah."

"Was it your copycat who did it?" I press.

Trent's expression remains calm as he responds, "Why are you so concerned about it?"

"Because you told him to do it. You orchestrated it. And because you are under my care, that makes it my responsibility."

His gaze locks with mine as he leans forward and murmurs, "You need to realize something. This is far beyond your control. Mine as well. We all are the pawns of the Dark One, and we will do his bidding regardless of our desires."

"Who did it?" I probe. "Who crucified her?"

A smile slowly creeps over his expression. "I told you the mystery would thicken, did I not? First the copycat—now this. Who knows what we'll do next."

"Who?" I retort. "Finley? Pazuzu? Parker Barrow? Who are you working with?"

He leans back in his chair and snickers. "I am so pleased that Detective Navarro has involved you. That was one thing I missed out on with my crimes: seeing investigators fumble over themselves as they tried to find me. Running through a labyrinth that is constantly changing. The more they speculate, the more the maze mutates and the further they fall into the maelstrom. Finley? Pazuzu? Parker Barrow? They're all red herrings that are too tempting to resist."

"So none of what you told me or Navarro is true?"

He shrugs dismissively, the grin on his face growing.

I reach into my pocket and remove one of the pages of song lyrics that I found in Trent's file. I unfold the paper and place it on the table in front of him. The title "Cuckoo Bird" stares up at him tauntingly.

"Here's a speculation," I add. "I think you want all of us to believe that you're working with the copycat so that you can get the satisfaction of twisting the knife in our backs, but in reality, I don't think you have a single fucking clue who it is. You said it yourself that imitation is the gallows of novelty. And these lyrics sound more like jealousy than flattery. I think you despise this person for trying to imitate you. *You* have not been corresponding with the copycat; the copycat has been corresponding with you. Boasting to you. Taunting you. Twisting the knife in *your* back. That package that was sent to you? You did not request that. That was the copycat rubbing the crime right in your face. And you know that it's going to happen again. The copycat is only going to get better. Refining the craft that you thought you mastered. How must that feel for you?"

Trent is silent for several moments, his expression hardened and unchanged.

Finally, he replies, "What about my mother then? Tell me, my little head shrinker, how does she fit into all of this?"

"It's like you said—she's nothing more than a red herring."

He smiles. "You're playing with fire, you know. Take it from me—the flames feel good right until the moment you get burned."

TWENTY-EIGHT

Detective Navarro follows me into the mailroom at Pantano as the bomb squad packs up their equipment. There's an opened package on the table nearest them, almost twice the size of the one sent to Trent a few weeks before.

Warden Moreno is speaking to someone on his cell phone, but soon after we enter, he hangs up and hurries over to us.

"This is Detective Navarro," I tell him.

Navarro shakes Moreno's hand and asks, "Did the bomb squad have to remove anything from the package?"

"No," Moreno says. "Everything is as it was when they opened it."

"Good," Navarro replies, walking over to the table as he slips his hands into nitrile gloves.

"I have to make another phone call," Moreno tells me. "You good here?"

"Yeah."

Moreno leaves and I join Navarro at the table. He inspects the exterior of the box first, specifically the shipping label that's on the top flap.

"This one also has the Stanley Palmer house as the return

address," he says. "I'll have to check with the post office to see which distribution center it came from. At least that will give me some idea of where the copycat is located."

He opens the flaps and carefully looks inside before removing a folded piece of paper.

"Is this like the note he left before?" he asks.

"Yes," I say.

"Let's see what he has to say this time." He opens the note slowly so as not to tear the page. Aloud, he reads, *"My Underworldly Lord, I know you only said one, but I couldn't deprive myself the double pleasure. May this harvest bless you and please Larua. Your humble servant."*

"Double pleasure?" I murmur.

Navarro looks into the box for a moment before putting both hands inside and removing two ziplock bags full of dark red fluid. He inspects them briefly, then places them on the table.

"Both look like hearts..." he says grimly.

I come over to the table to get a closer look, and sure enough, two human hearts are sealed tightly within.

Navarro reaches into the box again, removes two more bags packed with organs, and places them on the table.

"That's a liver," I say. "The other is a stomach."

Navarro continues to remove bags from the box while I identify the organ inside of each.

Another liver. Two spleens. A second stomach. And two uteruses.

Finally, he removes two sealed specimen cups filled with blood.

Navarro inspects the labels on the cups briefly and scoffs, "This son of a bitch is something else..."

"Why is that?" I ask.

He shows me the labels, and I see two names scribbled in ink: Jamie Cannon and Sophie Bennett.

"How much you want to bet those are the names of these victims?" he responds dejectedly.

"That's awfully risky of him."

"It's awfully cocky, is what it is," adds Navarro. "He knows we're drawing blanks and he's rubbing our goddamn faces in it." He sighs and places the cups next to the bagged organs on the table.

We stare despondently at the evidence before us. Both of us silently ruminate as we try to make sense of it.

After several moments, Navarro murmurs, "This one is incredibly calculated. To take the time to dissect his victims and pack everything as cleanly as it is? He's patient and he's skilled."

"That's one deviation from Trent's crimes," I add. "Trent's were so haphazard and barbaric. His passion was the killing itself and what he did with the body afterward. The copycat's different. His passion revolves more around the reveal of the body and the deception it incites. Same means to very different ends."

"Yeah..." Navarro mutters.

"Where do you think these two new bodies are?" I ask.

"That's the thing. I don't think he's dumped the bodies yet."

"What makes you say that?"

"We would have found them before this was delivered."

"Maybe he didn't dump them along the interstate."

Navarro shakes his head. "I don't think so. The theatrics are part of his motivation. He wanted us to open the package first. To build the suspense for when he does dump them. And I'll tell you another thing: I do not think this package is for Davis; it's for you and me."

"The letter said he requested it though."

"It implied it, for sure," he says. "But the copycat had to know that we would intercept it before Davis ever got his hands on it."

"So the whole point is just to screw with us?" I respond.

Navarro nods. "It certainly seems that way."

"You still think Trent is involved somehow?" I add.

"I do not know…" he mutters. "But I have an idea for how we can find out."

I glance at him quizzically. "What might that be?"

"Bring him down here and show him what he's been asking for."

"Show him the package?" I retort, dumbfounded. "What's that going to accomplish?"

"I want to see his reaction when he sees all of this shit," he answers. "And I want to ask him myself where the bodies have been dumped. See if he knows as much as he claims he does."

"You know as well as I do that he's not going to tell you that. Or he's just going to make something up to screw with you."

"What he does or does not tell me is beyond the point," he says. "His reactions are what I want to see."

"I don't know—" I say, but just as I prepare to refute this further, Moreno returns to the mailroom.

"Jesus Christ," he remarks when he sees the evidence laid out on the table. "What is all of that?"

"Organs from two new victims," answers Navarro.

"*Two* more? I didn't know you had found any new ones."

"We haven't. Not their bodies, at least. But we've got two sets of the same organs found in the first package. Sure as hell seems like there's two more victims somewhere."

"What a goddamn mess," Moreno groans contemptuously. "Was there a letter in this one too?"

"Yeah." Navarro grabs the note from the table and reads the message to Moreno.

Moreno shakes his head and scoffs. "Bunch of freaks…"

"I want to bring Davis down here," Navarro adds. "I want to show him what the copycat is sending him and I want to see how he reacts. See how involved in this he really is."

"That letter sure makes it seem like he's extremely involved."

"I'm not so sure," Navarro retorts. "And Dr. Fletcher has even more doubts than me."

Moreno glances at me quizzically and asks, "Is that true?"

"Yes."

"Why would the copycat send him all this shit then?"

"To taunt me," Navarro answers. "And to distract us from the investigation."

"So this is all just some ploy?" Moreno asks.

"Potentially."

"Fine," Moreno says. "Let's get his ass down here and see what he has to say."

I'm not so sure. "Warden, I don't think that's a good idea."

"With all due respect, Dr. Fletcher, I am not asking if you do. We're not violating any of his rights by bringing him down here and showing him what this demented care package contains."

"That's not what I am talking about," I retort. "Showing him all of this is gratuitous. For someone with his perversions, he'll regress to an even worse state than when he got here."

Moreno snaps, "I don't particularly care if it causes him to hang himself with his own pant leg. I am done letting this bastard play games in my hospital."

Seeing how adamant Moreno is about this, I ease my tone and reply, "I'm just as fed up with this as you are, but I think bringing him down here is only going to play into his game more."

"Your opinion is noted," he says dismissively. "But frankly, I don't think you're seeing this objectively."

"I beg your pardon?" I reply, struggling to hide my outrage at the implication. "How am I not being objective?"

Moreno glances at Navarro briefly before saying, "I'd prefer to have this conversation later, in private."

"No," I urge. "We can have this conversation now."

Moreno sighs. "You're too emotionally invested in this. I think your sympathies for Davis are clouding your judgment."

"My *sympathies*?" I retort, eyeing him scornfully.

"If I may—" Navarro interrupts. "If it wasn't for Dr. Fletcher's rapport with Davis, we'd be even further in the dark than we already are."

"I don't doubt that," Moreno responds. "But there's more to it, I'm afraid."

"More to it?" I retort. "How?"

Moreno glowers at me as a last effort to get me to acquiesce.

"Go ahead," I add. "Tell me what you think is going on here."

He sighs. "Ever since your therapist passed away, you haven't been yourself. You're not as focused on your patients or the unit. Small things are falling through the cracks. And don't take this the wrong way, but you look like you haven't had a good night's sleep in months."

I stare daggers at him, stifling all of the things I want to scream at him.

He continues, "I don't know if it's grief or if it's your involvement in this investigation, but something is taking a toll on you."

"Is that all?" I retort.

"Steph, don't take this personally."

I scoff, indignant. "Don't you dare patronize me. You want to question my judgment? Fine. Scrutinize the quality of my work? Go ahead. But do not treat me like I'm some pathetic, emotional housewife."

He reels back. "I wasn't trying to—"

"But you did."

"Look, I'm sorry," he says. "I just want to do what we can to keep this hospital safe. We can't go on having this lunatic sending these goddamn packages here."

"Fine," I say, losing my patience with him. "Bring Trent down here then."

Moreno shakes his head with annoyance, but he soon leaves the mailroom.

An awkward stillness settles between me and Navarro. I am too pissed at Moreno to say anything. Even if I could speak, I wouldn't know what to say.

"I apologize for inciting that," Navarro finally says. "I wasn't trying to cause problems between you two."

"It was bound to happen," I reply. "He's getting a lot of heat from the DOC ivory tower and the press about Trent."

"It's none of my business," he responds, hesitant. "I just want to make sure I'm not putting you in a tougher spot than you already are by consulting you so much."

"I'd be focusing on the copycat regardless, so I appreciate you including me in the investigation as much as you have."

"Well, unlike Moreno, I trust your judgment with this. I may not always agree with what you have to say, but it forces me to think outside of my habit trails nonetheless."

"Glad to hear my stubbornness hasn't driven you off."

He laughs, his voice echoing in the confines of the mailroom.

Hoping to deflect the conversation away from me, I ask him, "Have you had any luck finding Finley?"

"None," he says. "It's like she vanished into thin air."

I glance over at the table with the bags of organs on it. "You don't think she's one of these new victims, do you?"

"Jesus..." Navarro breaths with a shudder. "I sure hope not. Selfishly, she's the closest thing we have to a suspect. If she ended up dead, we'd be back at square one."

"What about Catherine Davis?" I add. "Any evidence or leads with her?"

"The coroner's still working on her, but he did finalize her cause of death." He pauses grimly before adding, "Blood loss."

"Ugh," I groan with disgust. "That's..."

"Fucked up," he adds. "His own mother, no less."

"Catherine was no saint herself. What happened to her is barbaric, but she's not guiltless. What she did to him as a boy is just as messed up."

He looks at me quizzically and asks, "You think that's why he did it? His original murders, I mean."

I shake my head slowly. "It's hard to say. He endured significant trauma as a child, but a lot of people do without becoming homicidal."

"Maybe what he says is true. Maybe he is possessed."

I roll my eyes and grin. "Certainly you don't believe in that superstitious nonsense."

He laughs. "I *am* Catholic. Raised by a woman who crossed herself anytime we drove by a church or a graveyard."

I snicker in response.

He adds, "In all seriousness though, I think some men are just born evil."

"Spoken like a true cop."

"You don't think so? After all the time you've spent with murderers and rapists, you think that everyone is inherently good?"

"I didn't say that either. If I've learned one thing from this job, it's that good and evil are not absolutes. They're context-dependent. What's evil in America may be good somewhere else. What's evil today may have been good a thousand years ago. Man is neither inherently good nor evil. Man is just an animal."

"Who knew you were so pessimistic," he replies in jest.

I grin. "Occupational hazard."

We share a laugh, forgetting that on the table before us are ten bags of preserved human organs.

The moment is interrupted soon enough, and a guard escorts Trent into the mailroom with Moreno following him.

"You mind waiting outside?" Moreno asks the guard, who steps out and closes the door.

Trent looks around the room confusedly before saying, "Where's this present you wanted to show me?"

"Over there behind Dr. Fletcher and Detective Navarro."

Trent ignores Navarro and makes direct eye contact with me. "Good to see you, Dr. Fletcher."

I nod, but say nothing in response.

"What's wrong?" he adds. "That fire get too hot for you?"

"You tell me," I say, stepping away from the table so he can see the package and its contents laid out on top.

"What's all of that?" he asks.

"Your present," answers Navarro.

Trent shuffles over to the table and gazes upon the display with a perverse awe. A grin emerges on his face as he says, "Looks more like a buffet to me."

I stifle a grimace, but Trent must sense my disgust because he adds, "Don't knock it until you've had a taste yourself."

"Your copycat left you a note," Navarro retorts. He grabs the paper and reads it aloud.

When he finishes, Trent murmurs, "Double pleasure, huh? Seems like he's gotten more than just a taste, wouldn't you say?"

"Did you know about this?" Navarro asks firmly. "Did you tell him to sacrifice two more people?"

Trent snickers. "A magician never reveals his secrets."

"So you *did*?" Navarro rejoins, watching Trent's reaction carefully.

Trent's eyes narrow. "Are you asking me to incriminate myself, Detective?"

"I am asking you to save yourself."

Trent's brow furrows. "From what?"

"From aiding and abetting charges."

Trent chuckles mockingly. "And what will that do? Add

another twenty years to my life sentence? I don't give a shit. Fire at will."

"It'll put you back in court. They'll re-evaluate your competency to stand trial, and if the psychiatrist determines that you are, in fact, of sound mind, then you'll be tried for these new murders. Your original crimes could be reopened as well."

For the first time since I have known Trent, he looks caught off guard. "You're full of shit. I have a legitimate diagnosis."

"Diagnoses evolve all the time," Navarro retorts. "Don't they, Dr. Fletcher?"

I wasn't expecting to be roped directly into the exchange, so I stammer, "Y-yes, of course."

"You can't just revoke my sentence," Trent interjects, his tone losing control and becoming more angered.

"Re-evaluations happen all the time," Navarro adds more confidently, seeing that his ploy is eliciting a reaction. "One minute the convict is in a cushy hospital like Pantano, the next they're in the Condemned Unit at San Quentin."

"You're a liar," Trent scoffs.

"Maybe," Navarro replies with a smirk. "Or maybe not. Do you really want to take that chance?"

"You piece of shit," Trent mutters, his body beginning to quiver as he struggles to control his anger. His face contorts as if he's trying to summon Larua from deep within his soul, and for several moments, I uneasily wait for what he'll do next.

Then, all of a sudden, Trent's eyes roll into the back of his head and he crumples to the floor in an unconscious heap.

"What the hell," I exclaim, hurrying over to him to see what's wrong.

Moreno joins me by Trent's side and we check his pulse and breathing. Meanwhile, Navarro stands nearby as he tries to make sense of what is happening.

"He's got a pulse," I tell Moreno.

"Still breathing," he adds.

"I think he made himself pass out," I say, smacking Trent on the cheeks to bring him back to consciousness.

"Goddamn lunatic..." Moreno grumbles.

Several moments pass before Trent finally starts to stir, and his eyes flutter open groggily.

"He was here," he whispers. "Did you see him?"

"See him?" I mutter. "Who are you talking about?"

"Larua..." he answers hollowly.

TWENTY-NINE

Three days after we receive the second package, the bodies of Jamie Cannon and Sophie Bennett are found on the shoulder of Interstate 5. Jamie's remains were dumped near Pyramid Lake, and Sophie's were left two hours north near Coalinga.

The discovery hits the news and social media like a typhoon. Everyone from journalists to internet sleuths jump on the bandwagon that there is a Bakersfield Vampire copycat terrorizing south-central California.

The coverage is ten times as extravagant as it ever was for the original crimes, people speculating wildly about who it could be and what is inspiring it. Immediately, Finley is targeted as a potential suspect, but then others who had a connection to Trent are thrown under the microscope. Musicians who played live with him when he toured. Record producers who worked with him on his albums. Anyone with an association with him is stripped down and scrutinized by the public eye.

To be honest with you, I find the coverage to be borderline perverse, as gratuitous and graphic as anti-abortion campaigns. People love sensationalism though. They always have.

As shocking as the discoveries are to the public, I am distracted by my own ruminations about Trent. Especially after the bizarre incident in the mailroom, I am wondering if he is no longer responding to his medication and either needs the dosage to be adjusted or a different antipsychotic drug altogether.

Later in the day, Navarro calls me with a breakthrough.

"The coroner found tissue underneath Catherine Davis's fingernails," he says. "We ran the DNA and got a hit on a guy from San Jose named Nelson Burch. He's been in and out of prison for most of his life. Burglary, assault, arson. You name it. He was even on the hook for a second-degree murder charge until the prosecution had to throw the case out because of a technicality."

"Does he have any connection to Trent?" I ask.

"Oh yeah," he answers, his voice assured. "He's a well-known SOS groupie. Even worked as a roadie on the last couple of tours. One of his assault charges came from an altercation when he was working backstage. He was high on meth and nearly beat another worker to death. Assaulted the security guards too when they apprehended him."

"Jesus... he sounds like a monster."

"He is. *Literally*. He's six-eight and weighs three-hundred-fifty pounds. Definitely capable of what he did to Davis's mother. I am heading up to Fresno now to interrogate him. See how Davis contacted him and maybe learn something about the copycat."

"I wouldn't hold my breath," I comment, trying not to sound too despondent. "I really don't think Catherine's murder is connected to the other three. Especially now that DNA was found on Catherine, but not on the others. The copycat is more careful than that."

"You're probably right," he replies. "But maybe he'll have some guesses as to who it might be."

"Maybe," I say, although I have my doubts. "You'll keep me posted if you do learn something?"

"You bet."

We end the call, and my brain starts churning about the copycat. Even though we have yet to find Finley, I am growing less confident about her as a suspect. Thinking of the physical and psychological state that she was in when I saw her at Pantano, I just don't know if she has the means or capability to pull off these murders. At least on her own. Maybe she is working with someone who is doing all of the dirty work, but there's no way she's doing it on her own.

Then there are the two packages and the notes left in each. These murders are not as much about Trent as we want to believe. Certainly the modus operandi is inspired by him, but he is not the intended target of the packages. Are they for Navarro, I wonder? If so, then why wouldn't the copycat send the packages to his home or the police station? Why send them to Pantano specifically? For Warden Moreno? For me?

I know I'm blindly speculating at this point, but my rational mind does think that we've been too insular about this. We zeroed in on Trent because it was the only lead we had, but I think we need to explore other, less obvious possibilities. Maybe Navarro is right—maybe Nelson Burch will lead us somewhere we did not originally see.

I spend the morning conducting one-on-one sessions with several of my other patients that I have been neglecting since Navarro first consulted me about the copycat. After what Moreno said to me in the mailroom, I know that he's doubting my attentiveness and competence. Even so, I resent the implication that I am too emotionally fragile to do my job. Yes, I am still actively mourning Dr. Maynard's death, but I am very diligent about keeping my personal life and my professional life separate from each other.

And the comment about me looking like I'm not sleeping

enough? Who the hell does he think he is? He can't just say "You look like shit" and use that as evidence for questioning my aptitude. Don't take this personally? As soon as he said that, he made it personal.

I am distracted in the sessions with my patients. I am listening to them talk. I am even taking notes of what they are saying. But I am not hearing their words and feeling their emotions as they speak. I feel trapped in this fugue of rumination. An inner monologue stuck on repeat.

By the time my one-on-one session with Trent rolls around that afternoon, I am chomping at the bit to talk to him. I want to see how he's doing since the day before, but I am also eager to ask him about Nelson Burch.

When the guard brings Trent to the room, he looks disheveled and exhausted.

"He didn't want to come," the guard tells me as he puts Trent into the chair and secures his shackles to the table. "I told him he did not have a choice."

I glance at Trent and his eyes are wide and trancelike. That vacant stare of an animal just before a truck plows into it on a dark, backcountry road.

"Thank you," I tell the guard.

He leaves, and silence falls hollowly between me and Trent.

Initially, I consider a subtle, gradual approach, but I am losing patience with delicateness and I decide to dive into the conversation headfirst.

"When did Larua come back?" I ask bluntly.

Trent shrugs and mutters, "He never left."

"So you were faking it before?"

"No," he breathes. "You of all people should know. Drugs do not eradicate that type of virus; they just mask it."

"When did you start hearing him again?"

"When you crawled into my head and roused up all the shit that I had buried in there."

"The abuse?" I ask, trying to clarify exactly what triggered him.

"No," he retorts sardonically. "All the *good* times I had when I was a kid."

I remain silent for several moments before responding. "I'm sorry about that. I hope you understand that I wasn't trying to hurt you. I know as well as anyone what it's like to have shit that you don't want to confront buried in your mind, but the only way to keep it from poisoning you is to get it out."

He smirks. "You know as well as anyone? Tell me: what have you endured that could possibly compare to what I've gone through?"

"I haven't," I answer, avoiding any kind of self-disclosure with him. "But I've worked with plenty of inmates who've suffered similar traumas. I can certainly sympathize with what you went through."

He rolls his eyes and scoffs. "Your sympathy doesn't mean shit."

I nod but say nothing. I want silence to squelch this conversation so I change the subject.

After several moments, I ask, "When did you reach out to Nelson Burch?"

Trent doesn't respond; he simply stares at me blankly. *Through* me, really. As if Larua is hovering over my shoulder.

"Trent?" I repeat. "Who is Nelson Burch?"

He grins ever so slightly, a subtle curl at the edge of his mouth. "The better question is, how do *you* know who Nelson Burch is?"

"They found his DNA," I answer. "On your mother."

Trent rolls his eyes and shakes his head. "What a goddamn noob. Can't trust anyone to do a job these days. Not discreetly, at least."

"So you told him to do that to her?"

He scrutinizes me for a moment before replying. "Are you asking as my psychiatrist or a police informant?"

"Your psychiatrist," I say.

"So what I tell you is confidential?"

"Yes." I hesitate briefly and add, "As long as it doesn't pose harm to yourself or others."

Trent shrugs. "Lucky for us, the harm's already been done."

His comment sends a chill up my spine, but I hide my discomfort and reply, "How did you contact him?"

"I didn't," he answers. "Not directly, at least. That was Finley. She was our Mercury."

"Your Mercury? What are you talking about?"

He sighs impatiently. "Our messenger."

"How? The letters you sent to Parker Barrow?"

He nods. "I told her to get in contact with him. He's a fucking lunatic, so I knew it wouldn't take much to convince him to do it."

"Was the crucifixion your idea or his?"

Trent scoffs. "Nelson is a moron. He probably couldn't even spell crucifixion."

"That's a horrible way to kill someone," I rejoin. "Your own mother, no less."

"No, it wasn't. If anything, it was too merciful. If I could have gotten my hands on her, I would've filleted her to the marrow and made her eat her own flesh."

His words haunt the air as I silently consider how I should respond.

Finally, I ask, "Did Finley help him? In either the abduction or the murder?"

Trent snickers. "Do you think Finley is capable of that? She can barely pull herself away from the gak pipe for more than an hour."

"People can surprise you," I reply.

"No, they can't. I expect the worst from people and they

always live up to that."

"Do you know where Finley is now?"

Trent eyes me quizzically. "Why do you want to know?"

"I am concerned about her," I answer. "About her safety."

"Yeah, well, you should be," he responds. "She can be real self-destructive, if her mood is right."

"Do you have an idea of where she might be?"

Dismissively, he answers, "Meth houses are a good place to start. Hospitals next. Then the morgue, if all else fails."

I look at him as sympathetically as I can. "You're awfully cavalier about someone you once cared deeply for."

"She was a means to an end. Nothing more and nothing less."

I shake my head slowly. "You don't really believe that, do you?"

"Everyone has that mindset," he retorts. "They're just too afraid to admit it. Even *you*. Look at what you're doing right now. Using this session to probe me for information. Even if you actually keep it to yourself, this has nothing to do with my treatment."

"That's fair," I say, not trying to deny his accusation. "But you're willingly going along with it, so I am curious: what are you getting out of it?"

He grins smugly and answers, "I'm your tapeworm."

My brow furrows quizzically. "What the hell does that mean?"

"You think you nourish yourself, when in reality you're nourishing me."

"How so?"

"You're my portal into the outside world," he responds. "My little rabbit hole through which I escape this place. Certainly you feel it here too? That claustrophobia. All these concrete walls pressing in on you? Making you wonder if this place isn't the bowel of the leviathan? Lucky for you, you leave every day.

You get proof that the rest of the world still exists. I, on the other hand, do not. A nuclear bomb could decimate the entire planet except for this one building, and I would never know the difference. That's how isolation drives men insane. We lose perspective on reality. Our minds create voices to stir the silence. Visions to shatter the monotony of the concrete. Fester in that long enough and those voices and visions become our reality."

The conversation continues to spiral in this enigmatic way until we reach the end of our session.

When I return to my office, I see that I have a missed call from Navarro.

I call him back, hopeful that his interrogation of Burch was productive.

"Any luck?" I ask as soon as he picks up.

"A little bit," he answers hesitantly. "He admitted to killing Catherine, but claims that Davis had nothing to do with it."

"That's a lie," I say. "Trent just told me that he coordinated it through Finley."

"How? Those letters he sent to her address?"

"Yeah. He said she contacted Burch and told him how he wanted her to be killed and where to find her."

"Fucking lunatics..." mutters Navarro. "Did he say where she's holed up?"

"No. Does Burch not know either?"

"No."

"Figures as much," I say, frustrated. "Does Burch know anything about the copycat?"

"That's why I am calling, actually. He claims he does, but he wants to strike a deal to reduce his sentence and only if one condition is met."

"Dare I ask what it is?"

Navarro sighs. "He wants to meet with Davis face-to-face."

"*What?*" I am taken aback by the request. "Why does he want to do that?"

"Burch takes obsession to a whole new level," answers Navarro. "His apartment is a giant shrine to Davis and SOS. Every inch of his walls is covered in song lyrics, photos of Davis, newspaper clippings from the Vampire trial, and a bunch of Satanic insignia. He's even got an enormous altar that he said he used to sacrifice small animals."

"What the hell..." I breathe.

"It was the most disgusting thing I have ever seen," he adds. "It really wouldn't surprise me if *he* ended up being the copycat."

"I don't know," I retort. "Trent told me he wasn't. He said that Burch is as stupid as he is ruthless. Physically, he's more than capable of it, but intellectually? The copycat is just as cunning as Trent was. Maybe even more so."

"Yeah, that's true. What if he's working with Finley? Maybe she's the brains and he's the brawn?"

"Trent did not think so," I answer dismissively.

"And you believe him?"

"I don't know," I say again, hesitating for several moments. "I want to believe him, but most of what he says is covered in nine layers of bullshit."

"I hear you," says Navarro, pausing briefly in thought. "I hate to say it, but I think Burch is our best shot at this."

"Did he say why he wants a face-to-face with Trent?"

"Yes..." he answers, although his voice wavers with uncertainty. "He said he wants to look into the devil's eyes one last time."

"Jesus..." I say, thinking what a terrible idea this is despite the fact that I am actually considering it. "I don't know if Moreno will go for it. Bringing Burch into the hospital for some psychotic reunion? He hates that theatrical nonsense. Not to mention when we let Trent meet with Finley, it turned into a mess."

"He might if it means catching the copycat and ending this

mess that Pantano is snared in."

"True," I say, although I am doubtful. "I'll talk to him and see what he says. Keep working on Burch in the meantime. Moreno will be more likely to do it if Burch knows the actual identity of the copycat rather than a potential person of interest."

"Will do," Navarro replies.

After we hang up, my stomach twists in knots as I consider the proposition. Does Burch truly know something about the copycat, or is he just trying to fulfill some perverse fantasy by meeting up with Trent? I know that, ultimately, it is not my decision. It is Moreno's.

I waste little time and go to his office to talk to him. The room is as uninviting and sterile as a morgue. He's been the warden of Pantano for over ten years, and he still doesn't have a single decoration on the wall or his desk.

Having worked with him as long as I have, I know this is by design. He is an incredibly private person, and his hardened exterior is an image that he has meticulously curated.

That being said, his office still makes me uneasy.

"Thanks for meeting with me," I begin.

"Of course," he replies. "I've been meaning to talk to you about the most recent incident with Davis anyway. I wasn't trying to call you out in front of Navarro like that."

I have no desire to discuss this right now, but I know I don't have much of a choice.

"It's fine," I say. "I understand your concerns."

"You need to know that I trust your judgment, but this situation with Davis and the copycat investigation is taking up a lot of your time."

"I know. I feel like Trent has been pulling the wool over my eyes since he got here, and I guess I was hoping that I could rectify that if I helped find the copycat."

"Your role in this hospital is much bigger than one patient.

And I'm sympathetic about these new murders, but it is not your job. Consulting is one thing, but Detective Navarro is using you as if you work for the sheriff's department."

"I get that," I say. "But I don't see the two as mutually exclusive. Especially considering that the copycat is sending these packages to the hospital. We're involved whether we want to be or not."

"Fair," he replies. He pauses for a moment and adds, "Are you sure you're doing alright otherwise?"

"Yes," I answer curtly. "It's nothing you need to be worried about."

"What about Davis? Do I need to assign him to someone else?"

"Absolutely not. Any little bit of ground I have gained with him would vanish. Not to mention the time it would take for someone else to learn his idiosyncrasies."

Moreno holds his hand up to quiet me. "I am not concerned about his own good. I am concerned about yours."

I cannot help but scoff at this. "I will be fine. Nobody is better fit to treat him than me, and you know it. How many guys like this have I dealt with before?"

"I know," he says. "Fine. You can keep him on your caseload, but I need you to regain focus on your entire unit. Understand?"

"Yes," I reply.

"Good," he adds, relaxing in his chair a bit. "What did you need to talk to me about?"

I hesitate, knowing full well that he is going to hate what I have to ask him. "There is something I need your permission for. I know you will not be wild about it, so all I ask is for you to hear me out, alright?"

He sighs. "What is it?"

"Navarro has arrested someone for the murder of Catherine Davis. He claims he has information about the copycat, but before he talks, he wants to meet with Trent face-to-face one last time. He said if he cannot see Trent, he will not talk."

"For Christ's sake," he grumbles. "Why on earth does he want to see him?"

"He told Navarro he wants to look into the devil's eyes one last time."

Moreno scoffs. "Absolutely not. I don't care if he knows who assassinated Kennedy; I will not allow them to turn this hospital into even more of a freak show than it already is."

"What if we take Trent to him?" I suggest, but as soon as the words leave my mouth, I regret saying it.

"That is an even worse idea," he responds. "Davis does not leave this hospital under any circumstances."

"Fair enough," I say, quickly racking my brain for a more tolerable alternative. "What about a video call then? Low security risk, and it does not need to take more than a few minutes. Navarro gets what he needs, and it puts little strain on the hospital."

Moreno shakes his head with irritation. "Fine. But you are sitting this one out. I need you to start distancing yourself from this, alright? I will coordinate with Navarro and monitor the call."

"How am I supposed to distance myself?" I retort. "I'm buried neck-deep in it."

"That's exactly why I need you to step away. If you can't start removing yourself, I will have to do it for you."

"Excuse me?" I scoff. "What does that mean?"

"It means that if you cannot refocus, then I will put you on a leave of absence."

I glower at him, a million reactions pulsing through my veins. But I remain silent, squelching the urge to tell him off and get myself into even hotter water.

"Have I made myself clear?" he adds.

"Yes. You certainly have."

THIRTY

On the morning of the video call, I wait anxiously for Trent to return to the unit.

Every minute feels like an hour, and the longer I wait, the more I wonder if something has gone wrong.

Finally, I see both Moreno and the guard that escorted Trent down to one of the conference rooms emerge from the elevator. I do not, however, see Trent.

As they get closer, I see Moreno's exasperated expression.

I hurry over to them and ask, "What happened? Where's Trent?"

"He'll be fine," Moreno answers brusquely. "We had to sedate him, so he is resting in the infirmary for the time being."

"Sedate him?" I reply. "Why? What happened?"

Moreno shakes his head with a mix of anger and disbelief. "That son of a bitch," he growls. "He had no intention of telling Navarro a goddamn thing."

"Who? Burch?"

"Yes."

"What did he do?"

"He took a melted toothbrush and stabbed himself to death in the throat."

"W-w-what?" I stammer, the news taking me aback. It feels like the air has been punched out of my lungs.

"Yeah, I still can't believe it myself," he says, his voice hollow with shock. "Everything was going as well as could be expected for a couple of minutes, then all of sudden, Burch just started punching himself in the throat over and over again. It didn't even register with us that he had a shank in his hands until blood started shooting out everywhere. Son of a bitch bled to death before Navarro could even get him out of his chair."

My mind goes completely blank as I try to process what Moreno has told me.

"How—" I try to say. "Why—"

"He fucking planned it," Moreno retorts, his voice full of with anger. "They both did. You should have seen Davis as it was happening. Rooting him on, he was so excited. Pulled so hard against the shackles that they cut up his wrists. We had to sedate him just to get him to calm down."

"What the hell..." My ears are deaf to the sound of my own voice. "I-I don't even know what to say."

"There is nothing to say," Moreno replies, shaking his head. "Other than that is the last time Davis interacts with anyone outside of this hospital. And until further notice, he is on full restriction. Unless a goddamn fire breaks out, he does not leave his room."

"I... I am so sorry," I finally manage to say. "This is my fault."

"He had us *all* fooled," Moreno adds. "But not anymore. He'll receive the San Quentin treatment from here on out. Understood?"

I nod, but my stupor is too heavy to really register what he has said.

As soon as Moreno and the guard leave me, I send a text message to Navarro: *What in God's name happened?!?*

Several minutes pass before he responds with a video clip.

I go to my office and open the video. It is a recording of the call: Trent's image on one side and Burch's on the other. Burch is so massive that his shoulders and head do not fully fit in the frame.

"I fucked it up," Burch says, his voice so shaky that it sounds like the internet connection is bad. "I have shamed myself."

"You did well," Trent tells him. "Your obedience pleases the Dark Lord."

"If only I could have done more."

"There will always be more to be done. You did your service. Now, others must do theirs."

Burch stares into the camera silently for several moments, tears gathering in his eyes.

"It will be alright," Trent adds. "I'll see you on the other side."

Burch nods, and just as his eyes close shut, his shackled fists slam into his throat over and over until blood smothers the entire camera frame.

Meanwhile, Trent's body convulses against his shackles as he growls, "*Ave Satana! Ave Satana!*"

I am horrified by what I see, not simply because of the explicit nature of the video, but also because I realize just how much Trent has regressed.

I contemplate this for a while, considering some of the worst cases I have dealt with over the years. Trent's symptomatology is not the worst I have ever seen, he's not the most unreachable patient I've dealt with, but his mercurial nature makes it so difficult to recognize progress. It is almost as if he is in complete control of his psychosis, manipulating his own mind to best fit the situation.

I have to know more about what happened, so I send Navarro another text telling him to call me when he can.

Over an hour passes before my phone finally rings.

"How did this happen?" I say when he picks up.

"I don't know," he answers, stupefied. "He must have had the shiv tucked into his waistband. We tried to anticipate the worst, but *that*? I still do not believe it happened."

"It's beyond insanity," I reply. "Moreno thinks the two of them planned it."

"Sure as hell seems that way."

"Shit..." I breathe. "*Now* what are you going to do?"

"I don't know... Try to hunt Finley down, I guess. Burch did tell me that she fled Bakersfield as soon as she told him how to commit the murder. If nothing else, she will be charged as an accomplice to Catherine's murder. Maybe she'll have information about the copycat and be willing to make a deal for a lesser sentence."

"Christ, that is a long shot," I reply.

"Unfortunately, long shots are all that I have right now."

"I'm sorry," I tell him, feeling his despondency through the phone.

"It is what it is," he replies. "I just have to go back through the evidence and see what I've missed. There has to be something there that I am not seeing."

"I've been wondering if we are being too narrow in our approach to this. We have been so focused on Trent and any immediate connections to him that we've not looked very far outside the box."

"Maybe. But why would the copycat send the packages? To the hospital, no less, if Trent wasn't connected?"

"A distraction?" I answer. "Or a giant middle finger to you and the entire investigation? Like some kind of Zodiac ploy."

"If that's true, it has worked pretty damn well." He sighs and falls silent.

Did Burch's suicide shake him up that badly, I wonder, or is he losing hope with the investigation?

Soon, he adds, "Maybe you're right. Maybe I just need to widen the scope. The coroner did say that the copycat's technique for removing the victims' organs is very clean and skilled. *Professional* was how he put it. Perhaps he's someone who works in the medical field or, if nothing else, has had some type of training?"

"It is a possibility," I say. "I remember I had a classmate who got kicked out of med school because he was molesting cadavers."

"*Seriously?*" Navarro retorts. "That is fucked up."

"Yeah. It happens more often than you'd expect, actually. Same with mortuaries and coroners' offices. Necrophilia. Cannibalism. Some of the most perverted shit you could imagine."

"What the hell is wrong with people?" he says. Silence falls between us for a moment before he adds, "By the way, I want to apologize again if I got you in hot water with Warden Moreno. He told me that he doesn't want you consulting on this case anymore."

"You don't need to apologize. I've been more than willing to help. He thinks that it is interfering with my duties at the hospital, but it has yet to be a problem, in my opinion. Besides, you wouldn't have involved me if the copycat didn't send the two packages here. Moreno wants to think that Pantano has nothing to do with this, but it does. Frankly, I don't really care what he says; if I can help you catch this bastard, I will."

"Well, I appreciate that," he says. "I know you are going to do what you want to do regardless of what anyone says."

I laugh briefly. "You finally learned that, huh?"

"Oh, yeah. I sure as hell will not get in your way."

Navarro and I talk for a little while longer, but I soon

receive word from the infirmary that Trent is awake and asking to speak with me.

I'm reluctant to go down there. I'm not sure what he wants to talk to me about, but I can't imagine it is anything positive.

When I arrive at his room, Trent is shackled to the bed by both his wrists and his ankles. Immediately, I'm reminded of the image of the man inscribed in a pentagram from Heinrich Cornelius Agrippa's *Three Books of Occult Philosophy*, one of several volumes found at the Stanley Palmer house when Trent was first arrested.

Trent still looks groggy, but he is awake and watches me as I enter.

I stop at the foot of his bed and stare silently at him.

A grin emerges on his face. "You hear what happened?"

"I saw the video," I answer. "Is that why you wanted me to come down here? To gloat?"

He closes his eyes and sighs with contentment. "Death is a beautiful thing, isn't it? Especially when it is at your own hands."

"Did you make him do that?" I ask.

"In so many ways. People are so weak, don't you think? So eager to be manipulated. Nelson was the perfect puppet. Even being trapped in this shit hole, I could make him dance."

"Is that why you did it? For the fun of it?"

He snickers. "You still don't get it, do you? My fans are not Swifties or Deadheads. Their devotion and loyalty is not printed on some shirt or tattooed on their skin. It is pierced through their souls. They would die for me and he whom we serve."

"Why?" I reply. "What's your endgame?"

"Out of chaos comes the dancing star," he answers enigmatically. "Only through madness can you bring sanity to the asylum. If people would just relinquish their false sense of control, the butterfly could finally flap its wings."

I do not understand what he is talking about, and it makes me think that his psychosis has only gotten worse.

"How severe have your hallucinations been?" I ask.

With a wide smile, he responds, "I have never seen such a kaleidoscope until now. I used to drown the voices and visions with meth, but who knew what I was missing. *You* have opened my eyes, Dr. Fletcher. Psychosis is the catalyst of my enlightenment."

THIRTY-ONE

Despite Warden Moreno's insistence that I back away from the copycat investigation, I dive into it even more. I don't take Moreno's threat lightly though, so I need to make sure that I keep my involvement hidden from his view.

I spend hours searching the internet for news articles and social media posts about medical students expelled for deviant behavior, as well as undertakers and medical examiners fired for misconduct. My conversation with Navarro about the dissection techniques used by the copycat opened a wide avenue of possibility for me to explore.

One student from USC was kicked out a year ago for stealing preserved body parts from the cadaver lab. Then, there was an embalmer from Oxnard who was arrested for alleged necrophilia, but the charges were eventually thrown out. Lastly, I found stories about an assistant coroner in Fresno who was fired from the county medical examiner's office for suspicions of stealing organs and other nefarious acts. Supposedly, he was obsessed with cannibalistic serial killers like Jeffrey Dahmer and Albert Fish, and his lifelong aspiration was to open a museum dedicated to serial killers and mass murderers.

The latter catches my attention, particularly when I comb through his social media and find that he is also a fan of SOS. It's probably a long shot, but Fresno is close enough to the locations that the bodies were found to make him a person of interest.

I eventually call Navarro to tell him about the potential suspects.

"I was just about to call you," he tells me eagerly. "They found Finley."

My mind immediately jumps to the worst-case scenario. "What happened to her? Is she dead?"

"No, she's alive," he says. "LAPD arrested her for solicitation and possession a few days ago."

"What?" I respond with confusion. "Why did they wait so long to notify you?"

"She didn't use her real name when they arrested her. She told them her name was Parker Barrow. She's also chopped off her hair, so she was pretty unrecognizable."

"You said she was arrested for solicitation and possession?"

"Yeah. An undercover cop picked her and several others up on a beat known for prostitution."

"Jesus..." I mutter. "*That* was her idea of laying low?"

"I hear you," he says. "If I had to guess, she ran out of money and needed a fix. They found a dime bag with a couple of crystals on her."

"Ugh," I groan with disgust. "What a mess."

"I'm getting ready to head down there to question her."

"As much as I want her to be, I still don't know if she is connected to the copycat," I say.

"I know," he responds. "But I'm hoping that she might know something. We know she was communicating with Davis, so maybe he mentioned something to her accidentally."

"Trent doesn't say anything accidentally, but it is worth a try nonetheless."

"Is everything alright with him?" he asks. "I assume you called to tell me something."

"Yes. What you said about the copycat's dissection techniques got my mind going, so I spent some time looking through news articles on the internet. I found a couple of people who may be worth looking into. One guy in particular: Chad Shaffer. He was an assistant coroner in Fresno, but was recently fired for stealing organs from the lab. They think he was cannibalizing them, although nothing was proven. I searched through his social media, and it looks like he is an avid fan of SOS, not to mention a generally bizarre guy."

"He certainly seems like someone we should look into. Once I get back from Los Angeles, I'll see what I can find out."

"I can do some more digging in the meantime, if you want?"

"That's okay," he replies hesitantly. "You've already helped a lot, and I don't want Moreno crawling up our asses more than he already is."

"The hell with Moreno," I retort. "He's just tired of dealing with Pantano's associations with the copycat murders. We get enough negative press as it is, and this has made it ten times worse."

"All the more reason for you to keep your distance. At least, as far as Moreno is concerned. Internet sleuthing is one thing. But I can't have you knocking on doors trying to find suspects for me."

"Alright," I reply, acquiescing despite the urge to continue pressing him.

"I appreciate everything you have done so far," he adds. "This work can be mind-numbing, so it's nice to have someone to process with."

"I know what you mean. Spending as much time as I do around lunatics and psychopaths, I wonder how I haven't lost my own mind."

Navarro chuckles. "To do what we do for a living, we both have to be a little crazy."

We share a laugh, and as the moment lingers, I feel an earnestness in my core that I have only felt on the rarest of occasions. Instinct tells me to enjoy it, crave it even. A carnal desire as innate as breathing. Yet my mind won't allow it. As suddenly as it arrived, the hunger of attraction mutates into nausea.

I quickly fall silent, squelching all sensation within my body.

Navarro's laughter soon trails off as well, and awkwardness settles over the phone.

"You okay?" he asks, sensing something is off but not understanding what it is.

"Yeah," I say hollowly. "Just trying to make sense of everything."

My discomfort grows and I desperately want to disconnect the call. "Good luck with Finley," I add. "Let me know how it goes."

"Of course," he says, and before he can add anything else, I hang up.

I run to the bathroom and fall in front of the toilet. My insides twist upon themselves and I retch forcefully over the bowl. Nothing comes out though, and I dry-heave several times before my muscles ache and sweat pours down my face.

"What the fuck is wrong with me..." I say into the empty air, as if the answer is not already leering at me.

I know this has nothing to do with Navarro and everything to do with the baggage I've carried since my childhood. It's the same reason that I've never been married or even maintained an intimate relationship. My trauma has the half-life of uranium, and no matter how deeply I try to bury it, the radiation still manages to leach to the surface. It is the reason why I've buried myself in my work as much as I have. Lamenting a personal life is difficult if you don't allow yourself to have one.

And now that Dr. Maynard is gone, I have no one to help me contain it. I'm alone, waging this war all by myself.

Then I think of Moreno's concerns about me and his threat to put me on a leave of absence. He's wrong, I tell myself. I am stronger than this.

I steel myself for the day, and dive headfirst into my work as if Moreno is watching my every thought and move. I am not emotionally fragile. My competence has not been compromised.

Things go great for most of the day until Navarro calls me out of the blue in the afternoon.

"Everything alright?" I ask.

"Sorry to continue bothering you with this," he answers. "I've been trying to speak with Finley for the last couple of hours, but she says the only person she'll talk to is you."

"*Me?* Why me?"

"I don't know exactly. When she initially brought it up, I told her it was out of the question, but she's harder to crack than I expected. She said she would give us a full confession, but only if she can talk to you."

"So much for distancing myself from the investigation," I say.

"I know. If there was any other option, I would do it."

I sigh. "Moreno is going to lose his shit."

"I'll take care of Moreno," he says reassuringly. "How quickly could you get down here?"

"You need me to drive all the way down to Los Angeles?" I retort.

"Finley said she wanted to talk to you in person. No video conference or phone call."

"Jeez... How much do you think she really knows?"

"I'm not sure, but if nothing else, a full confession will guarantee that the charges for Catherine's murder will stick. We do not have any clear-cut evidence that connects her, aside from

Davis's testimony, of course. And that won't be worth a whole lot in court."

"Okay," I tell him. "I'll come."

"Could you get down here by tomorrow morning?"

"I should be able to."

"Thank you." He sounds relieved. After a brief pause, he adds, "I also wanted to apologize if I said something earlier that made you uncomfortable."

"No need to apologize," I say dismissively. "The situation with the copycat and all the peripheral bullshit is just wearing on me."

"I guess asking you to drive down to Los Angeles won't help, but I promise, it will be the last thing."

I laugh lightly, replying, "I seriously doubt that. To be honest, I would much rather work on the copycat investigation with you. The hospital and my patients are what are really burning me out."

"It sounds like you need a long vacation."

"Or a new career," I add in jest.

"I hear Fresno might be looking for an assistant coroner."

I burst into uproarious laughter, so much so that it takes me a while to regain my composure. When I finally do, I reply, "Wow, that was dark."

"Yeah... occupational hazard."

THIRTY-TWO

I've been having a recurring nightmare since Trent arrived at Pantano. One of those ones that feels so real it takes me a minute after I wake up to get my bearings.

Tonight it begins as usual with me gaining consciousness in a candlelit room. My brain is foggy as if battling the effects of morphine, so all that really registers is the heaviness of the air above me. It is this suffocating musk of wood smoke, candle wax, and sweat. As my mind clears, a stinging sensation radiates from my wrists and ankles to my core.

That is when I realize that I am naked, lying supine on some type of table with my arms and legs splayed outward and restrained with coarse lengths of rope. Panic immediately sobers me, and I struggle to no avail as I try to scream. I feel my lungs and throat strain with effort, but no sound comes out.

I try to look around the room as best I can. A crude chandelier hangs above me with dozens of candles spitting orange light. I hear a fire crackling in a hearth on one side of the room. Its warmth licks my bare skin on the nearest side, but it leaves my opposite flank prickly with a chill.

A shadowy figure lingers by my feet, the firelight dancing in such a way that it only illuminates the hard edges of a face. The bridge of a nose and the tip of a chin flicker between orange and black. And the eyes. Glowing embers in a halo of darkness.

My body goes limp. A paralysis caused by fear or submission, I don't know which.

The figure stands before me for several moments before drifting over to my side and the firelight illuminates the shadowed expression. It's Trent, his face serene despite the ghoulish nature of our surroundings.

His hand extends out toward me, and despite the urge to shrink away from him, I cannot. His hand glides through the air and stops over my chest. Hovering. As if he is imagining what I will feel like before he actually touches me. Soon, he lowers his hand until his palm is nearly grazing my breast. My skin prickles with anticipation as I brace myself.

"Don't be afraid," he murmurs, so imperceptibly that it is as if the darkness itself whispers to me. "You are with me."

My heartbeat races, yet the tension in my body abates. I cannot imagine what he plans to do with me, but his voice calms me somehow.

He remains this way for several moments before he steps away from the table and my skin goes cold again.

He soon returns with a small bowl. He dips his fingers into it and begins tracing something on my forehead. It is warm and wet.

"I anoint your head in sow's blood," he breathes, dipping his fingers into the bowl again and retracing the mark on my forehead.

I pay closer attention to the paths his fingers take, and I realize that he is drawing a pentagram.

"The sigil of baphomet blesses you," he adds. "May your pain bring us deliverance."

I whimper as tears form in my eyes. "Please don't do this," I manage to say.

"Shhh," he replies. "The decision has already been made."

He leans over me and places his lips on the center of my forehead, his mouth ice cold against my skin.

I try to retreat from him, but fear paralyzes me.

He soon breaks away from me. "I will be gentle."

He steps back from the table again, and I see him remove something from his cloak. It is long and slender, glistening in the firelight as he moves it over my torso.

"No—" I gasp, realizing it is a large knife.

He places his free hand over my mouth, and the metallic taste of blood rouses a surge of panic.

"You be quiet and still now," he says, taunting the skin of my stomach with the edge of the blade.

The knife crawls over my navel and, as he continues downward, I desperately try to pinch my knees together to protect myself.

He stops shortly after my navel though, murmuring, "I would never do to you what was done to me."

I whimper again, the tears welling to the point that I can hardly see.

"Pray for us sinners," he whispers. "Now, and at the hour of our death—"

Just as he says the last word, I feel an intense pressure below my navel, and then a burning sensation rips through my core and up into my throat.

That's when I wake. In my own bed, dripping wet from a cold sweat. My heart races and I pant uncontrollably.

When I finally calm myself down, I look at the clock with the hope that it's close to the time for me to get up and drive down to Los Angeles to see Finley.

The red glow of 2:36 AM seems to mock me and my heart sinks. I'm exhausted, but I don't want to go back to sleep. I don't want to fall back into that dreadful dream.

Despite the early hour, I get up and prepare for the day.

Because I have a Jungian attitude toward dreams, I dissect this most recent one, trying to find the symbolism and the cryptic messages of my unconscious mind. The most obvious explanation is that my work with Trent is simply wearing on me more than I would openly admit. Subconsciously, he terrifies me, and despite my attempts to repress this when I am awake, my resting mind desperately grapples with it.

I am convinced that there is more to this nightmare though. Jung believed that dreams were profoundly symbolic in their details, so I scrutinize the objects and elements that are present. Fire and flame. Darkness. The knife. All things that can be associated with death and destruction. Trent could represent an undertaker, or Satan himself. And what of the captivity in which he has me? Do I fear that the song he wrote about me—"Head Shrinker"—is true? Has he crawled into my head? Do I fear that he is manipulating me?

Then, there are the more disturbing sexual insinuations. Are my restraints symbolic of the unique trauma bond that Trent and I have inadvertently formed? Do I fear he has carnal desires toward me?

My thoughts continue to wander as I head out of town on Highway 101 and through the darkness of the central coast. I replay the dream in my mind a hundred times like a detective inspecting surveillance footage. Certainly, there is some detail that I am overlooking or misinterpreting. I can't figure it out though. My speculation only breeds greater uncertainty.

I hit a wall of traffic around Thousand Oaks, but my conscious mind is oblivious to it. I'm hypnotized by my thoughts. I spend several hours bumper to bumper, yet it barely feels like a few minutes have passed by the time I reach the county jail where Finley is being held.

I sit in the parking lot and let my mind wander until Navarro arrives. He looks just as tired as I feel.

"How was the drive?" he asks as we walk into the jail together.

"Easy. Couldn't sleep, so I got here early."

"I know that feeling. Before I became a detective, I worked the night shift as a patrolman. I could never develop a good sleep schedule, so I forced myself to function without it."

"Good to know I'm not the only zombie," I reply.

We head into the jail and go through the process of admittance before a guard guides us to an interrogation room. Navarro and I take a seat at the metal table as we wait for Finley to be brought to us.

"Anything in particular you want me to press her about?" I ask.

"See what she's willing to discuss first. If nothing else, try to get her to talk about her involvement in Catherine's murder. If she is responsive to you, then see what she knows about the copycat."

"Got it."

A few minutes pass before the door of the interrogation room opens and Finley enters. Her appearance is shocking. Her hair has been completely buzzed off and her gaunt frame makes her look like a skeleton in an oversized jumpsuit.

She stares at her feet as she shuffles to the other side of the table and takes a seat. Her hands and feet fidget uncontrollably, creating a white noise of jingling chains.

"Well, Ms. Keenan?" begins Navarro.

"I said I will only talk to her," she answers, her eyes still cast downward.

"You alright with that?" Navarro asks me.

I nod, knowing that he will be in the observation room next door.

"You just buzz if you need anything," he adds before rising from the table and leaving the room.

Finley and I sit quietly for a few moments after the door

closes. More than anything, I want her to initiate the conversation to see what she is willing to discuss.

Finally, she breaks the silence and asks, "How is Trent doing?" Her voice is so soft and weak that she sounds like someone on the verge of death.

"He is alright," I say. "Getting better every day."

"Good," she mutters, her face still cast downward.

"How are you doing?" I ask, making my tone as compassionate as I can.

She shakes her head, her lower lip and chin trembling as she fights off her emotions. "He told me he would love me again," she answers. "He told me my obedience would be rewarded."

"Is that why you helped him?"

She nods and glances up at me. Her eyes are bloodshot and tears have started to drip down her cheeks.

"Can you tell me how you helped him?" I ask.

She lifts her shackled hands to her face and wipes the tears away. "He wrote letters to me," she says. "He told me to contact Nelson and tell him where to find his mom."

"Did he tell you how he wanted Nelson to do it?"

She nods, the tears flowing from her eyes more freely.

"And you told Nelson?"

"Yes..." she answers, her voice catching.

"Did you help Nelson? Either with the abduction or the murder?"

"No," she says. "Trent told me to get out of town. He said Nelson would take the blame."

"And that's how you ended up down here?"

"Yes." She pauses, and in a matter of moments, her expression changes from mournful to angry. "He told me he loves someone else." She scoffs. "Can you believe that? I help kill his fucking mother and that is all he can say to me?"

"I'm sorry," I reply, hoping my compassion will numb the pain of the betrayal a bit.

"You will be," she says, her voice becoming more caustic. "I think it's you."

"I beg your pardon?" I retort, trying to hide my surprise at the accusation. "Is that what he told you?"

She eyes me hatefully. "No, but I'm not stupid. You're the only woman he has been around since he broke up with me. Who else could it be?"

"I know you don't want to hear this, but many of his fans who write to him are women. Maybe he has made a connection with one of them?"

"No," she replies. "It's you. You turned him against me. You wanted him all for yourself."

Gently, I say, "Look, Finley, I know you're hurting. He betrayed you in the worst way, and you're trying to make sense of it. But trust me: he does not have any affection for me. I think it is quite the opposite."

She shakes her head as she tries to control her anger. "Do you love him too?"

"Of course not. I am concerned about him as his psychiatrist, but I don't love Trent Davis."

Her gaze grows in intensity, but she says nothing.

"Is that why you wanted me to come down here?" I add. "To ask me if I love him?"

"It has to be you," she replies bitterly. "But you're going to pay. I'll make sure of it."

My skin prickles. "What do you mean?" I ask, trying to mask my uneasiness.

"He's been watching you, you know. Waiting patiently for the perfect moment."

"Who?" I ask, hesitant. "The perfect moment for what?"

She snickers. "The real killer, of course. You may not know him, but he knows you all too well. You'll be next, Dr. Fletcher. You will be his greatest sacrifice yet."

"The copycat?"

Finley grins, her expression a distorted mess of anger and joy.

"You know who the copycat is?" I prod.

"It doesn't feel very good to be fucked with, does it?"

"Who is the copycat?"

She laughs. "Larua, of course."

THIRTY-THREE

Warden Moreno comes down to my office once I have returned to Pantano from Los Angeles.

"How did it go?" he asks.

I sigh. "I'm not really sure how to answer that. She has completely lost her mind. She admitted to being an accessory to Catherine Davis's murder, but aside from that, everything was psychotic nonsense."

Moreno eyes me skeptically for a moment. "Detective Navarro told me what she said to you about the copycat. About you being his next target."

I roll my eyes. "We have to take that with a grain of salt. She is upset about losing Trent, and because she thinks it is my fault, she'll say anything to try to get under my skin."

"I hear you," he replies. "But we would be stupid to ignore it. I mean, look at how she coordinated Catherine Davis's abduction and murder. She cannot be that psychotic to pull that off."

"I really don't think she even knows who the copycat is. She sure as hell isn't coordinating the murders."

"What makes you so sure?" he retorts.

"If you saw what I saw and heard what I heard, you would think the same thing. She is right on the brink of a complete meltdown. She is not psychologically stable enough to coordinate crimes like these."

"So you think she was bullshitting you, then?"

"Of course she was," I answer. "She said the copycat was Larua, for Christ's sake."

"Maybe that's what the copycat calls himself," suggests Moreno. "In honor of Davis."

I shake my head vehemently. "No. She's trying to screw with the investigation the same way that Trent is. And we're letting her do it by entertaining this garbage."

"What if she *is* telling the truth? That is an awfully big risk to take."

"Well, it is mine to take," I reply with finality. "I have been dealing with murderers and rapists for over fifteen years; I am pretty sure I can protect myself from a psychotic drug addict."

Moreno's gaze softens in a way that I have never seen from him before. "I know you can take care of yourself. But there is a fine line between being tough and being stupid."

I scoff. "Don't patronize me, alright? If you knew what happened, then why did you come up here to talk to me about it?"

He hesitates, obviously knowing that what he has to say will anger me. Finally, he answers, "I think you should take some time off. Get away from this shit for a while."

I glower at him. Confused. Angry. Annoyed. I cannot even decipher what I am feeling exactly. After a moment, I say with contempt, "*That* is what you think I need? And what am I supposed to do? Take a fucking vacation? Bury my goddamn head in the sand and pretend that everything is alright while boxes of human organs continue to show up here?"

"Just relax—"

"No, I am not going to relax! Some monster is out there, and if I can do something to help catch him, I will."

"At the expense of your own health and sanity?"

I scoff. "What? Because I'm not sleeping like a baby with all of this shit surrounding me? Is that what you're talking about?"

"Yes, among other things."

"What other things?"

He sighs. "For one thing, you wear the same clothes for days on end."

"Give me a break," I reply, nearly laughing in his face. "Now you're going to criticize my wardrobe?"

"It's another sign of self-neglect, Steph. I don't know if it's the death of your therapist, the pressure of treating Davis, the stress of helping with the investigation, or some combination of all of those, but regardless of what's causing it, you're getting yourself into a fire you won't be able to get out of."

The more Moreno talks, the angrier I get. However, something about the last thing he says reminds me of a warning Trent gave to me a week ago: *you are playing with fire; the flames feel good right until the moment you get burned.*

Then, I think about my recurring nightmare. Despite my efforts to consciously filter the toll this situation is taking on me, is my unconscious telling me otherwise? Am *I* on the verge of some kind of breakdown?

"Is something wrong?" Moreno adds, jarring me out of my rumination.

"You're right," I reply, surprised that I am even admitting it. "This has been wearing on me and I have been too stubborn to acknowledge it. Dealing with Trent is one thing. But throwing the copycat into the mix is a rat's nest that I can't untangle."

Moreno is taken aback by my acquiescence, but he soon relaxes with relief. "Thank you for not making this more difficult than it already is. Hopefully this situation is resolved soon and we can get things back to normal again."

"I agree," I say, although I have my doubts.

"And just to be clear: time away from here is time away from the investigation too. No more consulting with Detective Navarro, alright?"

I have to fight the urge to balk at his directive, but I resist. I can spend my vacation how I please, and what he doesn't know won't hurt him. As the saying goes: ask for forgiveness, not permission.

"Got it," I answer.

I spend the majority of the day getting my duties temporarily reassigned. My colleagues are shocked to hear that I am going on administrative leave, but I don't go into details because the investigation is still active.

When everything is squared away at the hospital, I get in my car and call Navarro.

"Everything alright?" he asks.

"Yeah, Moreno put me on administrative leave."

"He did *what*?" Navarro retorts. "I am so sorry. I wouldn't have told him about Finley if I knew that was going to happen."

"It's okay. It was going to happen regardless."

"So, you aren't pissed about it?" he asks, surprised.

"No. Now that there's no way to fight it, I'm kind of relieved, to be honest with you. I can't remember the last time I took time away from the hospital. I was starting to feel like I was a prisoner myself."

"I didn't mean to go behind your back or undermine you. I was concerned about you, regardless of how credible the threat was."

"I appreciate it," I say. "Better to be safe than sorry, right?"

"Exactly."

"Are you still down in Los Angeles?"

"No," he replies. "I am heading back up to Bakersfield now."

"Did Finley tell you anything else?"

He hesitates for a moment before answering, "She had a meltdown a few hours after you left. They sedated her and took her to a psychiatric facility so they can stabilize her and get her evaluated."

"I saw that one coming. Now, I *really* question anything she said to me."

"You still don't think she knows who the copycat is?"

"No. If anything, my interview with her made me that much more confident that she does not."

"You may be right," he says. "I actually heard back from the Postal Service, and you will not believe which post offices the packages originated from. One from Palmdale and the other from Oban. Both are suburbs of Fresno..."

I don't respond as I rack my brain for the significance of the locations. Then, it suddenly dawns on me: Fresno is where that assistant coroner who was fired for stealing organs comes from.

"Chad Shaffer?" I reply.

"Yeah."

"Holy shit..."

"My thoughts exactly. I spoke with the Fresno medical examiner earlier, and he said that Chad was always a bit of a weirdo, but he caught him with a piece of a liver and that is why he got fired. I guess Chad told him that he didn't know it was a problem since no one had complained about it before. Apparently, Chad had taken dozens of organs over the last couple of years."

"What made them think he was cannibalizing them?"

"He said that Chad would sometimes bring bizarre things to eat for lunch. Funky-smelling stews and things like that. He would ask Chad what it was, and he would act all cagey and not tell him. Chad had hit some hard times, so the M.E. figured he was eating roadkill. Then, when he got caught with the human organs, he put two and two together. Chad never admitted to it, but the M.E. is pretty confident that is what he was making those stews out of."

"Ugh," I mutter. "What made him think he was always a weirdo?"

"I guess he was really aloof. Never made eye contact when he talked to him. Never spoke more than a few words to him. Dressed weird, too. Wore black eyeliner and lipstick. Listened to creepy music like SOS and Marilyn Manson. Read manga at lunch that was real violent and sexual. Just generally bizarre."

"If he was so weird, why did he put up with him?"

"He was very skilled. The M.E. said he was the best he had seen in twenty years."

"He certainly seems like he is capable of being the copycat. Definitely more capable than Finley."

"Exactly. I have to stop by the station first, but after that, I'll head over to Fresno to try to talk to him."

"You mind if I go with you?"

He hesitates, taken back by my request. After a moment, he says, "I don't think that is a good idea. Moreno made it very clear to me that he doesn't want you helping me with the case anymore."

I scoff. "Moreno can kiss my ass. My time off is mine. I can spend it however I choose. Besides, I am kidding myself if I think I can be home by myself and not think about the copycat murders."

"I really don't know..."

"You might be able to use me, especially when you talk to Schaffer."

He hesitates with thought. "That is true."

"And I know I would appreciate the company," I add, trying not to sound too flirtatious or desperate.

He chuckles. "I wouldn't hate the company either."

THIRTY-FOUR

My tastes are becoming more refined.

My palate more discerning.

I no longer eat any fig from the bough.

I pluck one. Hold it. Smell its flesh and scrutinize its ripeness.

If she isn't absolutely perfect, I put her back on the tree and pick the next.

The more selective I am, the more my hunger grows.

I froth at the mouth like Pavlov's dog.

My stomach aches to be filled.

But then I gaze upon a higher limb. I see a fruit so perfect, so ripe, that I thirst for its blood.

"Your eyes will be opened," He tells me. "You will be like God."

My hunger rises.

My stomach groans.

Yet I only want *that* fruit.

I only want to touch *her*.

To smell her skin.

To bite her flesh.

To feel her blood against my tongue.
To burn her soul.
But she's out of reach.
For the moment, at least.
I have to wait.
I have to watch.
Desire blinds me.
Starvation brings me to my knees.
But only my eyes may feast upon her.
For now.

THIRTY-FIVE

"So how long have you worked at Pantano?" Navarro asks me as we drive along Highway 5 toward Fresno.

"A little over five years."

"Did you work in corrections before then?"

"I started out as a psychiatrist at a medium-security prison outside of Sacramento. Then I was at San Quentin for a few years."

"San Quentin?" he comments, surprised. "Was that by choice?"

I laugh. "Yeah, believe it or not. I wanted to work with the worst of the worst, and I got my wish in spades."

"Why did you leave?"

"I was spending most of my time pumping inmates full of pills and not enough time doing cognitive psychotherapy. The whole focus was to keep them docile and compliant rather than actually rehabilitating them. When a position opened up at Pantano, I jumped at the opportunity."

"How have you liked it there?"

"It is exhausting work. Every patient is severely afflicted in his own ways, and it takes every ounce of mental and emotional energy out of me. But I love it. It's like an ever-changing riddle that I get to solve. I have a bit of the monkey brain, so I crave that challenge. That is partly why the search for the copycat intrigues me so much. It lets me decipher a whole different kind of riddle."

"You should have become a detective," jokes Navarro.

"Yeah, except you only get to hunt them down. I get to unearth what makes them tick. Dive into their minds and discover why they did the things they did."

"That is where you and I differ," he comments. "My only motive for learning about them is to catch them more quickly. Frankly, discovering what makes them tick freaks me out. It makes me realize just how fucked up the majority of people are."

"You don't find that intriguing?"

"No. I find it depressing."

He trails off and an awkward silence falls between us.

After several moments, I ask, "What about you? What made you want to work in law enforcement?"

"I grew up in the shitty part of Pasadena. Gangs and drugs and drive-bys were as much a part of my childhood as cartoons and PlayStation. My father ran a little market down the street. One night, some punks tried to rob him, and when he fought back, they murdered him. The police later found out that it was for a gang initiation. I was ten years old when that happened."

"I am so sorry..."

"It is what it is. Shit like that happened all the time in my neighborhood, and there was nothing that people like my mom could do about it. *That* was why I wanted to be a cop: to try to protect people like her."

"That's very admirable."

"Thanks." He pauses and sighs. "I have to be honest: most days feel like I'm bailing water out of the *Titanic*. The things that people do to each other? It makes you lose faith in humankind. I thought it was just an urban problem, but working in Soledad County has made me realize that crime is just as rampant in rural areas. I mean, these copycat murders are a perfect example. Murder in the city is tragic, but it is not sadistic the way the crimes out here can be. I think man is a fucking monster no matter what environment you put him in."

"Yet, you continue to do it," I comment.

He glances at me. "I'm a glutton for punishment, I guess."

"Have you thought about doing something else?"

"Yeah. But I wouldn't know where to start. Plus, as disillusioning as it is, it's the devil that I know."

Silence falls between us again before he adds, "I'm sorry. I don't mean to be so negative. Maybe I'm more exhausted than I realize."

"Too bad *you* can't take a leave of absence."

He grins. "I should. I'll let you investigate this case instead."

I smile at him. "That would not be as fun. I enjoy working with you."

He returns the smile and that feeling of attraction rises within my core. The excitement quickly turns into nausea though. That psychosomatic reaction that has crippled me into loneliness for my entire life. I try to fight it, to squelch the queasiness, but my stomach twists and I can feel its contents making their way into my esophagus.

"Can you pull over?" I say, panicked.

"Why? What's wrong—"

"Just pull over," I exclaim, reaching for the door to shove it open.

He slams the brakes and the car skids onto the shoulder of the highway. Before we even come to a stop, I throw the door open and vomit out of the car. My insides feel like they are plagued and my body is doing everything it can to purge itself of the sickness.

After a minute of heaving, the vomiting finally stops and I

hover out of the open door trying to catch my breath. Humiliation immediately overcomes me, and I want more than anything else to disappear into one of the cracks in the asphalt.

"You okay?" Navarro asks, his hand falling gently on my upper back.

I know I should be comforted by this, but his touch only causes me to shrink away from him.

"I'm sorry," he responds, pulling his hand away quickly.

I feel a pressure building in my face and tears well in my eyes. "*I'm* sorry," I murmur, choking the emotion back. "You've done nothing wrong."

"Just take your time," he says, his voice soft and compassionate.

I breathe as slowly and deeply as I can, hopeful that I can pull myself back together before I lose complete control.

After several minutes, I finally feel well enough to face Navarro. When I look at him, his eyes are concerned and confused.

"You doing alright?" he asks me.

I shake my head, contemplating if I should just lie to him and tell him that I get motion sickness from time to time.

"I can take you back, if you're sick?"

"No," I reply. "It's not that."

"What is it? You can tell me."

I sigh and look at him, trying to convince myself to not open up to him. The urge is too strong though, and I know that suppressing the truth will only make the condition worse.

"I like you," I say, feeling as uncomfortable as a teenager professing her love to her lifelong crush. "But things have happened to me that prevent me from acting on it. Things that prevent me from being intimate with anyone. Even the thought of attraction nauseates me. I know why it is happening, but I have no control over it. It has nothing to do with you. I'm just broken. I don't want to be, but I don't know how to make myself whole again."

"It's okay," he says. "I like you too, but I have no intention of acting on it unless you want to."

He reaches into the glovebox, removes several napkins and hands them to me.

"Thanks." I wipe my eyes and mouth. "For the record, this was not how I imagined this happening."

He chuckles. "We've not exactly had an ideal moment before."

I laugh. "You mean, people don't meet their soulmates through a serial murder investigation?"

"Not normal people."

We soon get back onto the highway and continue toward Fresno. The mood in the car becomes noticeably more awkward, but once we get into the city, we begin mentally preparing to confront Chad Shaffer.

Shaffer's home is in an older neighborhood on the south side of town. The houses are those simple brick ones that were so popular in the fifties. Most of the properties are overgrown and unkempt, exposing the neighborhood's age that much more.

When we pull up to his home, it looks as though nobody has lived there in years. The lawn is dead and infested with weeds, and the bushes are scraggly and dying. I also notice that the first-story windows and the front door are covered with plywood.

"Are you sure he still lives here?" I ask.

"This is his last known address, but it looks pretty vacant." He opens his door and adds, "I'm going to check it out. You stay in the car, alright?"

I nod and he gets out of the car.

I watch Navarro approach the front of the house from the walkway. He knocks on the plywood that covers the door several times. Then, he tries to peer into the boarded windows on the porch. After a few moments, he walks the perimeter of the house and disappears into the backyard.

A minute or so passes when I see a man hurry across the street from a neighboring house. He glowers quizzically at the car, but he must not see me through the tinted windows because he soon continues onto the property and heads toward the entrance to the backyard.

"Oh, shit..." I pull out my phone and start calling Navarro.

My heart thumps with adrenaline as I wait for the call to go through.

"Yeah?" he answers.

"Someone just crossed the street and is heading into the backyard."

"Christ," he says. "I see him."

He trails off, but he does not hang the call up and I can hear his interaction faintly.

"What the fuck are you doing on my property?" a muffled voice asks.

"I'm a detective with the Soledad County Sheriff's Department. Are you Chad Shaffer?"

"Hell no, I ain't."

"You said this is your property though?"

"Yeah," the man replies. *"I was renting the house to him before he trashed the shit out of it. Why the hell are you looking for him?"*

"I just had some questions I wanted to ask him about a case I am working. You don't know where I can find him, do you?"

"I wish. That son of a bitch bolted when he found out that the city was condemning the house."

"Why did they do that?"

"It's disgusting in there. Piles of trash. Dead animal carcasses. He stopped paying the utilities, so he was just pissing and shitting in one of the bedrooms. I have to gut the whole goddamn thing now."

"You mind if I take a look around?"

"Be my guest."

Navarro picks up the phone again. "I'm coming back around to the front. Did you hear all of that?"

"Yeah. Can I take a look in the house with you?"

He hesitates. "You sure you want to do that?"

"Yes," I say, hanging up the phone.

I get out of the car as Navarro and the property owner appear from the backyard. They are talking, but I cannot make out what they are saying.

Navarro motions to me as I approach.

"You don't look like no cop," the property owner says to me.

"I'm a consultant on the case," I answer. "What's your name?"

"Derek Tribbett."

Navarro adds, "Mr. Tribbett was renting this house to Chad Shaffer."

"Squatting is more like it," he corrects. "That piece of shit hadn't paid rent since he got fired six months ago."

"When did he abandon the house?" I ask.

"Week or two ago? It took the city that long before they finally came out here to do something about it."

"Any idea where he might have gone?"

He shakes his head. "Hell if I know. Wherever he went, he left in a hurry. Didn't take nothing with him as far as I can tell."

Navarro exchanges a look with me, his suspicions matching my own.

"What's this case you're working on anyways?" Mr. Tribbett adds.

"I can't share that unfortunately," Navarro answers. "But we appreciate you letting us take a look inside."

"No problem."

Navarro walks over to his car to grab a tire iron to pry the plywood away from the front door.

Mr. Tribbett asks me, "So if you ain't a cop, what do you do?"

"I work for the Department of Corrections."

His brow furrows with surprise. "You ain't a guard, are you?"

"No. I'm a psychiatrist."

He smirks. "Head shrinker, huh?"

His comment makes me hesitate as I immediately think of the song that Trent wrote about me.

"Bet you've dealt with some real sickos," he adds.

"No sicker than anyone else," I reply.

Navarro soon returns with the tire iron as well as pairs of nitrile gloves and medical-grade masks.

"Don't want to breathe whatever is festering in there," he says.

We put the masks and gloves on, and he gets to work prying the plywood away from the door.

It takes him a few minutes, but he eventually gets the doorway unobstructed and opened.

The mask does nothing to prevent the stench from punching me in the face, and we have to wait a moment before we can step into the house.

Once we're inside, I am immediately reminded of the crime scene photographs from the Stanley Palmer house after Trent was arrested. Garbage is piled in drifts against every wall. The ceilings are stained a pale brown color, and the walls are covered in graffiti.

"What the hell..." Navarro mutters in awe as he shuffles through the trash.

I am too horrified to speak. As if the garbage wasn't enough, I also see several animal carcasses strewn about the floor and hanging from the ceiling. Raccoons, skunks, and squirrels as well as cats and dogs.

I immediately conjure this image of Chad Shaffer as

LeatherFace from *The Texas Chainsaw Massacre*, and I half expect him to jump out from around a dark corner and attack us with an ax.

I follow Navarro through the house as he drifts from one room to the next. In the kitchen, large pots sit on the stovetop and counters, each containing a repulsive sludge that nauseates me to think about what they contain. Then, we reach the dining room, and this disturbing sense of deja vu strikes me. It looks exactly like the altar room that Trent used in the Stanley Palmer house.

"Holy shit," I mutter.

"We need to get a forensics unit out here," Navarro responds. "Now."

We get out of the house and Navarro calls the Fresno Police Department.

"What did you think?" Mr. Tribbett asks me.

I shake my head in disbelief. "I don't even know what to say."

"I've been a landlord for thirty years, and I ain't never had a house trashed out like that."

"When did you first suspect something wasn't right with him?" I ask.

"Maybe a month after he got fired and stopped paying rent. At first, I tried to cut him some slack because he had lost his job and he had been a good tenant up to that point. But as the weeks went on, he got harder to talk to until he stopped answering the door altogether. I gave him proper notice and tried to unlock the front door to go in, and that bastard had changed the locks. I called the police and they gave me a bunch of shit about tenants' rights and how I couldn't legally break into my own fucking house. He must have stopped paying the utilities around that time too, because about two months ago, they cut everything off. Gas, water, and electric. I hoped that sooner or later he would leave, but it didn't bother him none. Finally, the goddamn city got involved and sent code enforcement over here. Threatened to break the door down if he didn't let them in. When they saw the condition the house was in, they told me they needed to condemn it and that it was on me to fix! You believe that? I said I wanted to press charges, and they told me that there was no basis. No basis? He destroyed my goddamn house! They said I could take it to civil court, but a few days after that, that shithead disappeared."

"Did Mr. Shaffer show any signs of aggression or violence?"

Mr. Tribbett scoffs. "Did you see what he did to them animals? You tell me if that's a sign of violence."

"How about toward people?"

"Not toward me, but who the hell knows? Sure liked dead bodies from what I read on the internet. You don't think he was murdering people in my house, do you?"

"We don't know," I say, trying to not give him more information than is necessary.

"Is that the case you're working on? You think he might have killed someone?"

"We can't say—"

"You think he's the one copying the Bakersfield Vampire?"

"I really cannot say."

"Goddamn," he grumbles, exasperated. "I'm going to have to tear the whole house down after this."

"You don't have any idea where he might've gone?" I ask, trying to change the subject.

"Like I told you already, if I did, I'd be hunting that son of a bitch down myself."

"Do you know where he was from before?"

"He wasn't exactly a talker," Mr. Tribbett answers impatiently. "And I sure as hell didn't go over there to chat him up. All I know is he locked himself up in there for the last six months and did God knows what."

I continue to probe for information, but Mr. Tribbett tells me little more than he already has.

The forensics unit arrives quickly, and they begin to process the house for evidence.

Navarro goes to assist the technicians while I return to the car to comb the internet on my smartphone for leads as to where Shaffer was from or where he might have fled to.

I see that his social media accounts have been inactive for months, probably lining up with his termination from the coroner's office. If I had to guess, I would say that getting fired was the last straw for Shaffer psychologically and he had some kind of breakdown as a result. The question is: was it enough to make him homicidal? Simply based on the condition of the house, it seems possible. Mutilating animals alone is one of many hallmark signs of serial killers, but the fact that he had an altar room like Trent is even more convincing.

That being said, if he was as shut in as Mr. Tribbett claimed he was, then how was he getting out to abduct and murder those women? Was he doing it in the dead of night so that nobody would see him? Also, with him officially on the run, I wonder if the murders will stop, or if bodies will start showing up elsewhere?

An hour passes before Navarro returns, and his expression looks exhausted and exasperated.

"They haven't found anything obvious yet," he says. "They have to take those stew pots to the lab to figure out what the hell is in them."

"Anything that potentially links him to the copycat murders?" I ask.

He shakes his head. "It's too early to tell. The altar room is an obvious connection to Davis's crimes, not to mention the walls are covered in SOS lyrics and insignia. Sifting through all that trash is going to take a while though. We need to find him first. Any luck with figuring out where he went?"

"He's disappeared on social media."

"I'll see if our analysts can locate a cell phone or track recent credit card transactions. We'll put out an APB on him as well. If he left several weeks ago though, he could be anywhere."

"You think he'll do it again?" I ask.

Navarro hesitates. "It's hard to say. He needs a secure place to work, so I doubt he'll do it again until he's found a somewhat permanent place to stay."

"You would think he would at least stay along the Interstate 5 corridor, right?"

"Yeah, but that doesn't narrow it down a whole lot. Interstate 5 runs all the way from Mexico to Canada."

"Shit, I didn't think about that..." I reply dejectedly, pausing to think for a moment.

"Wait a minute," he says. "The packages that were sent to Pantano had the Stanley Palmer house as the return address, right? What if he is hiding out there? I know it seems too obvious to be true, but it's worth having someone take a look, isn't it?"

"I suppose."

THIRTY-SIX

Dead ends seem to emerge from all angles as the week progresses. The Bakersfield Police Department finds nothing at the Stanley Palmer house when they go over to check if Chad Shaffer is squatting there, and the Fresno forensics team finds no evidence directly related to the copycat victims or their murders. The lab did confirm, however, that the stew pots contained human DNA, but no matches have been made to the known victims. Navarro and I speculate that either there are more victims that have yet to be found, or the parts used were ones that Shaffer stole from the coroner's office.

The following week, Navarro receives word that a student at Bakersfield College, Shawna Bowman, went missing at a party over the weekend, and several witnesses thought they saw someone matching Shaffer's description.

He and I go to the campus to interview the witnesses and the friends that she went out with that night, but none of their testimonies are detailed enough to be helpful. One girl claims she saw Shaffer specifically, but her description doesn't even match him accurately.

"Her disappearance may not have anything to do with the

copycat," Navarro says when we are finished. "Aside from the fact that the witnesses were all intoxicated and their testimony is shaky at best, this new girl doesn't fit the copycat's M.O. All of the victims have been transients of some kind. Same with Davis's original victims. Why would he go after someone who is a part of various communities and well-known by others? Why not stick to victims who are less risky?"

"Maybe he knows her?" I suggest.

He hesitates. "I don't think so. I don't think who the victims are is necessarily important to him. It's what he does to them that matters."

"Maybe he wants a greater challenge? Abducting and butchering an invisible drifter is one thing; snatching someone whose disappearance will be noticed is a whole different level of difficulty. That was what was so terrifying about Ted Bundy. Girls were practically disappearing in broad daylight."

"That's more of a possibility. But why do that if the point is to copy Davis?"

"Maybe that isn't the point."

Navarro eyes me quizzically. "What do you mean?"

"I think we've been too restricted in our approach to this. At first, we were convinced that Trent was not only inspiring the copycat, but teaching him his ways. Maybe even using Finley to coordinate the murders."

"The letters in the packages would certainly indicate that."

"But what if that is just a distraction? What if this guy is like a magician using misdirection?"

Navarro shakes his head slowly. "I don't know. If that's the case, what's the trick? What's the true point of the murders?"

"To show Trent that he's better," I answer. "The packages were not meant to pay homage to him; they were meant to taunt him. To rub his face in it. With this new girl missing, the copycat is magnifying the difficulty and showing Trent that he can get away with it."

Navarro does not look so sure about my reasoning. "Does Chad Shaffer seem like someone who's mentally stable enough to pull off something like that? I mean, what you're talking about requires incredible patience and discipline on top of psychopathy. Shaffer wasn't fooling anyone at the coroner's office, so is it possible for him to do all this?"

"There's only one way to know. We have to find him."

Days pass with few meaningful leads. The Bakersfield Police Department works diligently to find Shawna Bowman, but there is no trace of her anywhere. Navarro and I do what we can to track down Chad Shaffer, but he too has vanished into thin air.

The only thing we have to go on is the last location his cell phone pinged from three weeks ago: a random section of Interstate 5 between Los Banos and San Francisco. When Navarro and I reach a point where we have exhausted most other leads, we drive out to the location to see what we can find.

The ping was not exact, only providing a one-square-mile radius in the middle of nowhere. The only thing out there besides pavement and desert is an abandoned rest stop. Nothing more than a small parking area with a covered picnic table and a pit toilet.

"Maybe he ditched his phone in the toilet?" Navarro suggests as we get out of the car. "I'll take a look in there if you want to start sweeping out here."

"Sure," I say, wandering over to the covered picnic table first.

Weeds have overtaken the area, even growing through cracks in the concrete pad. The only signs of human life are a couple of shattered beer bottles and dilapidated liquor shooters.

I scan the ground around the table, looking for footprints in the sand or anything else suspicious. A gust of wind kicks up, and sand slides across the surface of the ground as if being pulled by an invisible tide.

I hear the scraping of metal nearby, and I see Navarro opening the door to the pit toilet. Part of me expects to see him shrink backward from whatever he sees in there, but he shows no surprise as he creeps inside.

I scan the desert surrounding the area. The barren landscape extends to the east for miles like a beige ocean. Dust devils crop up and disappear at random, and the heat makes the air above the ground vibrate. It makes me feel microscopic.

The pit toilet door scrapes again as Navarro closes it shut. He comes over to me, unhurried.

"Find anything?" I call out.

He shakes his head. "Nothing. There's a chance he smashed the phone and threw it into the pit, but I didn't see anything in there besides rotting toilet paper."

"I don't know if that's good news or not."

"Good news doesn't really exist in this job," he says. "You find anything over here?"

"No. Old liquor bottles, but that's it."

Navarro sighs and scans the desert. I can only imagine what he's thinking about in these moments. Frustration. Disillusionment. Confusion.

Then, I see his hand rise and his finger point toward the distant sky.

"Are those vultures circling out there?" he says.

I squint against the glare of the sun and the heat. I cannot tell if I can see birds or if my eyes are playing tricks on me.

"I'm going to take a look," Navarro adds.

I follow him into the desert, picking our way through the cacti and dried-out brush.

"It's probably a dead coyote," he says. "But it doesn't hurt to check."

As we get closer, I see that the birds are not an illusion. They are vultures. Three of them. Circling in the same spot over and over as if they are trapped in the funnel of one of the dust devils.

The wind changes direction and fragments of sand fly into our faces. I turn away to let it pass, but Navarro continues on.

"You smell that?" he calls back to me.

"No," I answer, covering my face with my arm.

"Smells like something's rotting."

He picks up his pace, weaving through the cacti more briskly.

"You see something?" I ask.

He doesn't answer. I just see him hurry further ahead of me until he comes to an abrupt stop.

I hustle after him, trying not to slam my foot into a cactus by accident. Another gust of wind hits me, and that's when I notice the stench. It is distinctly the smell of rotting meat.

When I get within a few feet of him, I see what is causing the foul odor.

Before us are rocks placed in the shape of a gigantic pentagram. At each point, there is some type of dead animal placed in a supine position with its underbelly slashed open. They appear to be coyotes or foxes, but they are too mangled to tell. At the center of the pentagram is a rotting pile of innards that were removed from the animals.

Navarro glances at me, his expression smothered in bewilderment. "What do you make of this?"

I shake my head slowly. "It has to be Shaffer, right?"

"Seems that way. Question is: why?"

I think for a few moments before I recall the first package sent to Trent and the note it contained. The reference to the sacrifice and the five vertices of man. Is that what Shaffer was trying to do here? Some makeshift altar and sacrifice for Larua? Or was it an attempt to pay homage to Trent?

Navarro steps closer, inspecting the pile of innards specifically.

"I think this is all from the animals," he says. "Nothing looks remotely big enough to be human."

I watch him for a few moments, then ask, "What do *you* make of this?"

"It certainly links him to Davis..." he answers. However, he trails off as if he isn't so sure. "But does it make him the copycat?"

"How could it not?" I reply. "I mean, how many people are coming out to the middle of nowhere and doing something like this?"

"That's what I mean though. At none of the dump sites have we found something like this. No sacrificial imagery of any kind, actually."

"He references the five vertices of man and the pentagram in the first letter, right?"

This gives Navarro pause. Either he forgot about it or he hadn't considered it very carefully before.

"I don't know," he eventually says. "I don't think he's the copycat. He's obviously psychotic and maybe even trying to imitate Davis in some way, but this doesn't fit the three murders."

"I'm not so sure," I retort. "Especially given the condition of his house. The altar room? His obvious obsession with Trent and his music? Now this? It makes sense that Shaffer would take his obsession to such extreme levels."

"What about Shawna Bowman? None of the witnesses could accurately identify him."

"Maybe Shawna's abductor isn't the copycat?"

"Yeah..." he murmurs, his voice trailing off into the desert breeze.

He returns his attention to the pentagram. After a moment, he leans closer toward the rotting innards in the center.

"What are you doing?" I ask.

He doesn't answer as he reaches into his pocket for nitrile

gloves. As he puts the gloves on, he steps inside of the rock-formed sigil and kneels down by the organs.

"Shouldn't you let the forensics team do that?" I add.

He ignores me, reaching into the bloody pile carefully and removing what looks like a busted cell phone. He messes with it briefly, seeing if it will still turn on, but it shows no sign of life. He rises and steps out of the pentagram.

"You think that's his cell phone?"

"Either his or hers," he replies, opening a clear evidence bag and placing the phone inside of it. "We'll get forensics out here, but this is coming back with us. Maybe the SIM card can tell us something about this guy."

He starts walking back toward the car, but I remain where I am for a moment.

What the hell were you trying to do out here, I wonder? And what are you planning on doing with her?

THIRTY-SEVEN

Navarro and I watch eagerly as the forensic technology analyst tinkers with the cell phone. He tries to get it to boot up on its own, but after several failed attempts, he removes the SIM card and inserts it into his laptop.

Unintelligible strings of codes and commands scroll on the screen as the technician types. A window soon appears showing a folder with hundreds of files within it.

"That's the camera roll," says the technician.

"Can you open the most recent ones?" Navarro asks.

The technician scrolls through the folder for a moment, then highlights several files. With a double-click of the mouse, the files open and images start to appear on the screen. Several of them are selfies of college-aged girls at a house party. Others are the same girls at a sporting event. I recognize most of the girls depicted. They are the witnesses that we interviewed earlier, and, of course, Shawna Bowman.

"Christ..." Navarro says. "Is this *her* phone?"

The technician selects more files and opens them. Similar images appear. Nearly all of them show Shawna.

"It must be," the technician says. "I'll have to see what I can pull from the NAND chip."

"How long will that take?"

"Depends on how damaged the chip is," the tech answers. "It may take a few hours, or it may not be recoverable at all."

"I don't understand," I say, confused. "His phone pinged out there three weeks ago, and her phone last pinged at the college this past weekend. How is that possible?"

Navarro replies, "He must have ditched his phone out there, then took her there after he abducted her. We need to get forensics out to that rest stop ASAP. Comb the desert and find out what's in that pit toilet." He pauses for several moments before he says to the technician, "Keep me updated on what you find out, alright?"

The tech agrees, and Navarro and I leave the cyber forensics lab.

"You think she's still alive?" I ask.

"I doubt it," he answers hollowly. "It's been days since she went missing."

"Don't you think we would have found her remains out there?"

He glances at me somberly. "We still might."

"What if he took her somewhere else afterward?" I add. "I know that's a remote area, but San Francisco and Sacramento are only a few hours away."

Navarro shakes his head in disagreement. "I don't think he took her to that rest stop alive. I think whatever he did to her, he did it somewhere else and ditched her phone out there after the fact."

"She could still be alive," I counter, trying to maintain my optimism.

"She could be," he responds. "But it's more likely that she isn't." He sighs with exasperation. "We need to see what forensics finds out there."

"Can't we search nearby areas for him? I mean, we know he's been to the rest stop in the last few weeks. He must be hiding somewhere near there."

"Like San Francisco or Sacramento?"

"Yes!" I exclaim, growing frustrated with his dejection.

"You know how many people live in those cities? That'll be like looking for a needle in a stack of needles. Besides, if he was somewhere that densely populated, we would have gotten a hit on the APB by now."

"What about the Coalinga National Forest west of the interstate? He could be hiding out there where no one will see him."

"I appreciate your enthusiasm, but we're not going to aimlessly wander the woods looking for him."

"It's not aimless," I interject. "You sure as hell aren't going to find him hiding at the bottom of that pit toilet. We need to stop trying to trace his steps and start anticipating where he will be next."

"We have to go where the evidence takes us—" Navarro tries to say before he is interrupted by the ringing of his phone.

He glances at the screen, and I see the color wash out of his face completely. He flashes the screen at me so I can see who's calling.

WARDEN MORENO

My stomach leaps into my throat.

Navarro picks up the call. "Yeah?"

I cannot hear what Moreno is telling him, but I see Navarro's posture sag as he listens and I know it must be something terrible.

"I'll be there as soon as I can," he soon says and hangs up.

"What is it?" I ask anxiously.

"Another package," he replies, the dejection smothering his face even more. "A smaller one like the first, so as far as he can tell, it's only for one victim."

"Do you think it's Shawna?"

"Maybe. I'm not sure if I should hope it is or not."

"Goddammit," I grumble, my optimism for her well-being draining from me.

"I'm going to head over there now. Why don't you go home and I'll let you know what I find?"

"I'm not going with you?" I retort.

"You're supposed to be on a leave of absence, remember? You shouldn't even be helping me with the case. Moreno will lose his shit if you show up to Pantano with me."

"Yeah, you're right..." I murmur. "What do you need me to do in the meantime?"

"Go home and get some rest."

"Rest is the last thing I'm going to be able to do," I respond. "I can stay here and wait for the tech to finish processing Shawna's cell phone."

"You don't need to do that. As soon as he's done, he'll let me know. I know you want to help, but the best thing you can do is rest so that your brain stays fresh. We can't both be running on fumes."

"Alright," I say, seeing that he's not going to budge on this.

We walk out to our cars together, and I watch him as he pulls out of the parking lot and heads west toward Pantano.

I sit in my car for a while, losing myself in my thoughts. I understand why I can't go with him to the hospital, but I am annoyed by it all the same. I wonder if they will find something similar to the other two packages, and if they don't, what will it be instead?

Then, I start to wonder if Chad Shaffer has more of a connection to Trent than just a fanatical obsession with him. Does Shaffer know Trent personally? Has Trent been corresponding with him from prison? I wonder if Navarro will try to speak with Trent again once he has seen the package?

The more I think about it, the more my body pulses with

energy despite the fact that I haven't had much sleep in the last week. I can't just go home. I have to do something.

I pull out of the parking lot and hop onto northbound Interstate 5. With this new package being delivered, it's only a matter of time before the rest of Shawna's remains appear. My gut feeling is that Shaffer is somewhere in the general area of that abandoned rest stop and that stretch of the interstate is where we will most likely find Shawna's body.

Neither Trent nor the copycat have been discreet about where they have dumped the bodies of their victims, so as I drive, my eyes toggle back and forth between the median and the right-of-ways of both sides of the interstate. Nothing out of the ordinary jumps out at me. Certainly not the discarded remains of a murdered young woman.

I drive for an hour before coming upon the abandoned rest stop. There are several Soledad County Sheriff's vehicles parked in the lot, and I assume that the forensics team is continuing their search of the pit toilet.

I drive past the rest stop, continuing along the interstate for another ten miles. I see nothing other than a couple of broken-down cars and bits of trash blowing in the breeze.

When I reach the point at which Interstate 5 bends sharply northward toward Sacramento, I pull off onto a nondescript county road and stop my car. To the west is the Diablo Range, a small series of fire-scarred mountains that make up the eastern flank of Big Sur. As I look at the mountain range, I think of what Navarro said about Shaffer being a needle in a stack of needles and the general futility of blindly searching for him.

I jump back onto the interstate and head south toward Bakersfield and Pantano. Fatigue begins to settle in, and the dotted white line separating the lanes lulls me into a hypnotic state.

I don't know how long I've been traveling when I see a figure walking on the frontage road alongside the interstate. At first, it looks like any regular hitchhiker. Soiled clothing, disheveled hair, hitched gait. As I get closer though, I see that it's a woman. A younger woman at that.

When I pass her, she does not stick her thumb out to try to get me to stop. She keeps her head down and trudges along as if she never saw me.

It's only a minute or so after I pass her that I realize what she was wearing. Her blouse in particular.

I hit the brakes and pull the car onto the shoulder. I find a spot where I can cross the right-of-way, then I speed back in her direction on the frontage road.

That can't be *her*, I think as I go. I'm exhausted and my eyes are playing tricks on me. Another package was sent to Pantano, so I know she can't be alive, yet I could have sworn I recognized that blouse from the photos on the SIM card.

I come over a small hill, and I see her figure off in the distance. I slow down, not wanting to startle her, whether or not she is Shawna Bowman.

As I approach, she doesn't seem to notice my car. She simply continues trudging along the road as if trapped in a fugue.

I stop the car twenty or so yards ahead of her and step out onto the pavement.

"Shawna?" I call out.

The young woman's head snaps upward and she halts in place. She looks like a deer frozen by a car's headlights.

"Shawna Bowman?" I add with disbelief.

She doesn't say anything. She only remains motionless on the roadway.

"I'm working with the police," I tell her. "We've been trying to find you."

She doesn't respond, but after a moment, she crumples to the ground in a sobbing heap.

I run over to her, still not sure if she is who I think she is.

When I get within a few feet of her, I know I recognize her blouse from the photos that were pulled from her cell phone.

I stop and kneel beside her. "Are you Shawna Bowman?" I try to ask.

She sobs so heavily that she cannot speak, but she nods her head over and over again.

"It's okay," I tell her. "You're safe now."

THIRTY-EIGHT

I eventually convince Shawna to get into my car and I race down the frontage road until I can find a flat spot in the right-of-way to jump back onto the interstate.

"Do you know who abducted you?" I ask her.

She shakes her head. She is no longer sobbing uncontrollably, but tears continue to drip slowly down her cheeks.

"Do you remember what he looked like?" I add, trying to remain calm despite the urge to rapidly fire a hundred questions at her.

She shakes her head again.

I pull out my cell phone and show her a photo of Chad Shaffer. "Was it him?"

She glances at my phone and her eyes grow wide. "Yes," she murmurs, the emotion choking her voice.

"Where did he take you?"

"I don't know," she answers. "He put me into his trunk and took me somewhere there." She motions through the passenger window in the direction of the Diablo Range.

"Did he take you to a house?"

"No... it was like an old barn."

"Do you remember anything about the barn or the area it was in?"

She doesn't answer for a moment as she thinks. "There were some trees nearby, I guess."

"How did you get away?"

"He untied me and told me not to leave the barn until I couldn't hear his car anymore. I thought he was going to lock me inside or burn it down, but he didn't. I waited for a while after I couldn't hear his car. The door was open and he was nowhere in sight."

"He just let you leave?" I try to hide my skepticism.

She nods.

"Do you know why?"

"He said he was too weak. That he couldn't go through with it."

"Go through with what?"

The tears well in her eyes as she answers, "Sacrificing me." She pauses, emotion overcoming her briefly. "He said he admired him and wanted to be like him, but he was too weak to do it."

"Who did he want to be like?"

She shakes her head. "I don't know. He only referred to him as *he*."

Shaffer must have been talking about Trent, I think, but if he is the copycat, then why was he able to kill the other three but not Shawna? What stopped him?

After a moment, I ask, "Did he take you to an abandoned rest stop at any point?"

"No, just the old barn."

He must have performed the animal sacrifices at the rest stop after he abducted her and left her at the barn, I think. But why? Is that part of his usual ritual, or was he building up the nerve to do it to her? It didn't make sense. How was he able to kill the other three so easily and skillfully, but not Shawna?

Plus, why did he let her go knowing that she could probably identify him? Is he on the verge of a breakdown, or is he not the copycat at all?

As soon as I get cell phone coverage, I call Navarro.

"Everything alright?" he answers.

"You're not going to believe this, but I found Shawna Bowman. Alive."

"What?" he exclaims. "What do you mean, you found her? Where?"

"Walking the frontage road along I-5. Shaffer took her out to some abandoned barn near the Diablo Range. I'm taking her to the hospital in Bakersfield now."

"Jesus Christ. How did she even escape?"

"He just let her go, I guess. He told her that he was too weak to sacrifice her."

Navarro is silent for a moment. "That doesn't make any sense... How was he able to kill the other three but not her?"

I hesitate briefly. "I don't think he's the copycat. I think he wants to be, but I don't think he actually is."

"What about the animal sacrifices at the rest stop? Or all the shit we found in his house? You're thinking he was just pretending?"

"Unfortunately, yeah," I say.

He sighs heavily. "I'm going to send a team out to the area to see if they can find him or the barn he took her to. Once I'm done here, I'll head over to Bakersfield to talk to Shawna."

"Jesus, I almost forgot you're at Pantano," I reply. "What did you find?"

"Same stuff as the other two. A heart. A liver. A stomach. A spleen. A uterus. And a specimen cup of blood with the name Andrea Osborn printed on it."

"Did he leave a note again?" I ask.

"Yeah," Navarro answers, and I hear a piece of paper crinkling over the phone. "*My underworldly lord, you plague me and I plague you. The killing. The feeding. What you began, I am only perfecting. What I've buried inside will bury you too. Into the flames we shall go together. Your humble servant."*

"What the hell..." I say, the words reminding me of Trent's own lyrical style in his songs. "That has a different tone than the other two, don't you think?"

"A little bit. I was thinking maybe the copycat was being literal about burying something incriminating inside the box, but there's nothing as far as I can tell."

"If only we were that lucky," I say. "I don't know. There's something ominous about that note. *'Into the flames we shall go together'*? What do you make of that?"

"Maybe it's some weird Satanist thing," he suggests. "Some reference to them both going to hell when this is all over. Or if the note is meant for me, it might just be another misleading dead end."

"I guess..." I reply, trailing off in thought.

"There is one difference from the other two packages," he adds. "The return address isn't the Stanley Palmer house."

"It's not? What is it then?"

"Some random address in Cholame," he answers, "758 Bitterwater Road."

I almost drop my cell phone and my heart immediately begins to race. "Say that address again?" I reply.

"Seven-five-eight Bitterwater Road. Do you know where that is?"

"Yeah," I reply, my brain spinning wildly. "That's *my* house."

"What?" he exclaims.

"Yeah, that's my goddamn house. How does that son of a bitch know where I live?"

"Is everything alright?" Shawna asks, concerned.

"Sorry," I tell her, squelching my panic as best I can.

Navarro replies, "It's public record, I guess, but not that

many people know you're helping with the investigation, right? Davis and Finley are the only ones not connected to corrections or law enforcement that I can think of."

"What the hell..." I try to keep my composure so as not to alarm Shawna any more. "I didn't actually believe what Finley said at the jail. Maybe she knows who it is after all."

"Either that or Davis told him."

"How's he communicating with him then? We've looked through the mail logs and haven't picked up anything aside from how he communicated with her."

"I don't know," he answers. "I'm tempted to talk to him before I leave though."

"Don't waste your time. You know he's just going to jerk your chain."

"For all we know, the copycat's identifying *you* as his next target."

"I can't talk about this right now," I interject, doing everything I can to keep my composure. "I'll see you at the hospital."

I hang up before he can say anything else. I need to keep my cool so I don't freak Shawna out even more, but when I look over at her, I can see she's worried.

"Everything's going to be alright," I say to her. I'm trying to convince myself as much as her.

She eyes me anxiously. "Was it the Vampire copycat who abducted me?"

"I'm not sure," I answer, wishing I hadn't had the conversation in front of her. "It's possible."

"Oh my God..." she breathes, emotion overcoming her.

"You're safe now," I reassure her. "We're doing everything we can to catch this guy, you have my word."

She watches me closely and sniffles. "Is he going to come after *you* next?"

"He knows I'm helping with the investigation. He's just trying to scare me."

"*Are* you?" she asks.

I stare through the windshield as I absorb her question. I do not know her from anyone else, yet I cannot bring myself to lie to her.

"I'm terrified," I say, my voice wavering. "But don't you worry about me. My job is to deal with monsters like him."

She reaches over the center console and takes my hand in hers. Her skin is cold and clammy.

"Will you pray with me?" she asks.

I nod, although truth be told, praying is not my thing and the request makes me uncomfortable.

"Our Father," she begins, her voice calm in spite of the circumstances. "Hallowed be thy name. Thy kingdom come. Thy will be done. On Earth as it is in heaven. Give us this day our daily bread, and forgive us our trespasses as we forgive those who trespass against us. And lead us not into temptation but—"

"Deliver us from evil," I find myself murmuring, so silently that Shawna doesn't even realize that I spoke.

"Amen," she finishes.

THIRTY-NINE

I wavered.
> A moment of weakness.
> I could not deprive my body any longer.
> I had to eat. To satisfy the cravings if only for a moment.
> But my eye remains on her.
> Hanging from the highest bough.
> Taunting me.
> Teasing me.
> The sun ripening her flesh.
> But she is protected.
> Forbidden.
> By Him.
> And so I must wait.
> I must shackle the beast within.
> I maintain dominion over myself.
> But my eyes feast.

FORTY

I've been waiting in the lobby of Bakersfield Hospital for two hours before Navarro arrives. There are bags beneath his eyes, and he looks like he could fall asleep at any moment.

"Where is she?" he asks me.

"They're still examining her. They took her back over an hour ago, so it shouldn't be much longer."

"Alright."

"Don't take this the wrong way, but you look like you could use some coffee," I add.

He sighs. "By this point, I could use an entire pack of Red Bull."

"Come with me. I'm buying."

We leave the lobby and find a coffee vending machine. As the coffee pours, the aroma reminds me of the smell of the cheap coffee at Pantano.

"How is she doing?" asks Navarro.

"Better. She's still pretty shaken up, but the shock is at least wearing off. More than anything, the thought that she was almost the next copycat victim was what really freaked her out."

Navarro nods, his eyes wide from the fugue of exhaustion.

I hand him the first cup of coffee, and despite the fact that it is steaming hot, he gulps the majority of it.

"I think you melted half of your taste buds," I say, trying to get some semblance of a smile out of him.

He forces a slight smirk, but it quickly disappears.

"You doing alright?" I ask.

"Not particularly," he answers. "But there's not a whole lot I can do about it other than catching this prick."

"Do *you* think it's Shaffer?"

"I hope it is. Otherwise, I'm back at square one."

I nod slowly, and silence falls between us as my cup of coffee pours.

I grab the cup and take a sip before asking, "Do you want me to try to talk to Finley again? Maybe I can coax her into telling me who he is."

He shakes his head. "Finley's gone. I called LAPD on my way over here and they released her a few days ago."

"What? Why?"

"Don't know. If I had to guess, the jail was getting over-crowded, and they weren't going to waste space with a junkie prostitute."

"What about Catherine Davis's murder? I thought they were going to charge her?"

"It didn't happen in their jurisdiction, so they must have figured it wasn't their circus to manage."

"That's such bullshit," I scoff. "Where's the justice in that?"

"There isn't any. But you've worked in corrections long enough to know that justice is often absent in the justice system."

"Yeah, no kidding."

He sighs. "I'm just burned out. Sick of running down rabbit holes to no end."

I nod, but I don't know what I can say to him that will drag him out of his loathing.

"I guess it won't matter soon enough," he adds. "My sergeant is meeting with the California Bureau of Investigation to have them take over. I'll still be involved, but they'll head up the investigation."

I sense this weird mix of dismay and relief from him, and a hollowness emerges in my gut. I want to tell him to keep fighting. To not give up. That this is *his* case and he's the only one who can catch this guy.

But I know that's not what he wants to hear. I can see it on his face; he doesn't have the energy for it anymore.

Finally, I say, "For your sake, I'm glad."

I put my hand on his arm for a moment, and he glances at me and smiles.

I buy him a second cup of coffee, and we return to the lobby to wait to see Shawna.

A nurse soon approaches us and tells Navarro that he can speak briefly with her.

Before he goes back, he asks me, "You mind sticking around until I'm done?"

"Sure," I say.

I take a seat in the lobby and scroll through my phone aimlessly as I think. The biggest weight on my mind is why my address was used as the return address on the package. As much as I want to deny it, the only logical explanation is that the copycat really is threatening me. Maybe I should take Warden Moreno's advice and go on a vacation for a while? Get out of the state until they find the copycat.

Then I consider how disheartened Navarro is, and I start to wonder if we can turn this potential threat to our advantage by using me to draw the copycat out? The idea frightens me, and yet, it feels like the fastest way to figure out who the copycat is and save lives.

In my hypnotic scrolling on my phone, I stumble upon a news clip of a wildfire that has broken out southeast of San Jose.

It is a small fire—only twenty-five acres—but the report says that forestry officials believe it was started intentionally near the base of Diablo Peak. Immediately, my attention is caught, and I look at the map to see where in relation to Interstate 5 the ignition point is. The area itself is remote and nondescript, but it is only five miles west of the interstate, specifically the section where I found Shawna walking along the frontage road.

I know that cannot be a coincidence, so I pull up my text messages and forward the story to Navarro followed by a note: *I think this is where Shaffer took Shawna.*

I wait anxiously for a reply, opening GoogleMaps to look at the satellite view of the area.

After a few minutes, I see Navarro hurrying down the hallway toward the lobby.

When he reaches me, he says, "She confirmed that is where Shaffer took her. I bet he torched the barn to destroy any evidence that was there and now the whole forest is on fire."

"Do you think that's where the fourth victim is too?" I ask.

"It's possible," he says. "I need to notify the state patrol and the DOT. Maybe a traffic cam picked up his vehicle somewhere nearby and we can track where he's going. I'm going out to the burn area to see how much of the barn is destroyed and what evidence the firefighters might've found. Do you mind staying here and keeping an eye on Shawna for me?"

"Of course."

"Thank you," he replies, hurrying out of the lobby toward the exit.

After he leaves, I feel an uneasiness settle over me that I can't explain. Maybe it's the persistent stress of the investigation, or the looming possibility of the copycat coming after me next.

To distract myself from the anxious energy, I go to check on Shawna.

The door to her room is open, and I give it a light knock.

"Come in," she says.

When I enter, she is sitting up in bed. She has a couple of cuts that have been bandaged as well as a few bruises, but she doesn't look as bad as I expected.

"How are you doing?" I ask.

"Better... Just tired."

"I can only imagine," I reply, taking a seat in the chair near the bed.

She gazes off briefly, and I can see in her eyes that her mind is wandering.

"I still can't believe this happened," she mutters. "You hear about it happening to other people, but you don't think there's any way it'll happen to you."

I nod, understanding all too well what she's talking about.

"I should've been more careful," she adds. "We were having fun and I just lost track of how much I drank."

"What do you remember about that night?"

She shakes her head. "Not much other than we hopped from one house party to the next. I don't even know when I got separated from the group or when he grabbed me. I just remember waking up in a car trunk with duct tape wrapped around my mouth and my hands and feet tied... That feeling of complete panic and helplessness. I'll never forget that."

"Do you know how long you were back there?"

"Hours, but it felt like an entire week. Long enough to where I had no choice but to pee my pants several times."

"And he didn't let you out until you got to the barn?"

She nods.

"What did he do when you got there?"

"He dragged me out and untied the rope around my feet so I could walk. Told me he'd shoot me if I tried to run." She shakes her head and wipes a tear away from her eye. "I was too terrified to walk, no less run away. Nowhere to go either. Just pine trees everywhere I looked."

"Where did he make you walk?"

"To the barn. It was super run-down and looked like it would cave in on us at any moment. He tied me to one of the posts when we got inside. I could hardly see anything; it was so dark."

"How long did he keep you in there?"

"Days..." she says, tearing up. "At one point, he finally came in and untied me and told me to lay down on top of this splintery table he had set up in the middle of the barn. I couldn't move, I was shaking so badly. So he dragged me over to the table and forced me on top of it." She pauses, gathering her composure before continuing. "He tied my hands and feet to the legs of the table, and then he just stared at me while he chanted something in another language. Spanish or Latin, if I had to guess. I wasn't sure if he was going to rape me or torture me or what. All I knew was that I was going to die."

She stops, tears crawling down her cheeks. I grab a box of tissues and bring them to her. She dabs her eyes and slows her breathing to compose herself.

"When he finally stopped the chanting, he kept staring at me. I thought he was fantasizing about what he could do to me, but then he stormed out of the barn and left me like that for several hours. He'd come back in, stare at me more, then leave again. He must have done that five or six times before he returned the final time. He was grumbling about something, almost as if he was trying to argue with someone without me hearing it. I could make out a couple of things like 'You're too fucking weak' and 'Sacrifice her already'. But he never touched me. Finally, he untied my hands and feet and told me to not move until I couldn't hear a car engine anymore. I waited for a long time. Paralyzed with fear until I forced myself to move. When I left the barn, there was no one in sight. There was only a single road, so I just started walking until I got out of the forest and saw the interstate in the distance."

"Did he ever mention the names Larua or Trent Davis or Finley Keenan?"

"No," she answers. "He mentioned that he wanted to be like *him*, but he never said a name. I'm sorry I don't have something more specific to tell you."

"That's okay," I tell her. "You've been extremely helpful."

FORTY-ONE

Navarro doesn't call me until later that evening.

"It's about time," I answer. "Have you found anything yet?"

"Yeah..." he replies, his voice hollow. "We found Chad Shaffer... what's left of him, anyways."

His phrasing confuses me. "What are you talking about?"

Navarro hesitates. "He's dead, Steph. The bastard lit himself on fire inside the barn."

"What?"

"Yeah. It's..." Navarro can't find the words.

"I don't even know what to think right now," I reply. "Was the fourth victim in there with him?"

"That's the thing. There's no sign of her anywhere. As far as we can tell anyway. The firefighters are still digging through the debris, but it doesn't look promising."

"Holy shit," I mutter. "I-I don't know what to say."

"I don't either." He pauses, trying to gather his thoughts. "I think you were right earlier; I don't think Shaffer was the copycat." Navarro sounds dejected when he says this. "How are things at the hospital?"

"Fine," I reply, still stunned by the news. "I left about an hour or so ago."

"You left?" he retorts. "Why'd you do that? That was the safest place you could be, considering he knows your address. And now that we know Shaffer isn't the copycat, who knows if he's coming for you next."

"Just relax," I say. "I'm not dumb enough to go home. I got a hotel here a few blocks away from the hospital."

"Still. Being alone isn't safe. I'm coming back down there."

"What? Why?"

"Because I don't have a good feeling about this. He's been five steps ahead of us from the beginning and I don't feel comfortable with you being by yourself. Not with him potentially targeting you."

"I am fully capable of taking care of myself," I counter, annoyed with his implication. "Besides, you're the only one who even knows that I am in Bakersfield."

"So you think. For all we know, that fucker could have been following you for days. Watching you without you ever realizing it."

Immediately, my mind goes to the song lyrics that Trent wrote about me in "Head Shrinker".

"You still there?" Navarro asks, startling me out of my rumination.

"I appreciate your concern," I say curtly. "But you're being paranoid. I'll be fine."

"At least let me get someone from Bakersfield PD to keep an eye on you."

"Jesus, absolutely not. I don't need a goddamn bodyguard."

"It's just a precaution—"

"I don't care what it is. Do not send someone over here."

Before he can say anything else, I hang up.

Only a few seconds pass before he tries to call me again, but I ignore his call and send it straight to voicemail.

What the hell is wrong with him? I know he's only looking out for me, but this is ridiculous.

Another minute later, he calls me a third time and I silence my phone and let it ring to voicemail.

"For Christ's sake, leave me alone," I breathe.

I don't know if he feels some sense of chivalrous duty or what, but I am starting to get really fed up.

When he calls me a fourth time, I turn my phone off entirely.

He'll probably call in the National Guard. I don't need a babysitter. What I need is space to decompress and absorb silence.

I try sitting in my hotel room, but as twilight settles in and the room darkens, it feels as though the walls are pressing in on me and this suffocating sense of claustrophobia overcomes me.

I need air. I know I should probably stay in the hotel room, but I can't help myself. I have to get out of here.

I step out into the hallway and put the Do Not Disturb sign on the door handle. The corridor is empty, and the only sounds are the muffled tones of televisions playing within the other rooms. I remain motionless for several seconds. The empty white walls and the geometric carpeting take me back to the living room of my childhood home. Sitting on the couch watching *The Shining* with Michelle. Standing there, I feel like I have been transported to the Overlook Hotel, and at any moment, those creepy twin girls will appear in their powder-blue dresses.

I walk down the hallway and exit the hotel through the side door. The air still feels heavy despite twilight fading into darkness. At least I don't feel claustrophobic anymore, so I proceed across the parking lot and make my way on the sidewalk down the main road in front of the hotel.

There are fast-food and casual dining restaurants lining both sides of the road. Gas stations and convenience stores. Big-box stores. Hotel chains. Their neon lights and vibrant signs fight the darkness that looms overhead. It's a stark contrast to Pantano, where the floors and walls are so plain it makes your eyes hurt.

When you've spent as much time as I have in correctional facilities, you start to wonder if you're an inmate yourself. Intentionally shutting yourself off from the outside world. For what? To help people? To rehabilitate criminals? To treat the mentally ill? Am I really accomplishing any of those things, I wonder? Or is it like Navarro described law enforcement—am I just bailing water out of the *Titanic* with a soup ladle?

Maybe that's why I've engrossed myself so much in the copycat investigation. Because it feels like I can actually make a difference. Saving innocent lives as opposed to salvaging shattered ones.

Of course, every meaningful lead we've had thus far has led us nowhere.

Suddenly, a cold sweat breaks out all over my body and I feel this sense that I am being followed. I turn abruptly, expecting someone to be within a few feet of me, but the walkway behind me is completely empty.

Don't let Navarro's paranoia rub off on you, I tell myself. Nobody even knows you're in Bakersfield except for him.

Despite this logic, I can't shake the sense of disquiet. The neon lights and bright signs seem to dim, and all the shadowed corners and alleyways between buildings turn as black as pitch.

I hear whispers in the back of my mind. *I only want to touch you. To smell your skin. To bite your flesh. To feel your blood against my tongue. To burn your soul.* I know I am imagining this, but it feels like someone is directly behind me, whispering the words into my ear.

I *am* being followed, I think, more a confirmation than a suspicion. I turn again, anticipating that single moment of terror before I am incapacitated somehow.

But no one is there.

I am alone in the darkness.

He's out there somewhere, I know it. Watching me. Waiting for the perfect moment. Who knows how long he's been stalking me? Was he sitting in the hospital waiting room with me? Did he follow me up and down Interstate 5 when I was looking for Shawna? Has he been trailing me long before then?

I turn and run as fast as I can back toward the hotel. What was I thinking, coming out here by myself? What was I thinking getting involved in this case at all? I should have minded my own damn business. Kept my nose out of shit that wasn't mine. Yet the copycat has made it my business from the start. Sending the packages to Pantano? I have been the target all along. But why?

When I get back to my hotel room, I don't even try to go to sleep. My heart races as if I have been injected with adrenaline, and my mind is focused on every little noise from the hallway of my hotel.

I spend the entire night in a heightened state of paranoia. Why would I be the copycat's target, I wonder? My best hypothesis is that it's a former patient of mine. Someone whose transference caused him to become obsessed with me. I've treated nearly a hundred inmates in my career, but only a handful really worried me in that way. Most of them had decades-long sentences, especially those at San Quentin. Whoever it is has to be someone who was up for parole soon. Maybe someone I treated at the prison in Sacramento when I first started my career. Or maybe someone who had a short-term stay at Pantano while they awaited trial.

The latter thought reminds me of Brian Wyer. He came to Pantano two years ago when he was charged for murdering his girlfriend. He was granted temporary insanity and sent to the hospital to be further evaluated by me.

Brian was a bizarre guy, especially when it came to his

interactions with other people. He liked me, however, so it wasn't too difficult to get him to open up. He was mournful about his girlfriend's death, and if I didn't know any better, I would have believed that he was innocent. The investigators had a bunch of evidence against him. Most of it was circumstantial, but when the pieces were all together, it made Brian look extremely guilty.

After a month of working with him, he never showed signs of psychosis or serious mental dysfunction, so I diagnosed him with antisocial personality disorder. In terms of legal insanity, he was of sound enough mind to stand trial for his crime.

He was infuriated when he learned all of this. He accused me of colluding with the prosecution team and manipulating him so that he would appear sane and culpable. He never openly threatened me, but his tone certainly implied it.

His trial began a few months after that. We expected it would be quick, with a guilty verdict. In fact, the opposite became true. The most incriminating pieces of evidence weren't admissible because of procedural misconduct, and after several hung juries, the prosecution postponed the charges until more evidence could be gathered. Brian was set free, and as far as I know, the prosecution has yet to make progress toward a new trial.

I've not seen or heard from Brian since he was transferred out of Pantano, but I can't help but wonder if the copycat murders are his demented way of fulfilling his homicidal cravings while terrorizing me in the process.

I am trapped in this swirling introspection until the morning light begins to emerge.

Then, someone knocks on my room door and startles me into a panic.

A voice calls out, "It's Navarro. You in there?"

Navarro? I didn't tell him which hotel I was at. How did he know where to find me?

"Steph?" he adds.

Is that his voice? It sounds like him, but fear causes me to question my senses. What if it's the copycat? What if he's found me and is posing as Navarro to get me to open the door?

I tiptoe over to the door and creep up to the peephole. I hold my breath for fear that breathing alone will betray my location.

When I see Navarro standing there, I refuse to believe my eyes for several moments. My heart races and I begin to feel lightheaded. Am I *sure* that's him? Or is panic deceiving me?

"Steph?" he repeats, his voice more anxious.

That has to be him, I tell myself.

I leave the door chain in place and crack the door open.

I'm relieved. It *is* him.

"What are you doing here?" I ask, sounding annoyed so as not to reveal how terrified I actually am. "How did you even know where to find me?"

"I spent half the morning checking hotels near the hospital," he says. He looks weary but comforted when he sees me. "I thought something had happened to you when your phone went straight to voicemail."

"Yeah, I turned it off. I just needed to think for a while."

"Jesus," he grouses. "You scared the shit out of me."

"If it makes you feel better, I didn't sleep all night because I thought he was going to come after me."

"I didn't mean to freak you out, but you're going to have to be careful until we find him."

"Well, I spent my night trying to figure out who else it could be and I think I have an idea. A guy I evaluated a few years ago: Brian Wyer."

Navarro eyes me quizzically. "Why does his name sound familiar?"

"He murdered his girlfriend in San Francisco in 2020"

"That's right. What made you think of him though?"

"I evaluated his competency before the trial, and when I

determined that he wasn't insane, he was furious with me. I think the copycat has been targeting me this entire time. Sending the packages to Pantano. Putting my address on the most recent one. Brian's got a motive, and I know he's capable of murder."

"It's as good a lead as any," he says. "You can tell me more about him on our way to Pantano."

"Pantano?" I reply quizzically. "Don't tell me they got another package."

"No. We need to talk to Davis. I just heard from the lab that they found a hair at the bottom of the most recent package, and when they ran the DNA on it, it was a direct match to him."

"What?" I reply, shaking my head with confusion and shock. "How is that possible?"

"I don't know. That's why we need to talk to him. I'm thinking he mailed the copycat a piece of his hair to plant as another way of screwing with us."

"What about Moreno?" I counter. "He's going to fire me when he finds out I'm still helping you with the case."

"I already spoke to him. I told him about the DNA match and I asked to bring you along to help break Davis. He was furious, but I was able to talk him off the ledge and see it as the quickest way to potentially put an end to this."

"Great," I say, knowing full well that Moreno wouldn't acquiesce that easily.

"I'm sorry. I know I probably should've talked to you first—"

"Don't apologize. It's the right call. Considering everything that's going on, losing my job is the least of my concerns."

"He can't fire you. Not for this."

I glower at him. "You don't know Moreno."

FORTY-TWO

Trent is sitting in the small therapy room when we arrive at Pantano. He looks as terrible as he did when he first arrived months ago. There's a pallor to his skin and his face looks gaunt and starved.

"When was the last time he ate?" I ask Moreno.

"Not since you left," he answers. "Hasn't slept either."

"What!" I exclaim. "Why not?"

"He won't say. Something to do with you, I imagine. When I told him you were coming back to talk to him, he showed more life than I've seen from him in weeks."

"Yeah, well, we'll see how happy he is when he finds out what they found in that box."

Moreno unlocks the door to the therapy room, but he stands in front of it and prevents me from entering.

"You and I need to talk when you're done here," he says grimly.

"I know," I reply with a nod, trying not to think about his implications.

He steps aside and opens the door.

As I enter, Trent's gaze locks on me and he grins broadly.

"Did you already start missing me?" he asks.

"No," I reply flatly. "We have something we need to talk to you about."

Navarro enters the room behind me and Trent sighs with disgust.

"Really, Detective? Haven't you heard that three's a crowd?"

Navarro ignores the comment and takes a seat across the table from him while I remain standing in the corner.

"This must be serious," Trent adds snidely. "So, what'd the copycat do this time?"

"You tell us," answers Navarro. "Your DNA ended up in the most recent package, so I'm guessing you know how it got there."

Trent eyes him suspiciously. "You're an even worse liar than she is. How would *my* DNA end up in there?"

Navarro removes a piece of paper from his pocket and places it on the table. "There's the report right there. See for yourself."

Trent leans forward as far as the shackles will allow and reads the paper. After a few moments, he scoffs. "How do I know you didn't forge that?"

"Why would I forge something like that?"

"My DNA being found in there would implicate me somehow, right? So what's the plan? Show me some bullshit evidence and make a deal with me to give up the copycat in exchange for immunity?"

Navarro flashes me a glance. "That thought honestly hadn't crossed my mind. I was simply going to ask you how your DNA ended up in the package."

Trent snickers. "Good luck trying to pull the wool over my eyes."

"He's not lying," I interject. "The lab found a hair sample in the package, and the DNA they pulled matched yours."

Trent rolls his eyes. "You think I sent my hair in the mail so he could plant it? Why the hell would I do that?"

"You tell us," responds Navarro.

"*You* probably planted it," Trent counters. "Trying to get me charged with this shit when you're too incompetent to figure out who it really is."

"So you're pleading ignorance? You have no idea how it got in there?"

"Fuck no," Trent exclaims.

"Yet you claim you know who the copycat is?"

Trent hesitates, his eyes flickering between me and Navarro.

"No more games," Navarro presses. "Do you know who the copycat is or not?"

"I'm not telling you shit. You've got no cards to play aside from some fake DNA report."

"Your DNA was found in the package. If you want to tell us how that happened, great. If not, we'll charge you as an accessory and let a jury decide."

Trent's eyes narrow. "Are you threatening me?"

"I'm simply telling you what's going to happen if you don't cooperate."

"I didn't give him my DNA!" Trent barks, trying to jump out of his chair. The shackles tighten and he jostles the table. "I didn't give him my fucking DNA!"

"Alright. Alright," I say, trying to de-escalate him. I turn to Navarro and add, "Can you step out and give us a minute?"

Navarro glares at me as if he thinks I'm crazy.

"It's fine," I assure him. "Just trust me."

Navarro hesitates as he thinks. Meanwhile, I watch Trent intently as he glowers across the table at him.

After several moments, Navarro stands and whispers to me, "Do not get close to him."

I nod, and he leaves the room.

I turn my attention back to Trent, who continues to stare daggers through the door.

"Why'd you stop eating and sleeping?" I ask, taking a seat across the table from him.

Trent returns to his seat, but his body is still tense with anger. "As if this place doesn't control us enough, I'm not allowed to eat and sleep when I want?"

"I didn't know if it had something to do with me."

He scoffs. "Don't flatter yourself. I'm doing it to exercise discipline over my body."

"Have you done that before?"

"Several times. The body has to be reminded that it must be subservient to the mind."

"I see. Do you think your copycat abides by that philosophy of self-control?"

"I don't give a shit what he abides by."

I pause, contemplating where to lead the conversation. Finally, I say, "He really did leave your DNA in that package."

"That doesn't mean a goddamn thing. I didn't send it to him. Hook me up to a polygraph if you don't believe me."

"I don't need a polygraph. I know you're telling the truth."

"Then tell that pig to back off."

"Not until you tell us who the copycat is."

He shakes his head. "I'm not doing that."

"Why?" I retort. "You won't, or you can't?"

Trent's brow furrows.

I add, "It's hard to reveal something when you don't even know what it is. You're acting like you got an ace up your sleeve, when in reality you're holding onto nothing."

He eyes me with silent contempt for several moments, and I brace myself for some type of violent outburst.

His reaction is the exact opposite though, and his expression soon cracks into a devious grin.

"Iron certainly sharpens iron, doesn't it?" he mutters.

"That's all we truly seek in this life: someone who can spar with us, hit for hit."

My brow furrows with confusion. "What are you talking about?"

"You and me," he replies. "We're cut from the same cloth."

"I am nothing like you."

"I don't know about that. Take Lucifer and God, for example. On the outside, complete opposites of each other, right? But without Lucifer, there is no need for God. And without God, there is no sport for Lucifer. They depend on each other for survival. That kind of dependence is what true love is. It's why I never loved Finley and it's why you seek love fruitlessly in your work. You and I were meant for each other whether you like it or not."

I scoff. "I am your psychiatrist. Nothing more and nothing less."

"Oh, come on. Haven't you heard that the only way to get rid of a temptation is to yield to it?" His gaze travels from my eyes down to my chest and back up. "I can only imagine what you must taste like."

A shiver runs up my spine, causing me to rise from the chair. "We are not having this conversation."

"Love hides in the strangest places. You either seize it by the nape or let it bury its fangs in you."

I ignore his prophecy, turning and proceeding toward the door.

"So long, my little head shrinker," he adds to my back as I step out of the room and close the door.

Navarro and Moreno are waiting for me outside, watching me eagerly.

"You alright?" Navarro asks.

"I'll be fine," I say, trying to shed my disgust with Trent.

"Did he tell you anything?"

"Yeah. Most importantly that he doesn't know who the copycat is."

Navarro's shoulders slump. "He actually told you that?"

"More or less. Yes."

He eyes me skeptically. "More or less?"

"I called him on his bullshit and he had nothing to say about it. Then he tried to change the subject by giving me this garbage about iron sharpening iron and how he and I challenge each other and give each other purpose. He also professed his love to me and practically raped me with his eyes."

"Fucking monster," Navarro murmurs. "So you really don't think he knows who the copycat is?"

"No, I don't."

"I don't understand. How would the copycat have gotten a sample of his hair then?"

"I don't know, but I'm telling you, Trent doesn't know who it is."

Navarro hesitates. "Are you *sure* about that?"

"If I had any reason to doubt it, I would. Lord knows it would be our best shot at figuring out who it is. But I can read Trent; I'm certain he doesn't know."

"What about Brian Wyer? Is there any chance he's been communicating with Davis?"

I glower at him, agitated. "How many times do I have to say it? Trent doesn't know who the copycat is."

"Alright," Navarro says, backing off.

I turn to Moreno and ask, "Has Trent been taking his meds?"

"As far as I know," he answers.

"Well, he's talking in circles again. I need to re-evaluate his dosage."

Moreno eyes me strangely. "I'm sorry, Steph, but you're not treating him anymore. I took him off your caseload when you left."

"When were you planning on telling *me* about that?" I retort.

He sighs impatiently. "That was one of the things I wanted to talk to you about after this."

"*One* of the things? Dare I ask what other bombs you wanted to drop on me?"

He glances at Navarro briefly as if the two of them have discussed this. "You need to step away from the investigation. *Actually* step away. With the copycat targeting you now, it's the only way to keep you safe."

"Safe?" I reply with skepticism. "I feel like that's way riskier. What safer place to be than around a cop?"

"We can speak to the sheriff and get one of his deputies to keep an eye on you, if you want."

"I don't want a damn babysitter. What I want is to work the case and help find this monster."

"That is not your job," he retorts more firmly.

I shake my head with frustration. "So what happens when packages of human organs continue to show up here? We're all just going to bury our heads in the sand and pretend it's not happening?"

Moreno doesn't respond to this. He just silently eyes me for several moments.

Finally, he says, "This is neither a negotiation nor a request. We've had this conversation before. Your work here is suffering because of this. I need you to take a vacation. Get out of town for a few weeks. Recharge yourself so you can do *your* job again."

"Or what?" I counter.

"Christ..." He sighs, rubbing his brow. "Do I really need to give you an ultimatum?"

"Yes. What's going to happen if I don't step away from the investigation? Are you going to fire me?"

He hesitates briefly, then answers, "Yes."

I scoff. "That's how much you respect me and my work? As soon as I challenge you, you're ready to shove me out?"

"Dr. Fletcher," he interrupts firmly. "Do you understand the potential repercussions if you do not comply with my request?"

I so badly want to tell him to go fuck himself, but I acquiesce instead.

"Yeah," I reply. "Message received loud and clear."

Before he or Navarro can say anything else, I head for the exit of the hospital.

He is so full of shit, I think as I go. I'm not sure what this is truly about, but I know it has nothing to do with my safety or the quality of my work at the hospital. When push comes to shove, Moreno is a self-preserving bureaucrat. I don't know how my involvement in the investigation threatens that, but clearly it must.

Navarro soon chases after me and catches up outside of the hospital.

I turn on him and ask, "Did you really speak to Moreno about me?"

"Look, I'm sorry, but I can't continue to put you at risk."

"That is such bullshit," I rejoin. "This was my choice. You haven't forced me to do anything."

"That's beside the point. You're his next target; I can feel it. You need to get out of the state for a while. Lay low until we catch this fucker."

I shake my head, but by this point I am too fed up with the situation to argue about it anymore.

He adds, "For what it's worth, I appreciated all of your help."

"I'm sure Andrea Osborn and the other victims appreciated it too."

FORTY-THREE

She knows something's wrong.

She's not sure what, but she feels it in the air.

Her ears are pricked. Her body is still.

She stares into the darkness.

Watching.

Waiting.

Listening.

I shrink into the night. Movement can only betray me.

What does she see?

What does she hear?

What's her instinct telling her? Flee or fight?

I can smell her fear.

I can taste her angst.

Her panic floods my veins and sends me into fits.

But I stifle the urge.

I bite my tongue.

I will taste her soon enough. I will crawl inside of her and tear her innards out.

She searches the night. Her eyes flicker.

Seconds become moments. Moments become minutes.

Then she turns and continues on.

It must have been the wind, she tells herself. The whispers of the dark.

I linger in her wake.

Creeping.

Slithering.

Closer.

Closer.

Until her shadow is mine.

FORTY-FOUR

As frustrating as it is to feel like I have been banished, it gives me no other choice than to get away from Pantano and the copycat investigation for a while.

I go home, pack a bag, and drive northward without any particular location in mind. Oregon, Washington, maybe even British Columbia? Who knows?

In truth, I can't remember the last time I aimlessly traveled the countryside of the western coast. Probably when I was studying for my undergrad or even earlier. That alone makes me realize just how engrossed in my work I have been over the years. Always reaching for the next carrot in front of me. Medical school. Psychiatric residency. The Sacramento Medium-Security Prison. San Quentin. Pantano. Each rung I climb putting the next one in my sight.

I avoid the interstates as I go, Interstate 5 in particular. The obvious reason aside, I share the late Charles Kuralt's attitude toward the interstate highway system, that *it makes it possible to go from coast to coast without seeing anything or meeting anybody*. I take all of the state highways and county roads instead, absorbing the beauty of central and northern California as I go. Independent hotels and mom-and-pop motels become my new home. Some days, I only travel twenty miles to get from one small town to the next. On others, I press cruise control and cover hundreds of miles.

Despite my physical separation from Pantano and Navarro, I keep a close eye on my newsfeed for updates on the copycat investigation. My general curiosity aside, I am aware that I am still a potential target. If nothing else, I want to know if other victims emerge and, if so, where they are found so that I can be extra vigilant and avoid the copycat's path.

The day after I leave Pantano, the fourth victim's body finally emerges on the shoulder of Interstate 5 near Coalinga. Subsequent stories report that the medical examiner positively identifies her as Andrea Osborn, the name that was provided on the blood specimen cup in the most recent package.

A few days after Andrea is found, a fifth victim appears around Los Banos.

I have to battle urges to call Navarro to snoop for information about the new victim, but after my most recent conversation with Moreno, I know that I am on extremely thin ice and need to keep my distance. If something comes up that I truly need to know about, I am sure he would call.

The further I get from Pantano, the more my head clears and wanders beyond the confines of Trent and the copycat killer.

The memories of my childhood are the first to surface. The fragmented scenes of my trauma. Of Michelle. Of all the terrible things she did to me and all the things I did to myself as a result.

I don't avoid them though. I let them play in my head, knowing the only way to truly purge their toxins is to sweat them out.

Then I think about Dr. Maynard. How I miss her. How I wish she was with me now. How grateful I am to have had her in my life. All the things she gave to me without even realizing it. Without demanding anything in return. Her selflessness knew no bounds.

My thoughts make me realize that it isn't her absence alone that is so difficult to overcome. It's the fact that I never got to thank her. To show my appreciation. To say goodbye.

One day she was alive and thriving, and the next she was gone.

I have never cried so freely in my life.

Several times, I have to pull over onto the shoulder of the highway so I can let the emotion pour out of me.

But I'm dealing with it. I can feel it in my bones that the burden is slowly abating.

Despite this healing, sleep continues to elude me. The times that I do fall asleep, that nightmare of Trent sacrificing me in the Stanley Palmer house sneaks into my brain and jostles me awake. If anything, it makes me realize how much my work with Trent has been affecting me. I can only hope that time away and fresh air will help me cope.

FORTY-FIVE

She chose to flee.
    She must have heard me.
    How did she hear me?
    I was so patient. So quiet. So calm.
    But this one is good.
    She darts through the trees without a sound.
    Fuses with the night.
    A master of her environment.
    The most dangerous game.
    Her cunning tantalizes me.
    Iron sharpens iron.
    The more I chase, the more my hunger grows.
    The more I need to feed.
    But I will have her.
    She will be my Mona Lisa.
    She will be my Starry Night.

FORTY-SIX

A sixth victim is found between Stockton and Sacramento as I drive into Oregon.

Coalinga? Los Banos? Sacramento?

He's moving north, I think. Slowly. Carefully. But northward all the same.

Hundreds of miles separate me from this most recent victim, yet I can't shake the feeling that he lingers in my wake. A predator tracking a faint scent.

If he dumped this sixth victim a day or two ago, then he could easily be in northern California by now.

Stop being paranoid, I tell myself. This is exactly the reason you needed to get out of town and away from Pantano. When you're confined by the whitewashed walls long enough, you forget how vast and colorful the outside world actually is.

Focus on the landscapes.

The forests.

The mountain vistas.

See how healthy and lush the countryside actually is.

I stoke this fire in my conscious mind, yet the faintest chill of paranoia remains.

He's behind you, whispers the darkness of my psyche.

Run.

Run.

Run!

FORTY-SEVEN

I cannot see you, but I smell your fear.
    I taste your terror in the air.
    You are good, but I am better.
    I will find you.
    I will slither up behind you and set your soul on fire.

FORTY-EIGHT

I try to force myself to enjoy my trip.

I go to Crater Lake and it doesn't even look real.

Wizard Island looks like it has been photoshopped onto the water.

The Cascades are a facade that will tip over if the wind blows too hard.

I am here, and yet I'm not.

My mind is in California.

My soul is trapped in Pantano.

The breeze licks the nape of my neck and I nearly jump out of my skin.

Where are you, I wonder? How close to me are you now?

FORTY-NINE

I couldn't resist.
   I had to feed.
   The cravings were too great.
   The prey too easy.
   But she wasn't you.
   None of them are you.
   I will not sleep.
   I will not stop.
   Not until I have you.
   Not until I own you.

FIFTY

I see the Badlands.

I see Mount Hood.

But I don't really see them. I don't truly experience them.

I am in a fugue of his creation. I move through a fog that engulfs only me.

Then, my cell phone rings and jostles me awake.

I am startled to see that it's Navarro.

Maybe he has good news, I think. Maybe they know who the copycat is. Maybe they even caught him.

"Hey," I answer enthusiastically. "How are things going?"

"Hi," he replies, his voice hollow. "I'm sorry for bugging you, but I thought you should hear this from me before the news outlets get a hold of it. We just confirmed the identity of the fifth victim. It's Finley Keenan."

"What?" I yelp in disbelief. "I don't understand. How is that possible?"

"We're not sure. Last we knew, she was in Los Angeles, so how her body ended up two-hundred-fifty miles away is beyond us."

"Jesus. Does Trent know?"

"I'm not sure if Moreno has told him yet."

"Is the copycat still sending packages to Pantano?"

Navarro hesitates before answering. "I'm sorry, but I can't discuss that with you. I really shouldn't have told you about Finley either, but I felt you deserved to know."

"Are you thinking she knew who it was?"

"It's possible. I can't imagine it was a coincidence that she threatened you and then the copycat put your home address on the package."

"I agree," I say, although I don't tell him how paranoid I have been these last few days.

"Are you still in California?"

"No. Oregon. Probably head up into Washington tomorrow."

"Good. It doesn't seem like the copycat has gone any further north than Sacramento, but you never know. Just keep an eye out, alright?"

You don't even know, I think. I haven't slept a wink because every bump in the night puts me into cardiac arrest.

"I will," I tell him.

An awkward silence falls between us for several moments before he adds, "I hope you know that what happened at the hospital last week wasn't personal. I really enjoyed working with you... as much as you can enjoy working on a murder case with someone."

I smile. "I appreciate that. I'm realizing that it was for the best. I haven't taken a break like this in decades. You probably won't recognize me the next time you see me."

"I'm glad to hear that."

"When this is finally over, maybe we can grab a drink and talk about something other than dead bodies and the criminally insane."

He chuckles briefly. "I hear the Dodgers are having a hell of a season this year."

"Ehh," I murmur. "On second thought, let's stick to dead bodies."

We share a good laugh together before he tells me to take care and hangs up.

I continue driving toward the coastline to visit Haystack Rock, and despite the fact that the copycat is still on the loose, talking to Navarro has settled my nerves a bit. Maybe I can finally have a personal life when this is all over? Maybe I don't have to be alone anymore.

The closer I get to Haystack, the more I wonder if I should just quit my job entirely and do something else with my life. Get out of the messed-up world of corrections and work with civilians. Maybe work at a family clinic and help people who are not so psychotic. Or maybe I should get out of psychiatry entirely. Certainly the skills I've acquired over the last decade are transferable to other industries and professions. If nothing else, I could go teach at a university. Maybe get into psychopharmaceutical sales. Who knows? Just anything that keeps me from feeling as trapped as I have.

Haystack and the surrounding Cannon Beach are gorgeous, and I spend several hours simply walking along the shore and absorbing the views. Forgetting everything that is going on in my periphery. Trent. The copycat. They all become distant white noise.

I consider getting a hotel room in town, but it's crowded with tourists so I decide to continue north toward Washington and find a place to stay along the way.

FIFTY-ONE

You hide in plain sight.
    In broad daylight.
    Among the living.
    You think you're safe, but dusk will betray you.
    Darkness is your enemy.
    In your periphery I will wait.
    I will follow from a good safe distance.
    I will haunt your wake.
    Your scent remains on my tongue.
    From the beach.
    To the parking lot.
    Into town.
    Will you stop here, I wonder?
    Are you secure enough to sleep?
    To close your eyes and trust the night?
    I hope so.
    I'll be your magic beam.
    I'll bring you your bloody dream.

FIFTY-TWO

As I pass through Sunset Beach, I see someone hitchhiking on the shoulder of the highway. It looks like a younger woman. She's not disheveled like many vagrants I've seen so far, and when she holds her thumb out, a sense of anxiety tears through my core. I immediately think of the copycat and the types of women he targets, and although we are hundreds of miles away from where the most recent victim was discovered, I can't help but fear for this woman's safety.

I slow down and pull the car off onto the shoulder ahead of her. I glance in the rearview mirror and see her hurrying to catch up to me.

When she gets close, I roll my window down and poke my head out.

"Where you headed?" I ask her.

I can see on her face that she is relieved to see me. She answers, "Seattle."

"I'm probably not going all that way, but I can take you across the Columbia River at least."

"Thank you. I'd appreciate that."

She hurries over to the other side of the car and hops into the front passenger seat.

I wait for a gap in traffic and pull the car back onto the highway.

"What's your name?" I ask. "I'm Steph."

"Caroline," she says.

"Where are you coming from?"

"Santa Rosa."

"You stay there long?"

"No, just passed through. I'm heading back from Burning Man."

"You've been hitching all the way from Black Rock?" I ask.

"Yeah," she answers with a smile. "No better way to see the west coast than beating the pavement."

"Wow, I'm impressed. I'd be too scared to do that. Especially as a woman these days."

"You come across some weirdos for sure, but for the most part, people are decent."

"That's good."

"So where are *you* headed?" she asks.

"I don't really know, to be honest with you. I just got in the car and drove. I haven't taken a vacation in a long time, so I'm winging it."

She smiles. "Letting the wind take you wherever it wants you to go?"

"Yeah," I reply. "Something like that."

Silence settles between us briefly, so I ask, "Do you hitchhike often?"

"No. Maybe once or twice before, but only out of necessity. Car breaking down in the middle of nowhere. I wasn't even supposed to do it this time, but after Burning Man, I just felt inspired to see the landscape. To really see it, you know?"

I nod. "Sometimes it feels like you're imprisoned by everyday life."

"Exactly!" she exclaims. "People weren't meant to be cooped up in skyscrapers and cubicles. They're supposed to be free amid nature. The sun on their backs. The stars lighting their way. Civilized society has taken that away from us."

"I never thought of it that way." I pause as I contemplate her perspective further.

"You said you haven't taken a vacation in a while," she adds. "Do you mind if I ask what you do for work?"

"I'm a psychiatrist for the Department of Corrections in southern California."

"Wow," she replies. "I'm impressed. I'd be terrified to work in a prison."

I glance at her briefly and think, yes, you definitely would be.

FIFTY-THREE

I can taste your breath in the air.
    I can feel your heartbeat on my skin.
    Do you know it's me?
    Do you see the wolf beneath this fleece?

FIFTY-FOUR

I really enjoy Caroline's company, so I end up taking her past the Columbia River and over to Adna, Washington where I eventually leave her.

I wish I could have taken her all the way to Seattle, but she insisted. I'm glad I could take her as far as I did. I know she is not afraid of hitchhiking, but I get the impression that ignorance is bliss for her. How I wish I could be that carefree, but I've seen the dark edges of humanity too many times to be that idealistic.

From Adna, I go east toward Mount Rainier. I am amazed by how different a world central Washington is from California. I can only imagine how captivated the early frontiersmen were when they finally made it to this area. No wonder they risked life and limb for an opportunity to settle it.

Two days pass as if the concept of time ceases to exist. The further I get away from Pantano, the more peaceful my mind becomes.

FIFTY-FIVE

They have not been my finest work.
    Plein air is a different beast.
    The elements.
    The lighting.
    The publicity.
    But it's a rush I've never known.
    A drug injected straight to the brain.
    The danger of being seen.
    The thrill of being concealed.
    I've had the fix.
    I get it now.
    I will overdose on her.
    It will be my finest hour.
    She will be the perfect drug.

FIFTY-SIX

I receive another call from Navarro just as I am passing through Spokane. My heart jumps into my throat, and although I am hopeful he has good news, I have a feeling he doesn't.

"Where are you?" he asks, his voice clipped and rushed.

"Spokane—"

"You need to get to a police station. *Now.*"

"What? Why?" I reply, suddenly panicked. "What's going on?"

"He's following you."

Adrenaline surges through me.

"What! Who?"

"The copycat," he says. "Get to a police station."

Confusion takes me over. My mind is trapped in a whirlwind.

"How... how do you know?"

"There's no time to talk," he answers. "I'll explain later. Just get to a police station. Do not leave until you hear from me."

The urgency in his voice terrifies me. "Was it another package?" I ask.

"Just go!" he exclaims, hanging up the phone abruptly.

What is going on? What makes him think that the copycat is following me? How would he even know that? Do they know who it is and they're tracking him? Have they known this whole time and they've been using me as bait to draw him out? That has to be it, I think. *I* have been the bait. Nothing else makes logical sense.

I stomp on the gas pedal, all the while searching for the nearest police station on my smartphone. There's a state patrol office a few miles from my location, so I bob and weave through traffic to get to the exit ramp.

FIFTY-SEVEN

You're running.
  Why are you running?
  The game has only just begun.
  Even if you find a hole to dive into, I'll find you.
  I'll quarter you and roast you on a spit.

FIFTY-EIGHT

I watch the traffic in my rearview mirror as if the copycat is right on my tail. I don't see any cars making erratic moves to keep up with me, but I'm convinced that he is behind me somewhere. Did he bug my car, I wonder? Does he have some other means of tracking me?

My heart races as if the gas pedal is directly controlling my blood flow. I pant uncontrollably, so much so that my vision becomes fuzzy from hyperventilating.

"Calm down," I murmur to myself. "Just breathe."

I can practically hear him over my shoulder.

Yes, calm down, he says. Adrenaline makes the meat taste gamey.

I take my exit and tear down the ramp. I ignore my surroundings, honing in on the directions from my smartphone.

A right at the light.

Merge into the middle lane.

Continue for three miles.

Make a right at the upcoming light.

Continue for a mile.

Make a left at the stop sign.

Your destination is on the right.

I don't even stop in a parking spot. I simply kill the engine in front of the entrance to the state patrol office. Despite my panic and fear, I don't get out of the car. My blood is pumping so hard that it feels like my head is going to explode at any moment.

"Relax," I tell myself. "Just get inside."

Stay out here, he says. Let me show you what you fear.

I look into the back seat, expecting to see his fiery eyes.

I see nothing though.

I am alone.

"Pull yourself together," I whisper, controlling my breathing as best I can.

It takes several minutes for me to calm myself down, but when I do, I get out of my car and hurry into the station.

You can run, but you can't hide.

I'll be waiting for you.

I'll smoke you out and eviscerate you.

There's a state patrolman standing behind a counter at the front of the foyer. As soon as he sees me, his eyes grow wide with concern.

"Can I help you, ma'am?" he asks.

"Someone's after me," I tell him frantically. "You need to help me."

No one can help you. You squirm in my palm.

"Hold on," he says, hurrying around the counter.

"He's following me," I add.

"Who is following you?"

"The copycat, goddammit!"

If only you knew who I am.

I am hiding in plain sight.

I am coiled beneath your nose.

My legs suddenly feel weak, and just as the officer reaches me, I lose all strength and crumble to the ground.

The officer catches me before I crash onto the floor. "It's alright," he tells me. "Everything's going to be alright."

"No!" I retort, emotion erupting from me in a torrent of sobs. Tears pour from my eyes and I choke for air as if someone is strangling me.

Panic.

Please panic.

It feels so good when your arteries pulse like that.

Make it hard for me. Make me work for my dose.

"It's okay," the officer murmurs to me. "You're okay."

I try to focus on his voice and his touch. His arms are wrapped tightly around me and I surrender myself to his protection.

Do you feel that?

You're slipping out of consciousness.

You're falling into sleep.

Let the virus take hold of you.

Let it plague your soul.

"What is your name?" he asks me.

"Steph Fletcher," I manage to answer.

"Who is following you?"

"The Bakersfield Vampire copycat," I say. "I've been helping with the case and the detective just told me he's after me and that I needed to get to a police station as soon as I could."

"Okay," he replies. "Everything's going to be alright."

No, it's not.

I'm already inside of you.

I'm tearing you apart.

FIFTY-NINE

We remain like that for several minutes until I am calm enough to control myself. The officer takes Navarro's phone number from me and gives him a call.

I can't believe it, I think. That monster has been following me this entire time and I never knew it.

The officer returns to me and says, "He's on his way up from California. He wants you to stay put until he's arrived."

"Jesus, he's coming all the way up here?"

"That's what he said. He's sending someone from the Washington Bureau of Investigation to meet with you in the meantime."

"Can you call him back?" I reply. "Tell him he doesn't need to do that."

"He insisted," the officer says.

I nod, realizing that this is another non-negotiable.

The officer gets me some coffee and something to eat, and he stays with me until the WBI agent arrives.

"I'm Agent Hutton," he greets me. "You doing alright, Dr. Fletcher?"

"I'm better now. I just got really freaked out earlier."

"I don't blame you. If you're up for it, I'd like to talk to you about what's going on. See what you remember that might help with tracking this guy down."

"Sure," I say.

Agent Hutton and I follow the state patrolman back to a small conference room.

"Thanks for your willingness to help," he says once we're sitting down. "Why don't you walk me through your trip this past week? Any detail you can remember might be helpful even if it doesn't seem relevant right now. Where you went, what route you took, who you interacted with along the way, where you stayed."

"Yeah, of course," I reply with a nod.

I tell him everything I can recall about my trip and the events leading up to it. My involvement in the investigation. Moreno demanding that I go on a leave of absence. Everywhere I've been and how I've gotten there. As I talk, my brain feels scattered and my thoughts fragmented, but Agent Hutton never interrupts me to clarify a detail. He just takes notes vigorously as if every mundane fact could be the key to finding the copycat.

I have no idea how long I talk to him. It might be ten minutes or several hours; I really don't know.

When I finish my story, he continues to scribble notes silently for another minute or so.

Finally, he asks, "So you stayed clear of Interstate 5 the whole way up from Pantano to Spokane?"

"Yes," I answer.

"How did you get from Adna to Mount Rainier?"

My brow furrows quizzically. "I'm sorry?"

"Highway 6 is what cuts through Adna, but it doesn't connect to Highway 12, which is what you took to get to Rainier. Did you have to go south on I-5 for several miles to connect from six to twelve?"

"Oh... I guess that's right. Sorry. My mind got ahead of my

mouth a bit."

"No problem," he says with a slight smile. "Did you catch the full name of the hitchhiker you picked up?"

"No, she only told me her first name."

"I see. And where exactly did you drop her off?"

"Just outside of Adna."

"The west or the east side?"

I pause. "I don't remember for sure, but I thought it was the east side."

"Okay," he responds with a nod. "And you said she was hitching back to Seattle?"

"Yes."

"Did you see her actually go that way?"

"No... Do you mind if I ask why you're asking so many questions about her?"

He hesitates, and my initial skepticism grows into nervousness.

"Something didn't happen to her, did it?" I add.

"We're not sure," he says. "We found a body on the shoulder of I-5 east of Adna, but we haven't identified her yet. The M.O. appears to match the copycat though."

"Oh my God!" I exclaim. "And you think *she* might be this latest victim?"

"Maybe... Like I said, we haven't identified her yet."

"Do you have a photo of her? I can probably identify her."

He removes his smartphone from his pocket and pulls up a photograph of the victim's face. Sure enough, it's Caroline.

Immediately, I feel the tears well in my eyes and I have to take a moment before I can speak. "I had a shitty feeling about dropping her off. I knew I should have just driven her to Seattle."

Agent Hutton watches me, his expression impassive as he hands me a box of tissues.

"I'm sorry," I add as I dab at my eyes. "It's my fault. He was following me and he must have seen her."

Agent Hutton continues to show little sympathy. He eventually asks, "When did you notice that he was following you?"

"I didn't. I mean, I never actually saw him. Detective Navarro called me and told me that he was following me and that I needed to get to a police station immediately."

"I see."

I look at Agent Hutton questioningly. "*Was* the copycat following me?"

"That's part of what I'm trying to figure out."

"Listen, you can talk to Navarro when he gets here. All he told me was that the copycat was following me. He said nothing else."

"How do you think Detective Navarro knew that, if he's in California and you're up here?"

I shake my head. "I don't know. I assumed CBI finally figured out who the copycat was and tracked him by his phone. Navarro then asked where I was to see if I was in danger, and when I said Spokane, the copycat's cell phone must have pinged close by."

"That seems possible," Hutton replies.

"Well, can't *you* tell me?" I retort, my confusion building into frustration.

"My division only recently got pulled into this case, so we haven't been debriefed on everything they know yet. They simply told me to keep you company and get a statement from you while you wait for them."

"Listen, I've told you everything that I can remember. If he really was following me, then there's a chance he's still in Spokane. Call the division that's working the case in California and see what they know about the copycat. Maybe you can put an APB out for him and find him."

Agent Hutton nods slowly as he considers what I've said.

"Alright," he eventually replies. "I'll do that."

SIXTY

An enormous wave of relief washes over me when Navarro finally arrives with several CBI agents. When he enters the conference room, I run up to him and hug him. His body tenses, probably because my affection catches him off guard.

"What the hell is going on?" I ask.

He pulls away from me and says, "Why don't you have a seat and I can fill you in on what we know?"

"Okay."

I go back over to the table and take a seat. Navarro says something to the CBI agents before they leave and he has a seat across from me.

"Do you guys know who the copycat is?" I ask.

He nods. "We have a pretty good idea. Especially now with the newest victims."

"Agent Hutton told me about Caroline," I reply mournfully. "It's all my fault."

Navarro hesitates before saying, "There are others, Steph."

"Others? Are you talking about Finley and the one south of Sacramento?"

He shakes his head. "We've found three more, not including them or Caroline."

"What? Where?"

"One near Mount Shasta. Two in the middle of nowhere south of Eugene, Oregon. All found on sections of I-5."

My brow furrows with confusion. "I thought you said he was following me though? I wasn't near any of those places."

Navarro places a manila folder on the table and opens it. He removes a packet and puts it in front of me.

"What's this?" I ask.

"Photos taken from various traffic cameras along I-5." He points to one and asks, "Is that your vehicle there?"

I inspect the photo, and although it's pixelated, it certainly looks like my car. Then I see the time and location stamp.

"That can't be..." I breathe. "This camera is in Grants Pass, Oregon. I never passed through there."

He points to another photo. It shows my car more clearly at a location in Salem.

I shake my head slowly in disbelief. "I don't understand... How..."

He points to a third photo. My car just before it passes beneath an overpass in Portland.

"I'm so confused," I say. "I didn't travel to any of these places."

"You're sure about that?" he asks, his tone losing the softness that he usually has with me. "You're sure you didn't take Interstate 5 all the way up here?"

"I swear to God," I answer. "Why would I lie about that?"

"I don't know. That's why I'm asking."

I scoff. "Check my credit card transactions. The gas stations and restaurants and hotels that I went to. None of them were anywhere near I-5."

"There hasn't been a transaction on your credit card since you left Pantano."

"What?" I reply, outraged. "You've already looked?"

He nods.

My mind spins with uncertainty. "How did I pay for everything then?"

"Cash, I imagine. You withdrew several thousand dollars from an ATM in Bakersfield."

"What? There has to be a mistake."

"There's not," he responds. "You have been traveling all along Interstate 5."

My brain continues to reel, but then I remember all of the sites that I have visited along the way. "My phone! I took pictures of Crater Lake and Haystack Rock and everywhere else that I've been."

I reach into my pocket and scroll through my smartphone. When I click on my photos, my heart leaps into my throat. There is not a single picture in the folder.

"What the..." I breathe, closing all of my apps and reopening the photos folder. "My phone must have crashed," I add. "Everything's gone."

Navarro remains silent, watching me skeptically.

"I swear to God I visited all of those places."

"You understand why I don't believe that, right?"

I feel panic overwhelming me. "Does it really matter where I was? The copycat was following me the whole time, right?"

Navarro does not respond; he simply stares at me the same way he did with Trent when he was trying to interrogate him.

"Why are you looking at me like that? What the hell is going on? *Who* is the copycat?"

My question hangs in the air for a moment before he answers. "You are, Dr. Fletcher."

I feel like someone has struck me in the chest with a sledgehammer. My lungs are paralyzed and I can't find air.

"Wha..." I manage to choke out.

"*You* are the copycat," he says.

My brain feels like it is trapped in a vortex and thrashed about in a whirlpool.

He adds, "*You* murdered Caroline and the other three on your way up here. *You* murdered Finley and all those others in California."

My vision blurs and spirals. Nausea overwhelms me and I feel as though I will faint at any moment.

"You got careless. You sent a package from a post office in Eugene and they pulled the security footage."

"What!" I exclaim. "I wasn't even at a post office!"

He opens the manila folder again and shows me a series of surveillance photos.

He points at the images and asks, "Is that not you?"

I shake my head. "You're fucking with me, right? This is photoshopped or faked somehow. AI or something."

"It's not," he says. "That's you. And that's the package they received at Pantano a few days ago."

"That is bullshit," I snap back. "What are you trying to do? The copycat is out there somewhere, and you're accusing *me*?"

"I have to go where the evidence takes me."

"Evidence? What about Finley's threat and the copycat putting *my* address on that package? If I was the copycat, why would I do that?"

"I'll admit, that confused me for a while. But then I thought about something we've talked about a few times. How the copycat has been taunting us and rubbing Trent's face in it. What better way to do that than to indirectly identify yourself?"

"He's targeting *me*!" I proclaim, exasperation overwhelming me.

Navarro grins. "That's what you wanted us to think. And to your credit, it worked."

"When would I have gone out and abducted all of these women? I was either at work or with you. I helped you with the investigation, for Christ's sake. *Why* would I have done that?"

"You wouldn't be the first serial killer to get involved in her own investigation. Maybe you did it to see how close we were getting to you, or you did it to deflect suspicion and manipulate the investigation." He sighs, shaking his head. "And I bought it hook, line, and sinker."

"You're making a mistake. You know how often I was at Pantano. There is no possible way that I had the time to do this."

"That's the thing about insomnia. It puts a solid six to eight hours back into your day. Take it from me. I can't sleep for shit anymore, but boy, am I productive. I read more fantasy novels than a middle-aged virgin, but we all have our guilty pleasures. Mine is just different than yours."

I slam my fists against the table. "I didn't kill those women, goddammit!"

"We searched your house, Steph. As good as you were about leaving no evidence at the dump sites and in the packages, we found more than enough on your property. There's no point in lying about it. It's over."

My body trembles with anger, and it takes me every ounce of will to not leap across the table and strangle him.

But I don't.

I restrain myself and take several deep breaths.

"I want my lawyer," I utter. "Now."

SIXTY-ONE

I speak with my lawyer, Dana, over the phone and she tells me to keep my mouth shut until she can meet with me in person. Soon after, Navarro and the CBI agents escort me to Spokane International Airport where we board a private plane and fly back to Bakersfield so that I can be temporarily detained at the Soledad County Jail.

I don't utter a single word during the trip. I have accepted the fact that Navarro is convinced that I am the copycat, so I know if I try to explain myself, he will just find a way to use it against me.

I spend my hours of silence racking my memory for everything that he is accusing me of, but I don't remember any of it. Picking up the young women. Taking them back to my house. Murdering and dissecting them. Packing up their organs and shipping them to Pantano. Dumping their remains on the side of the interstate. Not a semblance of memory lives in my mind.

The longer I explore my memory, the more I think that Navarro is trying to set me up and gaslight me into believing that I did this. For all I know, *he* is actually the copycat and this is his last-ditch effort to avoid suspicion.

When we land in Bakersfield, they load me into a Department of Corrections van and transport me up to Soledad County. It is a surreal experience. Stepping off of that plane with my hands and ankles shackled like all of the inmates that I once treated.

As we take Interstate 5, I watch the desert landscape through the window as it monotonously passes by. This hollow feeling of despair settles into my core. Unless my lawyer can pull off a miracle, I know I will never see these vistas again.

The Soledad County Jail is old and musty. The deputies book me and I change into the bright orange jumpsuit. Seeing my street clothes piled on the floor makes it feel that much more surreal. And when one of the deputies sweeps them up and stuffs them into a bag, I feel my freedom being carried away with it.

My cell is confined and smells like fermented urine. A guard stands near the door at all times, even when I need to use the toilet.

So this is what it feels like, I think. The transformation from human to wild animal.

I don't know if I should feel sad or angry. More than anything, I just feel empty.

When Dana arrives, I am escorted to a small meeting room. The guard opens the door, and she is waiting inside with another woman that I have never met before.

Dana greets me as I shuffle inside. To the guard, she adds, "Can you unshackle her, please?"

The guard does as requested. My wrists ache when the steel unlatches. When I am unchained, I take a seat at the table.

Once the guard leaves and the door is closed, Dana says, "This is Roxanne, the criminal lawyer I was telling you about."

"Hello," I say.

Roxanne is roughly the same age as me and Dana, and if the setting were different, we might look like a trio of old sorority sisters getting together for cocktails rather than the defense team for an upcoming serial murder trial.

"How are you doing, Dr. Fletcher?" Roxanne asks.

"Fine, I guess. Considering the circumstances and all."

"Are they treating you decently?"

I nod. "As well as can be expected."

"Did they explain the charges against you?"

"Yes... although, to be honest, I have a hard time remembering them all. The ancillary ones at least. The first-degree murder charges are straightforward, but all of the evidence tampering and body disposal ones got confusing."

"Well, as you know, it's complicated. You've got dozens of charges filed against you by four different counties across three states."

"I know," I mutter hollowly.

A moment of silence follows, and Roxanne glances hesitantly at Dana.

"In order to best serve you, I need you to be honest with me," Roxanne says. "Did you commit these murders?"

I shake my head. "I truthfully don't know. If I did, I have no memory of them."

"You're sure?" Dana probes. "Roxanne is a terrific attorney, but in order to get you the best deal possible, she has to know the truth."

"That's the honest-to-God truth. I don't remember doing these things."

"Okay," Roxanne replies. "Because here's what we're facing. They have physical evidence from your house that conclusively links you to the earlier murders. Then, as you know, they have the circumstantial evidence implicating you for these last four."

"Yes," I utter. "I know."

"And you realize that both California and Oregon still have the death penalty? There have been moratoriums on them for over a decade, but the possibility of execution is still there. So I'm going to ask again. Do you remember murdering those women?"

The words *death penalty* and *execution* hover in the air like a foul odor. To think that she's using it in reference to me and my situation is unfathomable.

"No," I insist. "If I knowingly did these things, why would I have driven myself to the police station?"

Roxanne scrutinizes me, and an eerie sense of deja vu prickles every inch of my skin. That is how I analyzed Trent when he first arrived at Pantano. That is how I analyzed every patient when I first started working with them. Are you pulling my leg or not, I would wonder? Are you trying to manipulate me just as you manipulated your victims?

"Alright," she eventually says. "We're going to get a forensic psychiatrist in here to evaluate you. If we're lucky, we can plead not guilty by reason of insanity."

"*Insanity*?" I mutter, shaking my head in disbelief. "My whole career has been to treat the insane. How can *I* be insane?"

"I realize how difficult this must be for you to accept, but the evidence that CBI has against you leaves little room for reasonable doubt. Our only two options are to plead insanity or make a deal for more lenient sentencing. If nothing else, we'll get the death penalty off the table."

Emotion rises from my gut and constricts my throat and face. I lift my eyes upward when I feel the tears well.

"This is not happening..." I murmur to myself. "This is a nightmare."

"Dr. Fletcher," interjects Roxanne. "I need you to keep yourself together, okay? This *is* happening, and until you accept that, we cannot build your defense. Understood?"

I glance downward, and through the tears, I see her hardened expression. She looks at me with neither sympathy nor pity, yet I know that she is exactly the type of person I need on my side.

I nod my head in agreement.

"Good. Now, since you yourself are a skilled psychiatrist, do you have any ideas as to what would cause the memory loss that you're experiencing?"

"Jeez..." I pause, thinking. "Dissociative amnesia and transient global amnesia are the two that come to mind. Personality disorders often pair with those. Then there's bipolar disorder. PTSD. Schizophrenia."

"Have you ever been diagnosed with any of those before or have family history of those?"

Instantly, I think about Michelle and the trauma I endured from her when I was a child. Then, of course, there are the thousands of hours I've spent with the criminally insane, most notably Trent.

"PTSD," I answer. "I was sexually abused as a child."

I glance over at Dana. She looks mortified to learn this about me.

Roxanne simply nods as if this is no surprise to her. "Have you ever received treatment for that?" she asks.

"Yes. I've been going to therapy for the last thirty-plus years."

"Who has treated you? We'll need to have them testify."

I shake my head mournfully. "She won't be able to testify. She died about a year ago—" My throat tightens with emotion and I can barely squeeze out the last words.

Roxanne eyes me in silence for a moment. "I'm sorry," she says. "What was her name?"

"Dr. Lacey Maynard."

She writes her name down and asks, "Who have you been seeing since?"

"Nobody," I reply. "For the last decade or so, my relationship with Lacey became more of a collegial friendship than anything else. I'd vent to her about certain patients I was working with, and she'd give me suggestions for treating them. When she passed, I didn't think I needed to replace her." I pause, feeling the emotion tighten my throat again. "I didn't *want* to replace her."

"It sounds like she meant a lot to you," Roxanne responds, her voice the most sympathetic that it has been the entire conversation.

I nod. "You don't realize how much you need something until you don't have it anymore."

"Did you notice if her passing was affecting you in any way?"

"I stopped sleeping. I wanted to sleep, but I couldn't."

"Did it impact your work?"

"No. If anything, it made me dive into my work even more. Especially when Trent arrived, it was borderline obsession."

"Okay," she says. "I've got some forensic psychiatrists I've worked with in the past. I'll see who's available and we'll get you evaluated."

I nod, but my mind is incapable of making sense of anything right now.

Insane? How can I be insane? How can I be capable of any of this?

This is a dream.

This is a nightmare.

At some point, I will wake up in a cold sweat.

Terrified, but innocent.

Released from this horrific delusion.

SIXTY-TWO

I used to think routine was what kept us sane.

What curbed the chaos.

What squelched the pandemonium.

I couldn't have been more wrong.

Routine is what drives us crazy.

It's what makes every day feel like Groundhog Day.

It's what makes you lose all sense of time and space.

I don't even have a mirror in my prison cell to see how I have aged.

To see in my face how long I have actually been here.

Has it been a day?

A week?

A month?

A year?

A decade?

I cannot be sure.

My dissociative amnesia has worsened.

My memory is a wedge of rotting Swiss cheese.

My monkey brain has nothing to pick at, so it picks at itself.

Idle hands are the devil's workshop, they say.

My sanity has become the devil's plaything.

I am His Rubik's cube.

I am His Newton's cradle.

I remember when I first started studying mental health in my undergrad, abnormal psychology specifically. You learn about disorders and symptoms and causes, and you can't help but notice those things within yourself.

You know just enough to be dangerous.

You have just enough rope to hang yourself.

By the end of the class, you've diagnosed yourself with a dozen different disorders and spun your psyche into a pit that you can't get out of.

Christ, you don't even know what direction is up.

All you see is darkness.

All you feel is panic.

Hopelessness.

And the air is only getting thinner.

You get out eventually.

But the damage has been done.

The brain is not a muscle that rebuilds itself.

The psyche is not a bone that can be healed.

Sanity is a crystal glass, and when it breaks, it breaks for good.

We are beyond repair.

I am beyond repair.

A knock on the door of the therapy room startles me out of my thoughts.

A woman in a white coat opens the door. "Hello, Stephanie," she says. "I'm Dr. Barclay. I'm one of the psychiatrists here at the Chowchilla Women's Facility."

"Hello," I reply.

"Do you mind if we chat for a bit?" she asks.

I know this game better than any other inmate.

I was once the gatekeeper.

I was once the dungeon master.

Build her trust.

Make her believe that her efforts are working.

That her treatment is effective.

I will present myself as an innocent flower, but I will be the serpent coiled beneath it.

"Sure," I say, smiling.

A LETTER FROM THE AUTHOR

Thank you so much for reading *The Therapist*. I hope you were hooked on Trent and Steph's journey from start to finish. If you want to join other readers in hearing all about my new releases and bonus content, you can sign up for my newsletter!

www.stormpublishing.co/sa-falk

If you enjoyed this book and could spare a few moments to leave a review, I would greatly appreciate it. Even a short review can make all the difference in encouraging a reader to discover my book for the first time. Thank you so much!

The premise for this book first came to me a few years ago as my agent and I were pitching *The Patient's Secret* to publishers. The first draft was experimental, particularly when it came to the narrative style and point of view. I spent three months working on that draft, and what resulted was anything but a masterpiece. We both decided I needed to go back to the drawing board and start over.

Initially, I was incredibly disappointed, but in hindsight, I realize that *The Therapist* would not exist had it not been for that first failed draft. Painters often create small-scale color studies to help them refine the vision for their large-scale pieces, and that was ultimately the purpose of that first draft. It also reminds me of what William Faulkner said about writing: "You have to write badly in order to write well."

I didn't begin the second draft until six months later, and

although I kept the general premise of a correctional psychiatrist copying her own patient's crimes, I completely changed the narrative and characters.

For years, I wanted to write a story in which I incorporated my long-time passion for heavy metal music, but it wasn't until the spring of 2022 that I saw how I could do that. I had read somewhere that the Nine Inch Nails album *The Downward Spiral* was mostly recorded at the home in which Sharon Tate was murdered by the Manson Family. Although the single "Closer" is the best-known song for its disturbing lyrics and gratuitous music video, the album as a whole depicts a man's slow descent into depression, madness, and suicide. It is appropriately dark for the setting in which it was recorded, and the band's lead vocalist and songwriter, Trent Reznor, has discussed how personal and deeply emotional the album was to him.

As soon as I read the backstory on this album, I started creating the character that would become Trent Davis.

Trent Davis is a mosaic of influences though. Trent Reznor is probably the most dominant, but I was also inspired by Marilyn Manson, Jonathan Davis (Korn), Maynard James Keenan (Tool, A Perfect Circle, and Puscifer), and Jim Morrison (The Doors).

In regards to Manson, I've always been fascinated by his public persona and attitudes toward American pop culture. His criticisms are thought-provoking, and although I don't always agree with what he says, I have a great deal of respect for his articulation.

The same applies to Jim Morrison and Maynard James Keenan, particularly in their songwriting. Morrison viewed himself more as a poet than a musician, and Keenan's lyrics are enviable in their style and creativity. Read the lyrics for Tool's "Vicarious" and "Aemina" and you'll see what I'm talking about.

As for Jonathan Davis, I've read a number of interviews in

which he describes trauma he experienced as a child and young adult. He was an assistant coroner as a teenager and saw first-hand just how awful people can be to each other. Songs that were of particular influence in my creation of Trent Davis's character were Korn's "Mr. Rogers", "No Place to Hide", and "Pretty".

If you've read *The Patient's Secret*, you'll notice that child abuse is a common element in my stories. I do not write about this lightly or gratuitously. When I was in college, I worked at a residential treatment center for children aged six to twelve who had experienced severe physical and/or sexual abuse. As you can probably imagine, many of these children were deeply afflicted as a result of these traumas. Even in my work as a teacher, I have worked with students who have experienced things that no child should ever have to endure, and I incorporate these elements as a means of exposing these injustices and calling upon greater action in treating victims and prosecuting offenders.

Along with this, I want to impress upon readers the importance and power of mental health treatment. Particularly in the wake of the COVID-19 pandemic, we must not only acknowledge the growing mental health crisis, but also take action to improve access and affordability. Dr. Fletcher's example is certainly sensationalized, but the ultimate point I want to make is that untreated psychological dysfunction can have catastrophic effects.

Lastly and most importantly, I want to thank you for allowing me to share my stories with you. Writers are nothing without their readers, and I hope that you will continue to go along for this ride with me.

S.A. Falk

KEEP IN TOUCH WITH THE AUTHOR

facebook.com/SAFALKauthor

instagram.com/safalkauthor

ACKNOWLEDGMENTS

As always, I am so grateful for the guidance and patience of my literary agent, Liza Fleissig. Her feedback on this particular project really pushed me as a writer, and if not for her influence, this book would be nothing more than a rough draft collecting dust on the shelf. As the saying goes, iron sharpens iron.

I also must express my appreciation for my editor, Emily Gowers. She has a terrific eye when it comes to crafting a narrative, and her ability to collaborate has made the editorial process as easy as possible. Thank you for everything you have taught me so far, and I look forward to our work on future projects.

Lastly, I have to thank all the musicians whose work not only inspired the premise of this book, but also helped me through my own dark times.